THE CULT
-Eve Not Adam

Tego Arcana Dei Series

Andrew Man

Book VII

The Cult – Eve Not Adam.

Copyright © 2025 by Andrew Man

Dedicated to
Daniel

Disclaimer

This story is a work of fiction, except the parts that aren't. Names and characters are all creations of the author's imagination or are used fictitiously and should not be construed as real. Any references to actual organisation, places, or events are entirely fictional. Any resemblance to real persons, past or present, living or dead, is both random and coincidental.

In the Tego Arcana Dei Series

The complete trilogy Books 1-3

The Man who Played with Time

Book 4 – AFTER THE FLOOD

Book 5 – EVE NOT ADAM

Book 6 – POSTLUDE

Book 7 – THE CULT

Contents

PART ONE

FINDING THE TRUTH –

MARCH 2024

1 – ARRIVAL 2024

Out of the darkness, there came light, as the plane came to a hover over a coastline of lush, green vegetation and a blue sea and sky as far as everyone could see. Down below, James could see Janet's house set back on the Old Bluff, surrounded by palm trees gently swaying in the wind. James carefully let the plane descend another hundred feet, looking for some signs of life. He felt the sweat on his hands knowing that in 2024 people should still be here.

Still no sign of Janet and no way to contact any people either. A chance impulse had told him this year would be alright; now he was not so sure. As his inner conflict went into overdrive, he realised turning back was not an option either.

"My God, James, are we really back above Montserrat Island in the Caribbean?" shouted Bee, as the two girls scrambled to look out at the scene below.

"Where are we, James?" asked Susan, as James the pilot, saw people running down the drive and waving at the plane to depart. Only then did James make a weary reply.

"Yes, this is the island of Montserrat and we are near Janet's house. Look, I'm being warned not to land in daylight. That will only make our arrival public," he explained.

"And the time, James? In which year?" Susan asked again into her voice communication to James up in the front of the plane.

"It should be sometime in mid-March 2024. We've made a huge jump through time and space from the future. I've done it before with Janet in 2023; now we need to wash all the toxic dust off before we can land," he explained, as the plane hovered and turned slowly to face the sea.

"James, where are we going now?" Susan exclaimed.

"Don't worry, I've done this many times before. We need to sit under the water for a few minutes while I reset our arrival to nighttime," he said, as the plane slowly descended into the shallows below the house on Lime Kiln Bay. Then it went dark again.

"Mummy, what's happening? Why didn't we land on that island?" asked Susan's daughter.

James thought back to their escape from the military on the island. He was wearing a navy peak cap, beneath which his eyes were heavily pouched and bloodshot. He reached down to move the dial into darkness and dragged a hand over his face. Then he took a few deep breaths as they waited.

"How much longer before we can go back?" asked Susan on the intercom as they looked at the bubbles rising in the water outside the plane. Finally, James responded.

"Right, hold on, everyone. We are a go for launch into the night." Everyone held their breath as the plane slowly rose out of the water and moved back towards the island again.

"James, I can see people outside with lights. Can we go down and land?" Susan asked.

"Yes, engaging landing now; we're going down," James replied as the craft slowly descended onto the drive in front of the house on the Old Bluff. Janet ran out, carrying a ladder to the rear of the plane. She was followed by another woman called Jana.

The two passengers in the rear climbed down, each carrying a large bag, when there was a huge flash above the house and everyone looked up at the sky.

"Looks like a storm is coming," Jana said, lifting one of the girls down onto the ground to join their mothers, and they all ran into the house. After that, Janet climbed up to speak to James, with the headset left on the rear seat of the plane.

"James, we cannot let the plane stay out here all night. Apart from the locals, we have a satellite that passes overhead most nights, ever since the incident before the pandemic."

"I understand. So, it seems they still want to keep a watch on this place after the event four years ago," James replied.

"Yes, but it's okay. I've arranged a place to hide the plane at the airport. You remember Sam, who was on the first mission to the island? Well, he's been stationed at Osborne Airport as an observer and has agreed to help us. We're having power cuts all over the island. So tonight the lights will be out over Gerald's and the airport is closed down," Janet said.

"Okay, what do you want me to do?" James asked.

"You fly north from here. I will call him to flash bright lights every minute to guide you in. He'll be there with his assistant to help you land and hide the plane from the satellites," Janet explained.

"Roger that. Sounds like a good plan. Stand back as I need to close your compartment before I leave."

"Wait, James. Sam will bring you back here after you land," she said and, climbing down, removed the ladder and stood back as the craft lit up and silently moved up above the house, heading north.

James let the plane fly the few miles to Gerald's until he saw the runway lights flashing. Then he noticed two people with high energy beams light up the plane and he knew where to land. Once on the ground, an airport bowser was attached to his plane and pushed the craft into an empty hangar. When he finally opened his cockpit canopy, he found he was looking at his partner on the island in the past. His name was Sergeant Sam, a member of the US Special Forces, who James remembered only too well.

"James, so we meet again," said Sam, but looking down, he saw a man flashing between life and death. He called his assistant to bring up maintenance staging close to the plane. Once done, Sam lifted James out of the plane and placed him on the top of the staging, then he pushed the stage out of the hangar. Climbing up onto the back of his Toyota truck outside, he carefully lifted the body onto the truck and laid him on a tarpaulin. Sam watched as James's body changed colour from grey to dark grey and shook his head.

Then, turning back to his assistant, he shouted, "Okay, you can close up and secure the doors of the hangar for the night. I'm needed to take the injured pilot up to Janet's house."

Sam quickly drove out of the airport, south to Olveston, through Salem, and up to the Old Bluff road. Finding the gates open and the lights at the house on, he drove inside as the front door opened and Janet appeared.

"Sam, where's James?" she shouted, as Susan appeared at the door. Her breath tightened, and her breathing stopped. Susan was visibly shaking – probably wondering whether he was dead or not.

"He passed out in the plane after he landed, so I put him in the back here," he replied, opening the tailgate as Janet came to look.

"No, no, he does not look good. Susan, can you give me hand and we'll carry him inside," Janet asked. With some help from Sam, they lifted James out and carried him into the house, across the entrance floor, and up onto a platform of wooden planks. Janet pulled back a huge curtain to show stone steps in the far corner leading down into the water of a pool.

"I had this covered over when I thought you were coming with the children. We will push him into the water to help him recover," Janet said.

"But won't he drown?" asked Susan.

"No, the water has some special powers that will help to heal his condition."

"Alright, but let's tie this orange rope from the lifebelt here to his body. We don't want him lost under the wooden cover you installed," Susan replied, still in shock.

"Yes, good idea. I've tied the rope around him and now we can push him down into the water."

They watched as James descended in a stream of bubbles and settled at the bottom of the steps, but still appeared unconscious.

"Let me hold the rope now. Please will you ask Jana to come and assist?"

When Susan left, she pulled back the curtain again and found Sam waiting there so introduced herself.

"Hello, my name's Susan. We came in on the flight tonight with James," she said, trying to make it sound like a normal airport arrival.

"Well, is James going to be alright?" Sam asked.

"Oh, must have been a bad reaction to the long flight. I'm sure he'll recover by the morning. How did it go with the plane?" she asked as she looked at the man more closely. Clearly American, but older than she expected, with facial hair that needed attention: too-neat lines and blunt sideburns. The skin under his jaw looked smooth, as if he'd never been in the sun.

"Yeah, safely locked away in a hangar. Strange, but the craft was dripping with water when it landed. Is that normal?"

The question threw Susan at first.

"Perhaps we passed through a shower on our approach?"

"Well, when I tasted a drop, it was seawater. You know I've watched many of the US army VTOL planes land, but this one never made any sound. That's strange if you ask me," he said in his Southern drawl.

Thankfully, at that moment, Jana rushed up looking for James, which let Susan thank Sam and after saying goodnight, he left the house.

Without waiting, Jana guessed where he was and ran to find Janet holding the rope with James still at the bottom of the pool.

"Come on, Janet, we need to pull him out. I need to touch his head to see what's happened," Jana ordered, as Janet pulled him up to the surface again.

Touching his forehead, she could see the problem immediately.

"My God, James is still wearing his medallion! He's been flying through time on the plane and somehow it also activated his medallion. Help me get it off him as quickly as possible," Jana asked.

Janet pulled James further up out of the water and Jana removed the medallion and put it in her pocket.

"Good, now we need to pull him out of the pool together. Come on, one, two, three heave." This left James lying unconscious beside the pool.

"Right, Janet, can you take his arms and I'll take his legs, and we'll carry him down to my bedroom. That was a great idea to put him in the pool, but I think James will be out of action for several days," said Jana, as they struggled to carry the man downstairs.

Once they laid James on the bed, Janet left, only to meet a worried Susan outside in the corridor.

"Is he going to be alright? You know that man Sam, he asked a lot of questions about the plane. Does he know you and James from the past," she asked, still looking frightened.

"Yes, with Jana's help, James should recover. Now let me help you and your children get settled in for the night. Is there anything I can do for you now?" Janet asked.

"Not really. Could we open a bottle of wine to celebrate our return? Once the girls are asleep, of course."

"Most welcome, Susan. Perhaps you can explain why you both arrived with only one bag of hand luggage. That's most strange as well. Please follow me upstairs," Janet replied.

Susan followed her up to the kitchen bar. Janet opened the door of a large US-size fridge, placed an opened bottle on the table, poured two glasses of white wine, and passed one over to Susan.

"Welcome home," Janet said, smiling at her.

"Is everything on the island okay? You've been back for over a year now, haven't you?" Susan asked, feeling that things were not going so well in 2024.

"The island is still suffering economically after the pandemic. More residents have left, and we still import most of our food, which is a problem from the volcanic eruption a decade ago. It's a challenge, but I think you will settle in. What about you two?" Janet asked.

"Well, if you really want to know what happened to us, we were thrown off the airbase. They only let us leave with two bags of hand luggage and the clothes we are wearing." Susan explained.

"And James, what happened to him?" Janet asked.

"I don't know. He was fine when we landed outside, so something must have happened after, when he flew on from here," she replied.

"I can only guess, from that flash in the sky, we were being watched by a military satellite. I think they tried to make him crash the plane when it took off again."

"Is all of that possible on this planet today?" Susan asked.

"Yes, it's a long story that I will explain later, so let's drink to yours and the girls' safe return," Janet replied and started to explain her plans that would be necessary for the next day.

2 – NUMBER 324

We flash forward to the RAF airbase in England, in 2031, to James, the pilot of the time-travelling plane.

People were starting to ask questions about Janet and Jana after they disappeared. Then Bee was begging me to take them back to Montserrat Island as well. The problem was with Susan, as she insisted on finishing her report of their experiences in another world. It was called Earth 2.0 and the RAF Base Commander wanted it submitted before the end of August 2031.

Slowly, it became clear that the best solution was to return them to the Caribbean island with Janet, but it was difficult to know exactly what date. There were two ten-year-old daughters to consider, and landing on the beach was not an option. I looked for clues from Jana, but nothing showed up until one day I fell in the shower. While sitting under the water, I saw the numbers 324 and knew that was clearly a message from her.

Getting a test flight had become much easier, so perhaps the technicians knew that the plane was going to be returned to the US.

After Susan's big day, an alarm was sounded on the base that gave me the opportunity to get Susan, Bee, and the children on the plane, and we finally left without too much fuss.

When we arrived near the island in daylight in the middle of March, I saw both Janet and Jana waving at me to leave. I thought they were worried about drones, so I went to land in the water of Lime Kiln Bay.

"We're going down, we're going down," Bee was shouting at me in fear on my headphones until we hit the water, and everything went dark. Then the children also started to shout with urgent cries for help.

It took me a few minutes to advance the time dilation by a few hours and the plane rose out of the water, into the darkness of the night.

I thought that everything was now safe for a landing at the house. Once the passengers had disembarked, Janet told me to take a short jump to the airfield that I remembered well. It wasn't more than ten miles, but as I approached the runway, I felt that I was being pulled apart by a strong force from above.

After that, I remember nothing until I woke up at Janet's house lying on a bed dressed in wet clothes, with Jana. Jana has been my soulmate for some years now and I have a baby son who she takes care of when I'm away. It took me two days to recover, mainly from being immersed in the pool.

"You know you were lucky to have survived, as it's clear some people didn't want the plane returned to the island," she said.

"Yes, and now Janet thinks they may have other planes that are leased out as well," I replied.

***

As James slowly recovered, Jana showed him more of her research about alien planes she had found online from videos on the laptop that Janet had given her.

"You need to understand this all started in 2022. That was the year before we returned, when a new law was passed by Congress wanting to encourage witnesses to come forward and talk about secret programs and UAPs," Jana said.

"Really? So what happened then?"

"All sorts of UFO whistleblowers came out of the woodwork, including one guy, David G or something. He told Congress of a long history to retrieve and back-engineer crashed UFOs. Even the locations were provided in a public statement."

"You mean they actually wanted to know where Janet had got her plane from?" James asked.

"Right, but he got targeted for this because of his allegations. He took the evidence to the office of the Inspector General that oversees the most sensitive programs. They found his allegations to be 'credible and urgent.'"

"You've got to be making this up, Jana!"

"No, his name was leaked to the press last year, and he went public in interviews on national TV. I even watched some of them online. As you would expect, most newspapers in the US did their best to ignore the story altogether."

"Okay, what happened after that?" asked James.

"They passed several amendments so that all government departments, including the Pentagon and CIA, were required to gather all UFO material and submit it to a central office."

"Everyone except NASA I guess?"

"Yes, NASA appointed an independent commission to investigate UAP matters. Just as surprising was the reaction of mainstream science, who saw the possibility that UFOs might represent extraterrestrial intelligence," replied Jana.

"But how and why did so many things change since we left?"

"That was all down to the Intelligence Agency's Advanced Aerospace Weapon System program that was set up with a rock star band to provide an explosion of interest in UAP matter," explained Jana.

"So, was this AA weapon system a UFO program?" he asked.

"James! I don't really know, but the DIA stated in clear terms it was a UFO-centric investigation," Jana replied.

"And after that it would have to be shut down…" said James.

"How do you know that? Well, it was almost, but not quite. After academics thought the UFO topic had gone mainstream, they slowed the momentum of additional hearings and finally stated that any more would cause harm to the Department of Defence and stopped any further hearings in public."

"And I suppose the NASA commission found no evidence to support any ET visitations or UFOs and we're back where we started," said James.

"Yes, although they do appear to have put together a database of all UFO encounters in the US, Europe, and Brazil. Sorry, but that's where we are in 2024," Jana said and then stopped as her baby started crying.

Jana picked him up and began to hum above his small cries. She started to move around the room, pacing a few steps forward and then back in rhythm to her humming, until he fell back asleep again. All the while, James was on the bed, looking at the videos on the laptop, and she joined him once more.

"Right, he's asleep again; where were we?"

"Any other research you found interesting?"

"Maybe. Do you remember the incident nine years ago when MH370 disappeared, and no one knows what really happened?" She started to explain, finding the videos on YouTube again, and James sat up on the bed to look closer.

"There was a video posted online four days after the plane disappeared, but no one took any notice of it. Everyone thought the orbs were UFOs. Then a satellite video was published three months later in 2014," she said.

"Right, Jana, but this all happened over ten years ago."

"Yes, but look at this, the orbs following the plane. See, they are defying gravity, not falling to the ground. Look, there's a clear heat signature from the orbs that is consistent with a monopole, having both a magnetic and a dipole effect to achieve anti-gravity."

"No, no, Jana, that's possible ten years ago."

"Well look, the orbs are creating space in front of them to run down a gravity well, probably using a laser or high-frequency vibrational effect to break through the fabric of reality. Are you with me now?" Jana asked.

"Are you sure this is a real video, not a fake?"

"Pretty much, because the guy who released them got a nine-year prison sentence in the US. These are copies of actual military satellite recordings with all identification removed except the time and date that you can see in the bottom left of the screen," she said.

"Okay, so how did this get on the internet?" asked James.

"He was a US signals operator, and sent copies to his friends in Taiwan, who released the data on Reddit," she replied.

"Alright, show me what finally happened to the plane."

"Right before the final zap on the plane, this is one of the strongest effects as the orbs converge on the plane with amplified energy. This breaks through the fabric of space time with some kind of entanglement effect. The plane goes from being there, to not being there, there," Jana said, as they both looked at the screen to see the plane had disappeared on the video.

"Jana, wait. Can you go back to just before the plane disappears? I saw a black circular shape in one of the last frames. That's interesting. It looks as if the plane was sucked into something like a mini black hole. It went into another dimension," said James.

"Yes, I think they tried to do that with your plane before you landed at Osborne Airport. Fortunately, that may have been blocked as you were wearing your medallion," Jana replied.

"So, if the US military has developed force fields, they can control space with a unity device, an icon construct that can tap into the negative energy of the universe. They must have developed super magnetic fields to create fusion power. When that's amplified to such a high degree, it can destroy a plane," James said.

"Possibly, but if all that happened nine years ago, think what they can do now in 2024," Jana replied.

"Sounds like they are using this technology that was reverse-engineered or found from crashed alien craft. From what I remember, in reports from the early 2000s, these craft were being used to take organs from cattle across the New Mexico border for years, weren't they?"

"Yes, not only animals but taking humans for scientific study. They also used these craft to transport children, and sow manipulation in war zones like Ukraine, where a lot of people have disappeared. Most of the UFOs seen out here today are probably our military, or might be from Russia or China. We don't know," Jana said.

"Right, and the problem of this unification of the forces is like opening Pandora's box. The real question is what will this do for our future and will it take humanity into oblivion," James replied.

"Come on, James, we can't solve this tonight, you still need to get some rest," Jana insisted, and James lay back on the bed to sleep.

3 – THE EMERALD ISLE

The house on the Old Bluff road was of a modern design, built more like a concrete bunker with the entrance and living rooms facing south, and bedrooms below overlooking Lime Kiln Bay.

The following morning, the two girls were awake as soon as it was light. They started playing in their bedroom with the toys they had brought in the hand luggage, forcing Bee to get up as well. Before long, the whole house was awake, but Susan was already upstairs in the kitchen making coffee and breakfast.

"Hello, everyone, you can come up and get some brekkie," Janet shouted to the noise downstairs, until Susan appeared.

"My God, I feel dreadful. It's as if I lost six years of my life."

"Yes, that's normal if you've flown overnight through time. Coffee and two Panadol are what you need," Janet replied, pointing to the breakfast bar. Susan sat down on a stool, looking very tired. Next to appear was Bee, with the two girls hiding behind her.

"Hello, girls, I'm your aunt Janet. You've come to stay with me on this Caribbean island. Your place is on the small table over there. I've got banana and cornflakes for you to eat for breakfast," she said.

"What are cornflakes?" asked Nut.

"Bananas are good," replied Mayati, and Bee took the bowls of fruit to the girls and then staggered back to the bar.

"Coffee, Bee? The aspirin are on the table."

"Sorry, but I feel as if I'm only half here? Can you add something stronger to my coffee, please."

"Of course, some of our local rum should help," replied Janet, smiling at the request.

Janet placed the bottle on the table, and Bee grabbed it and swigged the liquor down. Then topped up her mug of coffee and looked at everyone around the table.

"What? What the fuck are you all looking at?" she said. Bee was wearing the kaftan she arrived in and looked like a wreck.

"Bee, calm down, it's been a difficult time for us all. We need to get you some island clothes," replied Susan.

"Agreed, and listen up, everyone, because later this afternoon we need to go back to Osborne Airport to get you all properly checked in," announced Janet, to the astonishment of the two mothers.

"No, not possible, we don't have any ID," Susan replied, as her thoughts were screaming at more arrival demands.

"Oh! But you do. I have your British passports here," Janet said, handing over two old UK red passports to each of them. Susan and Bee took them and looked in amazement. Bee, on hearing the news, felt the air in her lungs, and tears form in her eyes. Slowly, she rested her arms on the bar and, composing herself, she replied.

"I don't think I can go anywhere today," she mumbled.

"Why do we have to do this today?" Susan asked.

"After I went back in England, having to renew my British passport, I made some enquires. I found these IDs for both of you, in anticipation of your arrival," Janet explained. "These passports cost me a lot of money. You can no longer arrive on any Caribbean island without some form of ID and that was only possible to fake with the old EU passports."

"So, I'm now Susan West, born in Liverpool in 1995. That's somewhere I've never been," Susan said, looking at the passport.

"And I'm Bee Norton, born in Manchester in 1994. Is this a joke, Janet?" asked Bee, still shaking in fear.

"Yes, I see mine expires in November 2024," said Susan.

"WTF, my expiry date is January 2025!" Bee announced.

"Wait, let me explain. You have both been invited here on real scientific projects that I have agreed to sponsor. Susan is here for a project with the Montserrat Volcanic Observatory and you, my dear Bee, are in much demand to revitalise the agriculture on the island. Do you understand? It's the only way you can stay here on the island."

"Alright, we understand. What do we have to do to pull this off with our fake IDs?" Susan asked.

"So, as long as the BA flight isn't late today, passengers should make the connecting flight to Monserrat that arrives this afternoon. I made a provisional booking on a flight to Montserrat today, so we need to plan for that before we leave for the airport," Janet replied.

"Wait, so we're not really going to Antigua, are we?" asked Susan.

"No, we're going to meet Sam at our local airport, who's got two more UK passports for the two girls. They can't legally enter any other way," Janet explained.

"You know, I think you're mad, Janet," Bee replied, laughing.

"Well, no more than you were coming back last night," Janet explained and then continued.

"Look, there's no way any government is going to admit where any of us has been for the last nine years. James brought Jana and me back to 2023. That was at the end of the pandemic and things were different then. I'm a resident here, so it wasn't a big problem. Since then, we've had time to plan for your arrival," Janet explained.

"All right, we understand, but we had no choice except to leave," replied Susan.

"Yes, when I read Susan's report last night about 'Earth 2.0,' I understood why you got thrown out of that RAF base in the future. If you want to live peacefully here in 2024, you must accept your new identities as Mrs West with ten-year-old Nut and Ms Norton with your daughter Mary. Is that clearly understood?" Janet insisted.

"Yes, Janet, we are most grateful for all your help. But what exactly are we going to do here? I think that's what's worrying Bee," Susan replied, trying to sound diplomatic.

"Alright, go and get the girls dressed and I will explain details when we have coffee; say in about an hour," replied Janet.

***

When they met later again, Susan asked about the status of the European Space Agency where they were both originally hired and first trained.

"Yes, that was an option I considered. While ESA has had some successes with the Horizon project, it has not developed as the members hoped. Much of the EU money has been taken up by a Russian invasion of Ukraine in 2014 that developed into a war two years ago," Janet explained.

"You mean the EU is at war with Russia?" asked Susan.

"No, not a war, but with Western sanctions against Russia. Now there are only two space players: the US and China. The Soviets have become a junior player. The ESA is firmly allied to the US, so if you went back to the ESA, they would almost certainly hand you back to work with the Americans. Is that what you want?" Janet replied.

"No, we just wanted to know what other options there might be," Susan said.

"Alright, I understand. You both have some very valuable experiences that any of these governments would dearly like to know."

"So, what's so special about the UK now?" Bee asked.

"Well, unfortunately, the UK has a new King Charles after the death of Elizabeth. Politically, the country is in turmoil. That means we can continue off the grid here on Montserrat for a while. We're far away from the many military disputes in Israel, Yemen, and the Middle East, and possible conflicts in Asia with China. You want to see what I have planned for you?" Janet said, passing them a copy of the *Montserrat Times* across the table.

"What have you done now, Janet? You've announced to the press that we will be arriving at Osborne Airport in the afternoon today, just before the St Patrick's Day celebrations!" Susan exclaimed.

"Yes, or you can hand yourselves in to the Montserrat Police at the airport as an illegal immigrant."

"We don't have any other choice, do we?" asked Bee.

"Look, this is for your own protection. Once you have entered legally, you will have the protection of the British Crown. Then it will become a lot more difficult for the CIA to abduct you back to the US for interrogation. A life of constant investigations with your children taken away to foster homes? Because if you go back to Darmstadt, that's what will happen," she said as the two mothers looked on in fear.

"Alright, we'll do it. Tell us, what do we need to wear?" asked Susan.

"You wear the same clothes as you arrived in: This is not a fashion show, except for Bee. She can't be seen in a kaftan. Otherwise, it will look like the white girl trying to teach the black man how to farm his fields. I'll get a pair of jeans and an old shirt of James's for her," said Janet.

"Alright, I understand," said Bee as she nodded.

"Susan, you need to take all the electrical stuff out of your bag. I will replace it with some British science magazines, tissues, and wet wipes! Right, let's show these people how this project will help the island," Janet finished, leaving them at the table with the coffee.

"Well, Bee, it looks like we're back to doing what we do best. Astro research for me and slash and char for you. How are you feeling?" Susan asked.

"Pretty shitty, and we don't have any handmaidens this time. And if we're expected to work outside, they're going to have to find us a nanny for the girls in the daytime," Bee replied.

"Look on the positive side and let's see how this works out for a few months. Come on, we need to prepare some lunch for the girls before we leave for the airport," Susan replied.

"And I need to get changed into some white man's clothes," Bee replied, laughing.

***

After an early lunch, Janet took them to her car parked outside. Bee sat in the back with their hand baggage and the two girls. Susan sat in the front, next to Janet. Jana went and opened the gates to the house, and they drove off down through Salem towards Geralds, where Osborne Airport is located. When they reached the tunnel, Janet received a call from Sam telling her where to park. There she saw him standing next to a white minivan with the word security and the Montserrat flag on the side. Janet opened her door and told them all to get out of the car, as Sam waved at the girls in the back.

"Hello, everyone, please take your bags and sit in the van," he said as Janet approached him, looking worried.

"Sam, is everything alright? I saw that the local flight today was at 4 p.m., so have we arrived a bit early."

"No, we are meeting a charter fight for the St Patrick's celebrations. Music artists, probably with lots of baggage, so we still have time to drop you off at the hangar, if that's alright with you."

"Yes, of course. I want to get that paperwork done," she replied and walked around to sit in the front of the van.

With that, San drove up to a security door and, using his pass, the gate opened and they went inside the airport. He drove around on a perimeter road until they reached a large semicircular building with green doors, partly hidden by trees. It didn't look much like an aircraft hangar but looked large enough to conceal a small plane. On the closed doors, Susan could see a sign that read 'Private US Property' with the US flag below.

Janet got out of the van as a man in white overalls approached her. They shook hands and he led her around to the back of the hangar. Susan was wondering if this was where James had hidden the plane when Sam interrupted her thoughts.

"We still have some time before the plane arrives from Antigua and can give you the passports for your two girls. These just arrived this morning, so please check that all is correct," Sam asked. Turning in his seat, he passed an old red British passport to Susan and another to Bee, who immediately opened them to see the details of their girls.

"No, no, this is impossible! How did you get a photo of Mary when we never... I mean, she has never been here," Bee exclaimed.

"Simple, Bee. Remember, there was a flash when we landed, and we all looked up at the sky. Your satellite imaging has improved a lot," Susan replied, looking at Sam and smiling.

"Alright, they needed to show the time and date the plane landed, so yes, we used that to help with your ID as well," Sam explained.

"The details for Mary Norton look correct, although you've had to fake her date of birth, but that's okay," Bee confirmed.

"Yes, it looks good for my daughter too. How did you get these fake IDs so quickly – does that mean the government here knows where they are from?" Susan asked, sounding worried.

"No, they are not aware. These passports are not even registered in the UK, if that helps. They only know you're science volunteers working for Janet and we need to keep it that way," Sam replied.

"So what do we do now?" Bee asked.

"Now we wait," Sam replied, looking at his mobile...

***

Meanwhile, Janet followed the technician to a side door in the hangar. He inputted a code and on opening the door, they entered inside.

"My name's Bob Schneider and we appreciate your cooperation, Mrs Romford, for returning the craft," he said with an American accent as she studied the man. He was a young man with his hair cut short and grey peppering on his sides.

"And where, Mr Schneider, are you from in the States?" asked Janet.

"I'm from Los Alamos in New Mexico."

"Well, I'm impressed that they sent someone from head office," she said as he turned on the lights and Janet gasped when she saw the plane standing stationary for the first time.

"We can start the handover procedure, if you will follow me."

"Yes, of course, go ahead." They walked around the tail of the plane and he looked at the fuselage carefully.

"I did a quick inspection this morning and the craft looks to be in good condition. There was sand in the landing gear that had to be washed out, perhaps from a landing in the sea," he said.

"Yes, that's standard operating procedure after a long flight. It was done every time at the RAF base; obviously not in the sea."

"Do you know the duration of the last flight that was made?"

"Err. Yes, the number of years travelled was six."

"Really? I don't know how that's possible."

"The technicians in the UK didn't understand how the plane flew at all," Janet replied.

"Alright. I inspected the passenger compartment and wiped it clean of all fingerprints and the same in the pilot cockpit, but I didn't find the logbook. Do you know where that might be?"

"Oh yes, that will be back in 2031 at the Group 22 base in the UK," she replied, smiling at him as he knew the conversation was going nowhere.

"Okay, let's go back and I'll let you sign the discharge papers. But you need to give me more details of the flights undertaken. Purely for my report you understand," he said, handing her a clipboard with a copy of the original lease contract.

"Please initial each clause of the release agreement and sign and date with your full name at the end," he asked. After Janet signed in all the places he indicated, she handed the board back to him and asked him to sign in the places as well.

"Do you mind if I take some images of the document, for my board of directors, you understand," she replied and when he turned away, Janet took a few shots of the plane as well.

"Thank you. Now I need the details and the dates of all the flights that you can remember," he asked.

"Yes, of course. It's quite a long list and dates six years in the future are meaningless, but if you're ready, here goes," she continued.

"After the craft arrived in the autumn of 2030, it was tested for several months at the airbase and my son took it on a first flight in November 2030," Janet explained.

"And your son is still there?"

"Yes, in fact, the plane made two trips from London to the Algarve in Southern Portugal, there and back in a day, where the pilot and passenger survived with no ill effects at all. Following that success, the plane flew to Montreal, Canada, and back in a day."

"Really? All right, go on," he insisted.

"In addition, the plane has made several flights to the island here. One to bring me and my assistant back to my home in Montserrat after the pandemic and the second to return with the two women and girls you saw in the minivan with Sam."

"Yes, they all looked in good health, but what about the pilot I saw last night? He appeared to have passed out."

"Yes, that was unfortunate. He was wearing a device that became activated, and he is now recovering at my house," Janet explained.

"I suppose that this device is classified?"

"Yes, that's the best way I can explain it," Janet replied.

"Alright, I can accept that. Now, do you want to know about the bond you posted? Under the contract, 50 percent is payable upon return of the plane undamaged and the balance after one year, depending on your continued cooperation. Let's say it takes me a week to complete the diagnostic tests, then I'll be willing to recommend that the first payment is released in about a month."

"Very good, that's exactly what the terms of our contract state and I would like the payment made to an offshore bank if that's possible?"

"I think we can accept that, if you give me the details."

"I need to agree that with my company in due course."

"Right then, I think we're finished, and I'll let you out to rejoin Sam and your colleagues," he said, shaking her hand.

"Oh, just one more question. I suppose the plane will be returned to your base in New Mexico now?" Janet asked.

"No, not straight away. It's an election year, and it will need the agreement of the new president to return the craft to the States."

"I see, and you don't have a pilot who knows how to fly the plane?"

"Correct. That's why we're being most reasonable with you. When I'm done here, and with the agreement of Sam, your pilot might take it out for a spin to recover your son as well," he suggested, smiling at her.

"Thank you, Mr Schneider, that's most considerate of you. If perhaps you are free for a dinner, you would be most welcome," Janet replied.

"I'm not sure if that's possible as I'm not really on this island, for security reasons, you know."

"Yes, I understand, anyway thanks again," she said and waving goodbye, she walked back to the doors of the hangar, where she found her transport waiting with Sam. For the first time in months, she felt quite pleased with herself.

***

As soon as she climbed into the minivan, he started to drive back towards the airport.

"So, it went well. You look pleased?" Sam asked.

"Yes, I signed the papers and he's going to recommend the return of 50 percent of our investment, but there were a lot of questions. Sam, it was like returning the car to a Hertz rental agency! He wanted to know all the past flights and thought there should be a flight log in the cockpit. Do you think they have more of these planes?" Janet asked.

"That's strange. Of course, that's possible, and no questions about the alien landing?" Sam asked.

"No. Nothing at all. As he didn't mention the topic, I wasn't going to say anything either," Janet replied. "But the good news is that the plane will be here until after the US election. He said they don't want it back before then. So how did it go with you?" she asked as they arrived at the exit gate again.

"It went well. We waited until the plane had landed and the musicians had left the plane. While they were unloading the baggage, we walked round to the door of the plane for a group photo. It was a risk, but I trust the pilot. There are several flights coming in this afternoon for the St Patrick's Day parade. Lots of people and noise here as they prepare for the celebrations this year."

"So, what happened after that?" Janet said.

"After that, they walked to the arrivals door," he said, showing her the image on his phone as he drew up behind her car outside.

"Now, you need to move your car up closer to the terminal and go inside to meet them. Janet, you need to move fast!" Sam said firmly and then drove off.

Janet moved her car and ran inside the airport building, only to find a big group of locals, all in green costumes, waiting to greet the arriving musicians. Some of them were singing and clapping in celebration. At the back, she recognised local press from the island's media, so she quickly turned into the airport shop, empty except for the local behind the bar.

"Well, if isn't Mrs Romford, come to meet your friends today. How can I help you, my dear?" Almost in panic, Janet looked around and her eyes alighted on two children's backpacks with the flag of Monserrat.

"Err. Can I buy those two bags for the little girls?"

"Yes, of course. That will cost you twenty dollars."

"Right, here you are," Janet said, handing over a $20 East Caribbean bill, when a young Montserrat police officer tapped her on the shoulder.

"Mrs Romford, can you come now; your friends are here at arrivals. I'll clear a path for you to meet them."

Janet followed the officer and the crowd withdrew, letting Janet come face to face with Susan and Bee. Knowing the press would be taking photos, they formally greeted each other with just a handshake. Then Janet bent down to give her gift to the two girls. After that, the police officer cleared a way for them to leave the terminal.

Once outside, Janet led them to her car in the parking, where they climbed inside and Janet left the airport as fast as she could.

"Well, that was a happy welcome to Montserrat," Janet said, trying to sound positive, and looking at Susan beside her.

"Yes, it was well stage-managed by your man Sam. I don't think anyone cared if we had valid passports. I hope we don't have to do that ever again," Susan replied.

"But you did get your passports stamped, didn't you?" asked Janet.

"Yes, of course. How did your meeting go with the man for the plane?" Susan replied.

"Better than expected, they are going to keep it here until the end of the year. Probably because they don't have a pilot to fly it."

"But you have handed it back to the US, haven't you?"

"Yes, Susan, you don't understand but I had little choice. I'm going to talk to James to see what he thinks we should do next," Janet explained. While looking in the car's mirror, she saw Bee and the girls were fast asleep.

That evening, Janet converted the images she took on her phone and sent copies to her investors confirming that the plane had been given back to the US and was awaiting a refund. She proposed a board meeting in London for the middle of April, by which time she hoped both Susan and Bee would have settled into their new life on the island. After that, she went to look in on James and Jana. Finding James still in bed but looking much improved, she sought his advice.

"James, they told me they're going to keep the plane here until the end of the year. Some lame excuse about it being delayed by the US election and hinted you might take it for a spin after doing some diagnostics. What do you think?" Janet asked.

"Sounds like a US trap to try to get their hands on Ben. Perhaps they know he flew the plane a lot more than me," he replied.

"Well, I've been helping James with that remote viewing device he found in London. We know a lot more about these people now we're back together," Jana explained.

"That they have other craft as well?" Janet asked.

"Yes, but how do you know?" replied James.

"Oh! The meeting was like returning a hire car and signing the release papers was a complete joke! So, I'm guessing they have done this before," she explained.

"That's the new public-private partnership we keep hearing about. Where the US outsources its black space ops to the private sector. Then, if there are any problems, NASA can claim ignorance," replied Jana.

"Okay, sounds familiar, so who's behind it this time?" asked Janet.

"That's what we're still trying to work out," James replied, sitting up in bed to show Janet the screen of the viewing device.

"This is your technician doing his diagnostics on the craft in the hangar," explained James.

"What, how can you see this from here!" exclaimed Janet.

"Jana can connect to the plane; after that, it's easy to watch his movements. So far, he's been trying to record all the flight movements we made...don't ask me why."

"But what if he deletes the coordinates to the Group 22 base, or my house in Windsor? How can you ever go back there?" Janet asked.

"Don't worry, Jana has already copied the details onto this device. So even if he deletes them, we can still input them again," James replied, and Janet looked calmer.

"Tell us, Janet, how did it go with the new arrivals at the airport?" Jana asked, changing the subject.

"Oh that! Yes, it went well, or at least there weren't any questions asked," she replied, sounding unsure of herself. "But Bee was freaked out by a group of locals who were waiting for a music group that came in on the flight before. They were dressed in green costumes with long black hair. You know, all singing and clapping, and now she says she can't face working on the project on the island."

"Don't worry; let me talk to her tomorrow. I remember her from that airbase in the future. She helped me find out where Nathalie was going on the black tablet," Jana replied, pointing to the device on the bed.

"Alright, so what can we do this time?"

"Perhaps you can find some plants in pots from the locals. Young plants like breadfruit, pineapples; I'll give you a list once I've spoken to her. Then we put the pots on the outside terrace and convince her to take care of them. Once she's involved, the plants will tell her what to do. She'll be back working in the fields in no time," Jana suggested.

"Alright, let's give it a try," replied Janet.

"We're invited to the Emerald City Fest tomorrow. Both James and I are going; do you want to join us?"

"Do think that's wise for James after his incident on the plane? Is he ready to meet crowds of people?" Janet asked.

"Yes, he has his medallion again and most carnival revellers are only happy with the food and the music. You should get out more, to meet people and continue a normal life again," said Jana.

"Alright, I can't promise, but I don't think the others are ready for a Caribbean carnival experience just yet."

"Right, we understand, don't we, James?"

"Anything else I can help you with?" Janet asked.

"Yes, could you open up a width of the pool so James can swim every day to help his recovery," Jana suggested.

"Consider it done; well, after all the celebrations are finished," replied Janet, and she got up and left their room, wondering what their conversation was really all about.

Janet remembered how the black tablet had been used to locate the Royal family in Canada and bring back a science paper that confirmed a comet strike on the planet sometime in 2030. But that had already happened. Susan had written her paper and been thrown off the airbase, so what was the point of it all? As she walked back to her bedroom, she noticed an eerie silence in the house, as if time itself was standing still.

4 – JANA

I remember being on that RAF airbase in England.

James and Ben were busy training with the hover plane, while Janet and I were planning how we could get back to her home on the Caribbean island. Thanks to the remote viewing device, we knew that although the pandemic ended in March 2021, quarantine was still in place for foreign travellers, and obviously coming back from the future, we hadn't been vaccinated.

When Susan and Bee arrived back from Portugal in August 2031, we knew there would be problems on the airbase and asked James if he could find a way to help us. We needed to return to the year 2023, when we expected the pandemic regulations would be lifted. After that, we both packed a suitcase, ready to leave at a moment's notice. Things had been made more complicated as my one-year-old baby had not been well for much of the summer, and I was desperate to leave.

Finally, James said he had permission to take the plane out the next evening and Justin came to take us to the craft for the short trip back in time, that James can better explain.

James didn't want to give our position away at the house. So, he decided to land close on the beach in Lime Kiln Bay. The front of the plane was partly underwater, but hearing on the intercom there was a lot of shouting in the back, he opened the rear door to let us out.

I told James later that we'd had to wade ashore. Ten minutes later, Janet went onto the intercom to say that the baby and all the luggage were ashore and James could leave. He closed the passenger door, raised the landing gear, and let the craft slowly drift down into deeper water in the bay.

Shortly after James and his plane disappeared, a large blue Toyota truck backed down to beach, stopped next to Janet, and out jumped a burly man dressed in a khaki uniform with a military cap.

"Mrs Romford, I presume," he said as if we had come out of Africa! The two embraced, smiling and laughing. This was the first time I met Sam. Now he's a good friend and head of airport security. He threw our luggage and handbags into the back of his truck and helped me climb up inside the cab with my baby, followed by Janet.

No one said a word about how we had arrived on the beach. There were no other people or boats in the bay, but reading his mind, he was very much aware of our arrival, the plane, and of James.

The next few weeks were a whirlwind of homecoming as Janet started to put her life together again. The first thing she did was to renew her British passport, which she found had expired. She saw it was possible to renew online, so I took a new digital photo that was accepted and, after sending her old red passport back, a new blue one arrived in less than two weeks. The house was large and spacious in places with amazing views of the sea. Janet gave me the master bedroom, for when James returns, she said, that gave me room for the baby cot and some space for him to play.

However, the best thing was the large indoor pool that was warm and clean to play in all the time. With Janet busy renewing her contacts on the island, I took to sitting on the top steps of the pool with my boy, watching small bubbles rise to the surface. In no time at all, with my baby on the step between my legs, we were feeling better, happier, and healthy. I asked what was in the water. Janet explained that the pool was fed from water that came heated from an underground source near the hills below the volcano. This water has lifesaving properties that you can even breathe underwater without drowning, or so she said.

I was also introduced to Lucy, a bright, bubbly local teenager who was happy to be the babysitter while we went out shopping. As I got closer to both Sam and Lucy, I realised they both were here on the island with James when the visitors arrived from the sky. Our only contact with the people still in the future was limited but made possible with the remote viewing device I brought with me. Janet and I looked at grainy images of Susan and Bee in the house on the airfield and we were concerned that this would not end well.

The next day, Janet announced that she would take a long trip to the US to discuss her business affairs with her company's investors. Reading her mind, I could see she really wanted to hand the plane back to the US authorities and end this investment. So, I prepared myself for living alone and spent many hours in her office acknowledging email requests and forwarding them to her iPhone.

Life was quiet at this time, and without any ID never left the house, except with Lucy to find fresh food. Sam dropped by from time to time for a beer and we became good friends. It was at that point that I decided to help James with his life, should he return in the next few months. Only then, I started to look at his dreams and memories from the past and remembered his interest in the MH370 event in 2014. The problem with the internet is that there are a million videos on YouTube that are of no interest, until I found a report on MH370 nine years after the event that made complete sense to me. Everything was there as we had experienced in the future: anti-gravity orbs following a plane and not UFOs, or whatever they call them now. It appears we have a new kid on the block who can't get enough of his newfound power and it all comes back to some top people in the US, but I'll tell you more after James returns.

When Susan returned from her travels in late 2023, she was very excited. First, she gave me a company laptop that she had at her office. To make it official, I've been appointed as Secretary to the Board of her Company in London. I have no idea what that means, but it gives me a good reason to be a resident on the island. Second, as a bonus, I was given a renewed passport for the Czech Republic, complete with a new photo we had taken at the house. Janet said I didn't want to know where that came from and explained she had someone working to find passports for Susan and Bee.

Reading her mind, she was pleased to have reached an agreement in the US to return the plane, but I was worried what that could mean, until the next day she explained.

"I've been invited to meet the new governor at a social event and will propose my project to sponsor two scientists. One in the field of physics to work at the observatory and the other to help increase the local food supply. The island needs to become less dependent on expensive imports," she said, before donning a regal gown. Having never seen such a costume before, I was impressed as she left in her car for a reception at Government House.

The next day, Janet summoned me to her office and asked me to find the latest Monserrat development partnership document on the

Gov website and a summary of the Advisory Committee on Montserrat Volcanic activity for 2023. She wanted them emailed to her to see exactly what we were up against before Susan and Bee arrived. I quickly found the reports, sent them to her, and waited. It was lunchtime before she asked me to join her for lunch, clutching a sheaf of papers.

I joined her at the kitchen bar where she had opened a bottle of wine with a frozen meal in the microwave and she explained.

"Did you know that Montserrat's economy has not recovered since the pandemic? 'There is very limited private sector investment for agriculture or fishing production, resulting in a high import ratio and dependence on imports for food security,'" she said, reading from the report.

"You know what that means in simple terms, Jana. The island is bankrupt and will go bust without more private support!" Janet exclaimed.

"Well, it's the same in my country in the EU. My Czech Republic belongs to this EU socialist club and has little money to manage the pandemic recovery. The country is not strong enough to transition to green energy," I replied, taking a glass of wine.

"Yes, well listen to this." Janet read more from the report.

"The GoM has expressed a desire for the Paris Agreement to be extended to them and are working to achieve Net Zero on this! Can you believe this rubbish written in a UK partnership summary," she said as the microwave pinged and Janet got the plates out for us to eat.

"Oh! It's chilli con carne today with rice, if that's okay. So, what do you think?" Janet asked as I nodded at the food.

"If they want to build wind turbines all over the island or solar panels, go ahead! They will be destroyed in the next hurricane that blows through, won't they?" I replied, taking a mouthful of food.

"No, these so-called experts are stupid, but not that stupid. It says here the island faces a vulnerability to climate change and extreme weather events. But it's been like that for the last twenty years I've lived on the island, so what's new? It's nothing to do with the climate, it's more likely to do with controlling the population. That's what they want. Do you think that's possible?" Janet replied.

"Yes, I found reports online of this strange group in Switzerland, almost like a cult. They are working on forming public-private partnerships with the United Nations. Something called Agenda 2030," I said.

"Hmm. I heard about them when I was travelling in the States. Some believe this climate change agenda is also a cover to depopulate the planet. Of course, this island would be much more valuable without any people to be supported," Janet replied as she cleared away our plates and prepared some coffee.

"So, you think that the GoM interest in NetZero for more regional funding might in fact want to reduce the local population?" I asked Janet.

"Not possible, but there's a disastrous situation at the US-Mexico border that looks to have been intentionally produced. Even under the current US administration, it's obvious that sections of the border have been dismantled on purpose to increase illegal crossings," Janet replied.

"You think that may affect us here? Look, I found online there's an interest in Central and South America with an intelligence-linked satellite company to turn the regions into equity and carbon credits," I replied, looking her fully in the face which made her spill her coffee.

"Then, astonishingly, every capital city of Latin America has eagerly signed an agreement, unaware of the strings attached to partnerships. The majority of municipalities in the region have made agreements with the same groups to join some project called GREEN Plus," Janet replied.

"From what I understand, this is a brazen attempt to assert foreign influence across Latin America and the region, including this island. The economy still hasn't recovered from the pandemic, the island is suffering a cost-of-living crisis, with low wages and unemployment, and in need of financial support," I replied.

"That's why I must go to the governor's office in Brades this afternoon, to make the case to fund these two science advisers. Can you tell me when they might arrive?" Janet asked more seriously.

"Oh! That's easy. Knowing James, he's most likely going to arrive during the carnival celebrations in March next year."

"You mean the St Patrick's Festival in March 2024? You saw that on your viewer thing?"

"Not exactly, just feel that it's the most likely. When the island is full of celebrations and visitors, and no one will notice two more."

"Alright, finish your coffee as I must dash to get changed." And with that, Janet got up, leaving me free to go and feed my baby boy. Half an hour later, Janet popped her head into my bedroom to ask how she looked, dressed in a grey business suit that I said would make a good impression.

"Did you read this year's volcano statement?" she asked.

"Yes, it shows a measurable increase in activity in the last year. They expect a further increase in unrest prior to the resumption of eruptive activity. Here you are; better take a copy with you," I replied, handing her the paper.

"Thanks, Jana, don't know what I would do without your support." And with that, she ran up the stairs to drive to her meeting in Brades.

Now all I have to do is work out how I can send the numbers 324 to James. My recommended month for his arrival in March 2024. Sounds easy, but he's still somewhere years in the future…

5 – SUSAN

From the moment we landed, I thought this was a mistake. Why did James bring us back to 2024? That gives us just six years before the comet impacts with our planet. Six years to do what on a Caribbean island that's about as far off the grid as possible on the planet.

I try to remember the last time I was happy; I mean really happy. I think it was when we first arrived at the airbase, and I started preparing my report. There was a military man in charge of security named Justin. He gave me an old laptop with a word processor to write my report. It was the summer in England, and we were living in an old house at the end of the runway with our two girls away from most other people at the base. The house had an amazing view of the Thames Valley below that flooded with water twice a day.

That was the last time I was happy.

I have started my work at the Volcano Observatory. It's about a ten-minute drive from the house, past Olveston House and up Hope Drive to a large white building sitting on top of a hill. Janet gave me a map and the old mini-Moke that comes with a difficult manual gear shift, but it's transport.

Anyway, I don't arrive much before 9 a.m. and leave at noon to be back in time for lunch with the girls, so not exactly serious.

The first time I parked, I went up the stairs and found the team inside. They all welcomed me, but really, I had no idea why I was there. Inside there were two Seismographs machines, but sadly not else much to see.

There is an observation room with a desk and a couple of screens with windows facing the volcano. Outside, on the viewing platform, I could see the ash damage in the distance on the Soufrière hills from the volcano ten years ago, but why was I here?

I walked around the observatory for two mornings, looking for clues, even climbed up onto the roof to check out the radio tower, but got nothing. Then on my third morning, I walked into the observation, and confronted the two young observers, ready for answers.

"How long have you two worked here?" I asked in a stern voice. They both looked at me as if I was a bit mad.

One replied that he was an exchange student from the UK, but the other man named Daniel confirmed he had been working there since 2022. He said he had come over with the new governor that year. I asked if they kept a daily logbook at the observatory and he got up and took me aside. We went to talk in a back room that was used to store reports and paper supplies, with a small desk and a chair.

"What dates are you looking for?" he asked, so I guessed and said early 2020. I knew the seismic monitors should have recorded any unusual events in February 2020 when the cylinder landed. Shortly after, he found the logbooks for the months of January, February, and March 2020. He placed them on the desk and left the room. I quickly ran through the logbook for January, found little of interest, so turned to the records for February 2020. All appeared normal until the twentieth of the month when the records suddenly stopped. Then blowing the dust off the book for March, this book looked unused as well. I stood up to be confronted by Daniel standing at the door with a mug of coffee, as he saw my concern.

"Found what you were looking for?" he asked, smiling, and handed me the coffee.

"There was no one up here for over a year," he explained.

"Yes, of course. The island was locked down with the pandemic. People were only allowed out to buy food and essentials, didn't that happen where you lived?" he asked. Obviously, that put me in a difficult position as I wasn't around at that time, so I ignored his remark.

But I was thinking. If the pandemic only started in the UK at the end of March 2020, why was the island already in lockdown at the end of February? Something didn't add up in this timeline.

So, I asked: if the seismograph machines were still running in February, would daily reports have been sent back to the UK from the radio tower, even if no one was at the observatory?

Daniel said he didn't know, but he knew where hard copies of all the seismograph reports for the past ten years were kept and that should include 2020. I left the coffee on the desk as he led me down to a storeroom in the basement. It was like going down the rabbit hole to another world of underground rooms and passages.

We found the printouts for January 2020 and February 2020, but then everything stopped. There were no more graphs until March 2021. Then observations started again – that was at the end of the lockdowns in the UK, or so he said. I took the recorded data for the first two months of 2020 back to my desk to study them in more detail.

I didn't bother with January, I just unrolled February 2020 in anticipation of my fears. The graph showed all the details with a massive seismic event at 3 p.m. on 19 February 2020, followed by a bigger event at noon on 20 February that went far off the scale. After that, there was nothing recorded at all. Nothing was recorded on the graphs of the seismic machines for another year. Perhaps the machines ran out of paper, or no one was allowed back after that. I started to wonder if this was due to the lockdown or more of something being covered up.

I rolled up the graph again and, checking to see that no one was watching, I stuffed the data into my backpack with my bottle of water and went outside. I remember saying goodbye to them for the weekend and everyone smiled except Daniel. He said a US tech team was coming on Monday to install a new dish at the observatory. It was a science project that would be on the local news, and they would want to meet me at 8 a.m. I left feeling a bit concerned at having been left out of the loop.

I remember driving back at breakneck speed, that probably wasn't that fast for an ageing mini. As soon as I parked outside the house, I ran inside to find James. He was sitting at the bottom of the pool with Jana holding a towel or a dressing gown. Looking around, the children were playing with Bee on a green carpet and looked at me in surprise, until Janet appeared and almost shouted at me.

"Oh good, you're back, because the governor called and wants to have tea with you at Olveston House at 4 p.m. Please, Susan, come to my office straight away," she ordered. I realised the bush telegraph on the island worked with amazing speed. I explained my discovery and showed her the data, but she wasn't impressed at all.

"What you may have done, Susan, is to put us all at risk. This might even expose where you have really been for the last decade. We need to prepare you for this meeting," Janet explained. She handed me an old mobile phone that she quickly took back. If you are going to drink with the devil, you need a long spoon. She went on to detail where we had been living, a fake life going back to early 2000.

"I'm going to let you look at all the reports as a guest on my PC concerning the fires on the island of Maui in Hawaii in August 2023. That's what you need to say at your meeting. This is where you and Bee were working and after your house was destroyed by the fire, you fled back to friends in California. This is all true and there is no longer any evidence of you ever being there; it was all destroyed by the fire. Then you met me and with all your work destroyed, we agreed to work together. You realise you will have to account for where you have been for these years, don't you?" Janet insisted. Although I wanted to object, I could see there was no way but to have a realistic alibi.

Two hours later, I thought I had a pretty good understanding of the fires in Maui and didn't like what I had found online when there was a knock on the door and Janet appeared again. This time, she was concerned about our lack of luggage. She had filed a baggage claim on the mobile phone for both of us with British Airways.

"You hacked the BA site," I mouthed, more in fear.

"No, there appears so much missing baggage with these airlines that you can report lost luggage online. Not all the bags ever get found, even if they never existed!" Janet replied, smiling.

"Here are hard copies of your baggage claim. Yours was a Samsonite blue bag and Bee had a smaller pink bag," she said and placed the papers in front of me. Before I could pick them up, Janet crumpled them in her hands and then handed the ball back to me.

"Smooth the pages out and keep them in your back pocket; you never know when you may need them," she insisted, smiling again. As I looked at the time, I saw I should be leaving. When I got up, she slipped the phone into the side pocket of my jeans and, giving me a kiss, wished me luck.

Walking outside, I thought how quickly we had moved from Earth 2.0 to something as just as unstable on Earth 1.0.

I got into the Moke and drove off, back towards Olveston House. After parking the car, I walked up towards the front of a tropical bungalow and thought this place looked quite posh. Realising I was still wearing my old jeans with a short-sleeve work shirt that was going to look rather out of place, I continued up the steps. The roof was covered with green vegetation, with a palm tree outside, that looked comforting. Once inside, I approached a young receptionist, who got up from her desk to welcome me.

"It's Mrs West, isn't it? I recognised your photo from the newspaper, with those two lovely girls at the airport," she asked.

That really caught me off guard, so I just nodded and smiled, but she went on. "Here to give your credentials to Sarah, are you? That's what all you celebrities must do, isn't it," she remarked.

"Actually, I've been working at the observatory and expect to get a reprimand, if you must know," I replied.

"Oh! Sorry to hear that. Sarah asked for a table at the end of the veranda; and as it's quiet, you won't be disturbed. If you will follow me then." She led the way out onto the veranda. Around a corner, at the very end, there was a table, laid with a pot of tea, two cups with milk and sugar, and a plate of biscuits.

Sarah stood up as I approached, and we shook hands. She was a short woman with auburn hair and a welcoming smile.

"Please sit down, Mrs West, and call me Sarah. It's good of you to come. In fact, it gives me an excuse to get out of the office on a sunny Friday afternoon," she said, beaming a smile at me.

"Look, if it's about the incident at the observatory today..." I started to say, but she held her hands to stop me.

"Oh! It's nothing like that. You're here to ask questions and I like that. Now, tell me as a scientist, what do you think of our Volcano Observatory?" Sarah asked.

"Well, err..." I stuttered.

"I know, it must be a bit Heath Robinson after your time at the CERN centre in Switzerland," she said, making it clear she had read my file.

"Well, I've got some good news, and the main reason for our discussion. A shipment arrived a few weeks ago. It's a new monitoring dish for the observatory and a couple of technicians will be setting it up on Monday morning," she explained, holding her hand up before I could reply.

"I know the office there is like a box. I've told them to get it painted, remove all the old papers, and put in a proper desk for your research. Does that make it sound better? Shall I pour the tea now?"

"Yes, of course," I replied, feeling a bit of an idiot.

"So, any questions?" she asked, adding milk to my cup before pouring the tea, as I must have looked a bit confused.

"Ah! I see you've forgotten the British ritual at tea time. We talk in silly pleasantries and then ask the real questions; that confuses most foreigners," she remarked, helping herself to a biscuit.

"And you wasted too much of your time on that dreadful Hawaiian island. Maui wasn't it?" she asked, smiling at me, as I started to feel most uncomfortable.

"Well, go on, tell me about what happened," she asked again more firmly. I was ready to burst and tell her the truth, that I was never on any Pacific island, but managed to force back my tears.

"Well, the fires started at the beginning of August 2023, and quickly spread to most of the town of Lahaina, where we were living. Bee, my colleague, and our two daughters were terrified, and we lost everything. Our possessions, clothes; in fact, we were lucky to survive," I explained.

"And the US authorities, did they help you?"

"Truthfully, not a lot. The state had set up evacuation shelters, but there were thousands of us trapped on the island and it took us over a month to leave."

"So where did you go?"

"First by ferry to the main island of Hawaii and then to Honolulu, where we found a plane to California. I still had friends there who put us up over Christmas," I explained, leaving out the details.

"So, when did you meet Janet?"

"It was purely by chance. She was in LA on a fund-raising tour for her UK company 'Clean Water Investments' and we told her we were desperate to get back to the UK."

"But you didn't go back, did you?" she asked, sipping her tea.

"No, because we signed a contract with her company to work here on Montserrat for two years, if the government will accept us."

"Yes, I see, and Mrs Romford filed papers for you both in February to work on the project. You know, Susan, it all sounds a bit strange to me? Leaving one tropical island to come and work on another in the Caribbean. I discussed the idea with the PM, and he has agreed to give you a chance, you will be pleased to hear."

"Thank you, that's good to know," I replied.

"Don't think we haven't checked on you. After some delay, the US agencies gave you both a good reference, even recommended that you continue your work, although I don't understand what Mrs Norton is going to do here?" For just a moment I had to think who this person was, and then realised she was referring to Bee.

"Right, I understand. She trained as a biologist in Scotland and continued her post-graduate studies at Cambridge. On the Pacific island, she cultivated over twenty acres of dry land by burning wet vegetation under a layer of dead branches. Burning the wood turns it into fertile soil. After that, she helped the locals grow tropical fruits, enough to feed two villages. That's what the Americans may be referring to," replied Susan.

"Yes, but it was all destroyed in the fires?"

"Mostly yes, but she's confident she can do this on some of the land I saw covered in ash from your volcano." I suddenly realised I hadn't touched my tea, so I picked it up and drained the cup.

"Very well. I'm happy to give you both a chance, but this island is quite different from the Pacific. I don't want any science reports, but would like to meet you here, from time to time, to keep me in the loop. If something happens of concern, you can call me direct. You have a mobile phone from Janet, I believe. Let's exchange numbers now," she asked, placing a new iPhone on the table. Having no idea how to this, I took mine out and handed it to her. Sarah connected the two phones and handed mine back.

"If there are difficulties up at the observatory, just call me," she said, indicating the meeting was over, and I stood up to leave.

"Oh! One more thing. Has your luggage turned up yet?"

I stopped and reached into the back pocket of my jeans, pulled out the two lost luggage claim forms, and placed them on the table. Sarah took one look at the BA logo, checked our names, and handed them back to me.

"It's nice meeting you, Susan. You do seem to have lost a lot of things in your life recently." Her phone rang, so we shook hands and she waved goodbye.

As I walked back towards the reception, I noticed three women sitting at a table at the other end of the veranda. A young local teenager with black curly hair looked at me and smiled. But one of the women with their back to me looked like Janet. I recognised her dress from earlier today at the house. I quickly turned away in surprise and when I reached the reception desk, the girl took one look at me and remarked, "Looks like you kept your job then."

A comment that I ignored and continued walking back down the steps feeling much more confident about my interview. I got into the mini to drive back to Janet's house on the Old Bluff road.

6 – BEE

I really wanted to leave that horrid RAF base in the UK and thought anywhere with Susan and the girls would have to be better. The flight back was frightening, although we had been on that plane after we returned to 2030, on the island off the coast of Portugal.

The last time I was really scared was when James helped us escape on the plane to the airbase near London with our two girls. It was there that I first met Jana. On the pretext of looking for James, I took the girls to the creche at the camp and found her there. She insisted we went to her house to look at a remote viewing device. It's like a tablet that can see our memories from the past. We drank some wine and on opening the tablet, I saw us back on the island where we landed with James. What I saw was so scary that I wet myself. Same happened here when we arrived here.

When Janet insisted, we went back to the airport. I was already upset after the flight, thinking that James was dead. These local men at the airport were all singing and clapping and made me think I didn't want to stay a day longer.

After the St Patrick's festival, Janet brought some workers who took up some of the wooden boards so that James and the girls could swim widths down the pool. The workmen also erected a barrier around the pool with a gate, so it was safe for the children. Janet took me out to the terrace on the side of the house with an incredible view down to a small beach far below. She was looking for some old swimming kit that her children had in the past. Only then did it hit me that she was a mother too, with Jasmine, her daughter, and her son Ben, who remains on the other side.

That's how I must think of it; we are in this place now and they remain in another dimension, six years in the future. Sad really, but that's how I deal with it. Of course, I never had much to do with her son, Ben. He was always around Michelle. They were two young people so much in love. I also miss the US soldier Anita, who did so many amazing things on the submarine, when we escaped from Amarna, but that's all lost in the future now.

With Susan working up at the observatory, I take the girls swimming in the pool in the afternoon. Janet found me a costume and some flotation aids to help the girls get confident in the water and it's been a great success. I don't know what's in the water, but I feel much more positive now after a few dips.

Janet told me she ordered some tropical plants last week that I can look after on the terrace when they arrive. Maybe things are not so bad after all.

Susan was asked to meet the governor today. She left the house before 4 p.m. and everyone else left later, when we were swimming in the pool. After that the children were tired, so they ate an early supper and I put them to bed. While I waited, I was looking online in Janet's office for more news when I heard Susan had returned.

"Hello, Bee? Bee, where is everyone," I heard her shouting until she found me in Janet's office downstairs.

"Here you are. You know, I think I saw Janet at Olveston House after my meeting," Susan asked.

"Possibly. She left with Jana when the girls were swimming."

"Oh! You're looking on Janet's computer," Susan said.

"Janet gave us both access as guests on her PC, so I've been looking at the latest videos on YouTube, like I used to do at Uni. So how did it go?" I asked, looking at her confident face.

"Sarah, the governor, asked a lot of questions, but it was okay, thanks to all the preparation Janet gave me. I'm not sure if she really believes our story, but it's difficult to disprove the Hawaiian fire because that happened."

That started to upset me because even if the events can't be disproved, we were never there and that still worries me.

"But did you tell her exactly where we were on the 8th of August, on Maui, because we both need to agree on this," I said.

Then I suggested: "Let's say we took the girls for a day out to a beach down the coast. We found the roads all blocked when we tried to return that night. Are you on the same page as me now?"

"Yes, of course. Don't worry, I didn't give too many details. So, you've been looking online at this event, have you?"

"Of course, it's horrific, destroyed the capital Lahaina. There are still 6,000 people living in Red Cross camps, set up as temporary accommodation. Susan, you need to be clear on this, because we were never there."

"Agreed. I looked online before, but only for a short time."

"Well, this is going to come up again, unless we keep to the same story. I've taken a few screenshots of the event and will put a folder on your desktop if you give me your password."

"Yes, my password is *susan1.0* if you can do that."

"Great, so what else happened over your cup of tea?"

"Well, err… She asked what you were doing on Maui. Obviously, she has checked both our past records online."

"Alright, how did you answer?"

"I said you had cultivated two fields of land with your slash and char and planted crops to feed local villages!"

"What, Susan! I never planted anything when we were in the future. Remember, we only watched the Amarna woman do all that."

"I know, but let me explain. She said that a new satellite dish is going to be installed at the observatory on Monday."

"Okay, but please tell me why this governor was ready to accept your Maui story. Can you remember her exact words?"

"Yes, she got a good reference from the Americans. They recommended that I continue my work," Susan replied.

"Really! So you see, they recommended you continue your work, not me. I'm just along as a sideshow. It's all about your work. I'm beginning to think the US authorities know about us but don't want to let the UK in on the secret," I said.

"Well, NASA must know there's a plane here on the island, locked up on US property. The governor can do nothing to find out, except by allowing you to work on the island," I replied.

"Perhaps, but this will give me the opportunity to understand what happened with the volcano before the pandemic. Sarah needs me to keep my job to see what this new dish can do after installation."

"Alright, and now that you have a mobile phone, she can see everywhere you go. You do understand that, Susan, don't you?"

"But how do you know about my mobile phone?"

"It's already been added to your home page, see here," I said, as Susan looked at the icon on the screen in surprise. Susan asked what she should do, and I told her to leave the phone at the house if she didn't want to be followed. Then I asked to check out the phone Janet had given her, and she handed it over.

"Oh! I remember this model. It was the iPhone 6 that we all had before we went off for training in the States. Yes, it's registered as a company phone to 'Clear Water Investments.' That's Janet's Company."

"That's what I told Sarah, and she wants to meet me at the same place for updates," Susan replied.

"I bet she does. Nothing moves in the Caribbean without Uncle Sam and she's not in that loop."

"So, what can I do?"

"You know what. This phone may be old, but it still has the basic features like sound recording. We used to record boring lectures at King's College in London. Why don't you take it to the observatory on Monday and see who turns up. This new dish sounds strange. You can record the conversations when they come to install the dish. Sarah didn't tell you what it does, did she?"

"No, I guess she has little idea. But how do I do that?"

"I'll show you. Go to Utilities, open Voice Memos, and say, 'Begin voice memo,' then press record. When you arrive on Monday morning, turn it on before you get out of the car. Then secure it in the top chest pocket of your work shirt and let it record. Hopefully, we can listen when you get back; it's that easy," I explained.

"Okay, maybe I practice when I next go out with Janet?"

"Right, because Janet's taking us to Mary's clothing store down in Salem tomorrow morning with the girls."

"And how are we going to pay?"

"She's going to give us both five hundred dollars to buy something more suitable for the tropics. She said she will leave us at the shop for an hour, as she's going to pick up a local girl, who we need to meet," I replied.

"Now that does sound mysterious," Susan replied, then added that she wanted to take a swim to clear her mind, and I went back to my research on the internet.

***

Next morning around ten, together with the girls, we piled into Janet's car and drove off towards Salem. When we arrived outside, everyone was most excited, but my heart sank as this wasn't anything like a boutique shop in England. It was exactly like a clothing store in the Caribbean! Still, going inside, the girls loved it, as they had never seen anything like this before. They couldn't believe all the colourful green costumes that must have been left over from the carnival, until they looked at the sweets and jars of candy.

After half an hour, we managed to find some regular beach clothes and t-shirts for the girls and with some help from the owner, we found some work shorts and shirts for Susan and me that mostly fitted us. Then it was time to find sandals and flip-flops for the girls, who were amazed as well. Having made our purchases with those Eastern Caribbean dollars, I couldn't help but notice that Queen Elizabeth II was on every note we paid with. To end our excitement of the morning, Susan bought us all ice cream cornets while we sat outside waiting for Janet to return, by which time the ice creams were finished.

As the car approached, we saw a young local teenager sitting in the front. Janet got out and opened the trunk where we put our purchases and sat in the back with the girls on our knees. After we drove off, Susan whispered this was the girl she had seen after her meeting with the governor. I found it odd that no one said a word except the girls who were giggling and laughing while they ate the sherbet lollipops I had bought them.

It's only a five-minute drive back to the house on the Old Bluff, so after parking at the front of the house, we all got out and Janet introduced Lucy, an old friend who was known to James in the past. We all shook hands, with a kiss for our girls, and collected our purchases from the car. Janet announced that Jana was preparing a BBQ for lunch and we went inside the house. It was clear to me that Lucy was amazed at the changes to the entrance hall. A part of the pool was now open and the rest boarded over as a children's play space. It was as if she had been here before in very different circumstances. We went downstairs and the excited children opened their clothes and put on shorts and their flip-flops for the first time in their lives.

Once we had all changed into more casual clothes, I went looking for Janet and Lucy, who I guessed would be preparing the BBQ out on the terrace in the sun. To my surprise, Janet had already opened a bottle of chilled white wine and handed a glass to us both. The girls followed us and ran to sit at a small table with picture books and crayons, and then the real surprises started.

"Come over here, you two," Janet asked as we looked down onto Lime Kiln beach that looked calm and deserted, except for a few birds.

"Four years ago, at the end of February, an alien spacecraft landed close on that beach. Over five hundred survivors, all looking human, were found just sitting on the shore," Janet explained.

Susan tried to interrupt, but Janet waved her to silence.

"There are only two people on the island, apart from James, who can remember this event, because by March, the island went into lockdown with the pandemic and all those people had left," said Janet, and I realised this was what we were really doing on this island.

"And who are those two people you mentioned?" Susan asked, as Jana circulated to fill up our glasses with more wine.

"Well, one was Lucy here, getting to know your girls over there at the table. The other was Sergeant Sam of the US Special Forces, now responsible for security at Osborne Airport. He has our full trust up to now," she replied.

"But, Janet, how could you not tell us this before?" Susan asked.

"Because, had you known the reality, you might have let the cat out of the bag and Sarah would have spotted it at once."

"She knows?" I asked.

"No, not everything, just suspicions. The previous governor left under a cloud and said he had no recollection of any such events. He was disturbed by what happened, so that's probably good for us," Janet replied.

"My God, Janet, that's most scary, because both Susan and I saw what happened on that island when we returned to the airbase. We don't want to see this again. Those people in the future are dangerous," I warned.

"Yes, we know that, and Jana has seen most of those images on her remote viewing device. But now is not the time or place to have a detailed discussion. This is a children's party today," Janet replied, smiling at Jana to start cooking the lunch. After that, I kept drinking the wine to try to forget everything that happened to us in the future.

As if that wasn't enough, Jana cooked shabar flat fish for the girls, as she knew they liked this fish. I was ready to speak out as I knew this was a freshwater fish, until I spotted the BirdsEye box and saw it was frozen. Susan and I helped the girls to eat at the table in the shade and Jana started cooking hot, spicy chicken for us grownups.

After we finished lunch, Lucy came to talk to me. I don't remember everything she told me, except that she had helped James remove most of the human aliens from the island. He had told her to visit the Group Airbase in England in 2030 and asked if I knew where it was.

I was going to lie, but then I saw her face and those big, brown eyes looking at me and I just burst into tears. Finally, I was able to compose myself and almost whispered to her that was where we had just come from. I just said you don't want to go there.

That was all I could say, as after I showed her where I was going to grow the plants on the terrace, I was away in the world of plants that I so love. It was then that she told me she would find a group of women to help me grow the plants on the island. Only they knew from the past the places below the volcano where the plants would grow and I saw that she was someone who could help me and my project. Then I realised she was still a teenager, so asked what year she was at school.

"Oh! I'm now in year nine and going to college next year to take the Caribbean Advanced exams. Janet has invited me to come over and stay for the Easter holidays. I'll have time to help get your project started and take care of the girls if you would let me do that," replied Lucy.

"Yes, that would be great," I said, smiling, as suddenly a big window of opportunity had opened, so I asked some more.

"We haven't seen James today; has he now recovered?"

"Yes, he had to leave on one of his trips abroad, but you have to ask Jana if you want to know more."

"Well, I hope he hasn't taken that hover plane," I mentioned.

"No, he doesn't need that. He has his medallion, to jump to other places. I think that's called teleportation," she replied and with that, we went back inside to find the children.

PART TWO
INVESTIGATIONS –
Spring 2024

7 – INTERVIEW

Justin Benbow of the Royal Marines was on leave at the Army and Navy Club in London. He'd been to the Royal Opera House with an old girlfriend, drunk too much champagne, and ended up back at her flat in Knightsbridge, after midnight.

His partner that evening was a tall, slim brunette named Pam. They had known each other since his school days. Now, she was a thirty-something-year-old freelance journalist, who usually asked too many questions to annoy him. On entering her flat, she kicked off her shoes and went to look for some chilled wine. Justin, meanwhile, slumped down on the sofa, waiting for her to return.

"Come on, Justin, you can tell me the story of what really happened on the island of Montserrat four years ago," she asked, opening the bottle of white and placing two glasses on a low table in front of them.

"Oh that, nothing much really. Over one day and back the next. The problem with the island's telecommunications was sorted and we came home," he replied, finishing his glass of wine.

"And you've been having nightmares ever since?" she asked knowingly, refilling both their glasses again.

"Yes, it was strange. A Caribbean island with a population of over 5,000, and we never saw anyone. No one, during the whole two days we were there. No people, no birds, or animals. Nothing at all," he said.

"Right, but that was during the lockdown, where all the people were told to stay at home. Same thing happened here in London as well, you know," Pam replied.

"No, this was more than a month before the lockdowns started here in the UK. When I came back, I tested negative, so I don't think the island was infected. Where was everyone?"

"You didn't see the people on the beach then?"

"What people! No," he replied.

"Really, Justin. I made a FOI request years ago, after you first came back. I received a copy of the previous governor's report a few days ago. It's mostly diplomatic gobbledygook. Refers to a boat land-ing with migrants from South America. That doesn't make much sense to me. Would you like to have a look at the report?" she asked.

"Not really. That must have happened later. Sometime after we left the island," he replied, feeling more uncomfortable.

"Last week, I followed up this lead and found he's now retired from the Foreign Office. When I tracked him down to a retirement home in Surrey, I was told he suffers from advanced dementia. Only receives visitors from the family and most certainly not anyone from the press. So, what do you think, Justin?" she asked.

"Look, Pam, it's those Queen's Regulations again, isn't it?"

"Except, it's the King's Regulations now, isn't it?" she replied, pulling her dress up to her knees, offering for him to stay the night.

"I sorry, but I've already drunk too much tonight, so won't be much use to you. I really enjoyed the opera and seeing you again. But think it's time I get back to my Club," he explained.

"As you wish, but the truth about this story will eventually come out, you know," she replied, standing up and smoothing her dress down again.

Justin went to the toilet before he left. He looked at himself in the mirror, a haggard face after years of denial. *That's what's still in my mind in the middle of the night, when I can't sleep* – he thought…

Why do I have to lie? What else do I have to lie about? Straightening his tie, he ran his fingers through his hair and, opening the door, he found Pam waiting for him with the door of the flat open.

"Thanks, Justin, for a great evening. I will be expecting your call the next time you're in London," she said.

"Definitely. Call you when I'm back from Scotland," he replied and, giving her a big hug, he walked to the elevator. Outside in the cool evening air, he found a London cab and was soon back at the club in Pall Mall.

***

The next morning, he was feeling hungover from the night before and ate a late breakfast in the dining room downstairs. The date was Monday, middle of April 2024, when a waiter came and asked him to come to reception to take an urgent telephone call. It was his commanding officer, who gave him new instructions.

"Justin, while you are on leave in London, we want you to meet with someone at the Home Office. You need to do this before you depart for your final training in Scotland. A confirmation will follow, and this is of national importance," he said, and the line went dead.

Later that morning, he received a hand-delivered formal notice to a meeting at the government offices in the afternoon. Justin looked at the official card and decided not to wear his uniform. He dressed in a navy blazer and his regiment tie, as he remembered the minister was a reserve officer in the army as well.

In the early afternoon, he was on his way to the meeting with the Home Secretary at the offices in Marsham Street, Westminster. As the taxi approached the impressive building, he had some doubts about this as he walked up to the entrance. He showed his invitation and was escorted upstairs to a modern office for the meeting.

"Justin, good to meet you at last. I've read your file, and I'm impressed with your past activities in the service. Come and sit down on the sofa and I'll explain what you're here for," he said, shaking his hand and leading him to a more comfortable chair.

"Thank you, sir. It's a pleasure to meet a fellow officer. But is this meeting to discuss military affairs or something closer to home?" Justin asked.

"While I'm responsible for our borders, visas, and immigration, we have a situation that's left over from one of our previous PMs. We need you to help us with that," he replied.

"I see. Is this something to do with the mission to Montserrat I was sent on before the pandemic?" he asked.

"Yes, I'm afraid it is, and your name is the only one that came up. Remember you worked with a naval officer on that mission, who went over to the US army? We believe she is active again."

"I understand, so this does have to do with the armed forces?"

"Yes, indirectly. The island in question has used the Chief of Police from another British territory on a temporary basis. The governor is now pressing for a new permanent Chief of Police," he replied.

"I see, so it's not a military appointment at all," Justin replied.

"No, but as I mentioned before, we need someone on the ground to keep us informed of how future events occur from a military perspective. We thought you would be the best person for that."

"So, who would I report to with this intel?" he asked.

"Oh, the governor of course. If you accept the position, your reports will go to our intel persons involved already. You must know there's an election coming and we expect to be booted out of power."

"Yes, I've followed some of that on the news."

"You can expect that the new incoming government will be the full version of a socialist power. They already promised to close all the steel plants in the UK and now want to shut down North Sea oil and gas. Of course, imported steel will mean fewer new warships and you can expect the army to suffer further cuts as well. So, I'm afraid a long commission in the Marines is, well, perhaps, looking more uncertain."

"Really? I had no idea this was coming so soon," replied Justin.

"They want to reduce our military capabilities so that we have little power to stop the civil unrest coming from different religious people in some areas of England," he proposed.

"You mean they want uncontrolled civil war to increase?"

"Not openly, but that's what some are thinking. That will enable them to force the next part of their plan. Which is to introduce Digital ID on all UK citizens, to gain complete control," he said.

"So, you won't see me in this office again, and we don't want to pass this island problem on to the new government. They appear to have more interest in building windmills," he explained, smiling.

"Yes, it's an interesting proposal. What's the timing on this appointment?" Justin asked.

"Nothing urgent. I understand you still need to complete your final training. In the meantime, your file will be sent to the governor for her approval. Your relocation should take place in early June at the latest," he said, standing up to show Justin the interview was over.

"You said the governor was a woman?" Justin asked as they reached the door and shook hands again.

"Yes, her name's Sarah. She's our best hope of keeping a lid on this delicate matter. Once we get her approval, you'll be provided with a full briefing," he said, leaving Justin with an older secretary, who showed him the way out.

Justin took a taxi to back to the Club in Pal Mall, that took almost an hour with all the ULEZ speed restrictions and cycle lanes.

When he finally arrived, he was stopped at the front desk by the concierge to sign for a large envelope marked "Private and Confidential." He took it up to his room to open.

Inside, he found a contract of employment with the Royal Montserrat Police Service, with a description of the structure and duties of each rank of the RMPS local police force. Instead of being offered the Chief of Police, it appeared his offer of employment was as the Superintendent of Police or "Sup Ops." On reflection, he thought this might be less of a political position and allow him to focus on the operations on the island. He was being asked to sign the document by return in a brown envelope enclosed when he found another paper marked "Confidential. Read and Destroy."

On opening the paper, he found it was a list of names of contacts already on the island, starting with the governor, Sarah. As he read down the list, he found the name of Sam, the navy seal he had worked with in 2021; now the head of security at the airport. Lower down the list was Janet Romford, entrepreneur and benefactor to Susan West, an astrophysicist. Her previous career was at CERN, Switzerland, and then the High-Altitude Observatory on the island of Maui (unconfirmed) followed by another English-trained horticulturist Bee Norton (also unconfirmed). It continued to people he had seen on the island – James Pollack, and the naval officer Elizabeth K, at which point, he burnt the paper in the metal wastebasket and then sat down to sign the contract.

When he opened the return envelope, he found a first-class ticket on the Caledonian sleeper that evening! Seeing it was leaving at nine fifteen from Euston Station in two hours' time, he quickly sealed the contract inside and rushed down to the reception to check out.

"Excuse me, but I need to check out tonight. I've been called up on an urgent deployment tonight," he blurted out, handing over the sealed letter to the concierge.

"I see. You are Marine Officer Justin Benbow, if I remember correctly," the man replied, looking at his screen.

"Yes, I need to catch the overnight sleeper to Scotland tonight."

"No problem, sir. Your account at the Club has already been settled. You won't be joining us for dinner tonight, will you?"

"No, I don't think I have the time. Please can you return the letter to the people who delivered it this afternoon," he asked.

"Of course. I'll call the delivery company right away. Perhaps you would like the chef to prepare some steak sandwiches and a bottle of our red wine to take on your journey," he offered.

"Yes, that would be great. I'll go and pack now and vacate the room in the next half an hour, then come down to take the sandwiches."

"No rush, sir. I'll arrange for a taxi to be waiting outside at 8.30 p.m. You'll have plenty of time," he explained.

Justin went back to his room and thought about what to pack. He never travelled in uniform and his blazer was a bit smart, so he chose a casual shirt and jeans, perhaps with his highland sweater, in case it was cold, he thought, and on top his green military jacket. After getting dressed, he placed the rest of his kit in an officer's heavy-duty holdall and, looking at the time, saw he still had some minutes to spare, so decided to call his commanding officer to confirm his travel plans. Finding his personal number was engaged, he was transferred to his Marine base, where he left a message. Then, taking his jacket and the holdall, he went back to reception to check out. There he found the concierge again, who passed a carrier bag over to him.

"I've given you our picnic basket, but you will need to pay an extra thirty pounds," he asked.

"That's alright, here you are," he said, giving the man a good tip, and asked about the courier.

"Yes, the man came already and collected it. Have a safe journey," he replied. Justin thanked him and went to find the waiting taxi outside. Shortly before nine, Justin arrived at Euston Station and walked inside to find the platform with the night sleeper. Showing his ticket to an attendant on the platform, he was told to look for a carriage further down. Finally, he found the first-class cabins, where he was welcomed by a female assistant who showed him to a twin-berth cabin.

"Look, I think there's been a mistake. I'm travelling on my own," he asked.

"No, the booking here clearly states a twin club room. Sorry, and there are no more single rooms available tonight," she replied, handing his ticket back to him.

Justin smiled, said thank you, and closing the door, she left him alone. Justin threw his jacket and holdall up onto the top berth and sat down to look at the contents of the picnic basket. Five minutes later, there was a knock on the door; when he opened it, he found Pam standing outside.

"Hello, James, found you at last," she said.

"What the hell are you doing here?" he asked.

"You said you were going to Scotland, so I followed you."

"What do you want?"

"I'll tell you what I wanted after you left me alone last night," she said as she entered and started to close the door.

"I'm going to fuck you all night! All the way to Glasgow, where I will get off the train," she told him.

"And what if I don't agree?" he asked.

"Oh! I've already got a story ready to publish. British Army officer visits minister at the Home Office in the dying days of the Tory government. Won't embarrass you away on manoeuvres, but the reserve officer won't like it," she threatened.

"You wouldn't dare, not after all these years. You know I can have you thrown off the train," he replied, when, with a sudden lurch, the train started to move forward, and Pam fell into his arms and they both kissed.

"Too late, Justin, we've left," she said, looking at the table.

"Oh! What do we have here? A picnic basket for two and a bottle of wine; excellent," she said, smiling, sitting down next to him.

"Calm down, Justin. It's only a one-nighter. I'll make sure you enjoy it," she said, squeezing his hand. Then she remembered the newspaper article that she thought would stop him dead.

"I picked up a copy of the *Evening Standard* at the station while waiting for you. Have a look at this photo taken on Montserrat over a month ago," she said, reaching for the paper, and she opened an inside page about international news.

"Says here two British scientists arrived at Osborne Airport on Montserrat island with their two ten-year-old girls," she said and then continued.

"They have been sponsored by Janet Romford. Susan West is to work at the Volcanic Observatory and the other, a Bee Norton, to develop horticulture." Justin looked at the names in disbelief.

"Well, I guess you know all about this," she said, but before he could reply, the door opened, and a ticket inspector saw them sitting together on the bed reading the newspaper.

"Tickets please," he asked in a quiet voice.

"Yes, of course," replied James, searching in his jacket for his ticket and handing it over to the inspector.

"Thank you, and the lady," he asked.

"Sorry, but she only joined just before we left and tells me there wasn't time to get a ticket before," Justin replied.

"Army, eh!" the inspector replied, looking at the bag on the top berth.

"You know there's a fifty quid fine for boarding a train without a valid ticket. Still, in the circumstances, I'll waive that if you pay her fare for travel in a club room," he asked.

"That will be £305 single, to Glasgow is it, love?" he said, smiling at her. James found his wallet and paid the cost on his credit card. After that, the inspector handed her the ticket and left the room. Justin looked at her and they both burst out laughing.

"Pam, how did he know you were going to Glasgow?"

"Because that's where you get off as well. I looked online and found that the only place for infantry training is the Garelochhead

Army Camp near Faslane. So, that's where you must be going. Didn't you get any military instructions?" she asked.

"*Err*. Not exactly. I called and left a message, but no reply on my phone so far," he replied.

"Forget it, Justin, can you lock the bloody door, and we can relax at last. Do you want to open the wine, or shall I do it?" she proposed, as he took off his jumper and thought life was not so bad after all.

*****

The sleeper train arrived in Glasgow just before six the next morning, and as they prepared to leave the train, Justin asked, "Can you take the picnic box; I'm not going to need that."

"Sure, Justin, and you'd better take my copy of the *Evening Standard*," Pam replied.

They climbed down from the carriage and stood together on the platform while Justin looked at the other passengers leaving the train.

"Thanks, Justin. I hope your training goes well. I guess I owe you three hundred quid?" Pam asked.

"No, that's my treat, after such a wonderful night. We must do it again," he said. They kissed for a final time and she left, walking down the platform in the early dawn, holding the carrier bag with the picnic box.

Justin looked at his phone and found no message for his new deployment. So, he started to follow her down the platform to leave the station. When he reached the station entrance hall, he looked around to see if any military personnel were there for his transport. In the distance, he saw a US sailor leaning against the wall smoking a cigarette and walked towards him.

"Hi there. I'm looking for transport to the training camp."

"Great, and who might you be?" he asked.

"I'm an officer in the Marines here for military training."

"Name please."

"I'm Justin Benbow, of the Royal Marines."

"Good, as we're on a fast operation here. You walk to the exit on the right where you will see a white van. I'll join you there," he replied, turned, and walked away. Justin did as instructed, found the van, and waited outside with his holdall as the sailor returned.

"Get in, get in," he shouted. Justin jumped into the van that drove away at a fast speed.

"Sorry about that, but I was parked illegally. It's great to meet a real British officer. Now, we're on a tight schedule to make the midday tide," he said, driving north out of Glasgow. Justin watched as the miles passed and they drove up past Loch Lomond and then west towards Faslane.

"You ever been on a submarine before?" the driver asked. Ten minutes later, they were stopped at the gates to the Faslane naval base. The driver showed his ID and Justin took out his military issued card and the gate opened to let the van enter.

"Look, I'm sorry but I think you have the wrong person. I'm here for training at the Garelochhead centre for infantry training. Not on some bloody submarine," Justin said forcefully.

"No, my orders were to meet and transport Royal Marine officer Justin Benbow to our submarine here. You need to complain to the captain of my boat, because we're inside the base now," he replied, as they continued down to the docks and stopped on the quay alongside a very large and impressive submarine.

"There she is, the *USS Albany*. She's a Los Angeles–class attack submarine, one of the best in the fleet. Come on, we need to get you onboard. Captain wants to sail at midday," was all he said.

When Justin climbed out of the van, he looked up at an enormous black sail tower above him, as he realised this was a very big ship. He followed the sailor, who walked across a small gangplank and disappeared down an open hatch behind the tower. Justin followed and a voice from below told him to throw his bag down and climb down the ladder. Once inside the submarine, they walked forwards through the control room, to the officer's quarters and arrived outside the captain's cabin.

"Right, I'll leave you here to see the captain," he said, when a young man appeared from inside to welcome him.

"Lieutenant Benbow, good you made it onboard. I have your commanding officer on the horn if you need to speak to him," he said, leaving the compartment free for Justin.

"Justin, sorry I didn't get back to you yesterday, but our American friends wanted this done as a covert operation," he said.

"Right, sir, but what about my infantry training?" he replied.

"Oh, that. You completed that course last week and are already commissioned in the Royal Marines as a full lieutenant."

"Thank you, sir, but what am I doing on a US submarine?"

"You are on your way to do some different training now. After that, you will take up your position on the island sometime in June. Do you have any more questions?"

"Yes, sir. I saw in a London newspaper a report that two British scientists arrived there over a month ago. Are they my local contacts?" he asked.

"I haven't seen that report, Justin. We are looking at a fast-changing situation there. You must take this operation step by step. As you know, this is of national importance," he replied.

"Yes, I understand, so I don't report to you anymore?"

"Correct. You report to Captain Castello whilst onboard his boat and the governor when you reach your destination. Good luck and safe sailing," he replied, as the line went dead. Justin opened his holdall and took out the newspaper when the captain returned to the cabin.

"Everything good with the army then?" he asked.

"Not really. Do you know what I'm doing onboard here?"

"No idea at all. We were only told last night to take you onboard. We do occasionally get Special Forces insertion requests."

"Well, I'm not Special Forces. I have a newspaper article here. It shows two scientists arriving on an island in the Caribbean a month ago," he said, showing the newspaper to him.

"Yeah, that looks like one happy family photo! If you've got a posting there, you should be a happy man," he replied, laughing.

"But why on a submarine, when I'm not due there for another month?"

"Look, I don't know what you Brits have got into, but it must be important. When I get some instructions to drop you off, I'll let you know. Until then, let's find you a place in the officer's berthing. I need to take this boat out of here in less than an hour," he replied, as Justin realised he had no choice but to accept the situation.

8 – USS ALBANY

With Justin onboard the nuclear submarine at the Faslane Naval Base in Scotland, he followed the Chief of the Boat down to the officer's racks where the men were sleeping.

"Well now, not sure what we're going to do with you, but you can stow your kit here for now," said Arnell, not happy about his insertion on the submarine at all.

"Right, follow me back to my chief's quarters where you can wait as we're sailing, and I'm needed in the control room for that. There are books on regulations in there you can read, and I'll get some coffee sent to you. Do not leave this room, understood?" Arnell ordered.

"Got it," Justin replied and sat back on the bench seat, wondering what he was going to do on a submarine for over a month. It was some two hours later before Arnell returned and sat down with him again.

"You may want to know that we have left the mainland and are proceeding underwater on a new mission. The captain has been given a list of our mission objectives and from now on we don't talk back to home when we're on a mission status," he explained.

"Right, so can you tell me what my mission objectives are?" Justin asked.

"No, we don't communicate, because that can give away our stealth advantage, so we pretty much operate autonomously until the mission is complete," he replied, looking at his watch.

"Understood. What duties do you want me to do onboard for a month?" Justin asked.

"Yeah, that really depends on what training you did in the Marines," he replied. Then an enlisted sailor put his head around the entrance and said, "Chow's up, Chief."

"Well, I know enough about navigation that in thirty days at fifteen knots, your boat can cover about ten thousand nautical miles. Our destination from Scotland could be anywhere from the Pacific Ocean to Antarctica," he replied.

"Correct, going on global routes. But we rarely do that as we may have other objectives on the mission. You want to join me and get some food so you can meet some of the crew?" he replied.

"Actually, I think I need to change into my uniform shirt and pants. Don't want to look like a tourist," he replied.

"Okay, I'll send someone to take you back to your kit. Then you may prefer to eat lunch in the officer's mess."

"Yes, I think that would be more appropriate," he replied. Justin changed and was led back to the officer's mess. There he was welcomed and pressed by the junior officers for his possible destination, that he declared was unknown or "classified." What he really wanted to know was if anyone would give him a job to do for the next month, so he sent out some feelers.

"I did a couple of tours in the Middle East where my training was with navigation and developments on the GPS. Any of you do that on this boat?" he asked, which was met with a big silence.

He realised no one was going to give him any help on this subject. After lunch, he was left alone, looking at the US flags and photos on the wall of the *Albany* commissioning in 1990. He was still wondering what he was doing when a sailor came to take him to see Costello in the captain's cabin.

"Come in, Justin, and pull the door closed. We need to have a talk. So far you have impressed the chief with your knowledge of voyage times and frightened my junior officers asking about GPS," he said.

"Sorry, sir, I was just trying to find something to do," he replied.

"So, do you know where we're going on this mission?"

"No, sir. Although I think you have to drop me off somewhere in the Caribbean, as my next posting is on an island there," he replied.

"Really, because I asked and have received some intel of your past record that I don't understand," he said.

"Okay, what do you want to know?"

"Let's start with your mission on that island," he began.

"It was a straightforward insertion with a joint US/UK team made up of US Special Forces with Royal Navy and me – the Marine on the team," Justin explained.

"You didn't know what to expect at the start."

"Right, but we knew the island was surrounded by a magnetic force field. The airport was closed and all sailings to the island stopped. This was a covert operation, so we took a twin-hulled dive boat and just sailed. The US mission was to retake the airport while we were tasked with destroying the force field."

"How did you plan to do that?"

"I was an enlisted man at that time with little idea of what to do. We were given some kit sent out by UK scientists. It was a simple weather ballon, two bottles of hydrogen, and a box of aluminium foil!"

"But it worked, didn't it? Can you confirm these names I received?" he asked, handing a paper to Justin.

"Yes, Sam was Special Forces, but I never knew the name of this other American. The navy lieutenant defected to the US army after the crisis, so no idea where she is now."

"Well, I asked and was told she wasn't available, same with the Special Forces man. Told he could not be moved, so they came for you. Can you explain why you're needed on my ship?" he asked.

"No idea. I only took the posting to the island after some political pressure. I realised after there were other forces at play on this island, like a semi-active volcano that has magnetic properties. Maybe we didn't destroy the field after all," Justin proposed.

"Lieutenant, none of this makes any sense at all, does it?"

"No, sir. That's why they made me an officer, so I couldn't talk to the lower ranks about this mission."

"And what happened after the field went down? There were images of people on the beach, weren't there?"

"Yes, sir. Migrants. But I can't confirm or deny that. It's classified by our Official Secrets Act, sir."

"Right, so do you know where we are heading now?"

"I have no idea. Except my duties on the island don't start until the beginning of June. If the time taken to sail from Faslane down to the Caribbean is only about fifteen days, this boat is going to be needed somewhere else for almost a month. Hypothetically speaking, of course," he explained.

"Very well, I'll let you settle in onboard before I can decide on what duties to give you. Until then, spend your time in the officer's wardroom and learn as much as you can about the operations of a nuclear submarine," he replied. Justin stood up and saluted, and then paused at the door as the captain spoke again.

"Don't talk to anyone else about this, Lieutenant," he said, and Justin replied with one word: "Understood." After that, he went to the officer's mess to find out when his "rack" would be available for him to sleep and found they were scheduled to an eight-hour rotation, so he could take his bunk in another hour. Then, having eaten, he returned to the officer's rack for his night's sleep.

***

The next morning, on his way to find breakfast, he saw men were installing something electrical in the wardroom. When he sat down to eat, Arnell, the COB, came to tell him the captain wanted to speak to him and he got up to leave immediately. Justin was hoping to find what duties he might do as he entered the captain's cabin and closed the sliding door.

"Ah, Lieutenant, come and sit down. After our discussion yesterday, and with the agreement of the COB, I've decided to give you access to some of our training files in the wardroom," he told him.

"Thanks, I'm sure that will be good on my career path."

"No, Justin, that's more of a cover story. You need to understand that we are constantly receiving intelligence updates on our mission, but we can't reply and break silence to reply. So, I've decided to give you access to one program concerning scientific updates, that I want you to read and give me your input on a daily basis," he asked.

"You can log on with the screen and keyboard in the wardroom and the following ID," he said, passing a folded note over to Justin. When he opened it, he saw *ID: pirate* and *password: Benbow,* which made Justin grin.

"Thank you, sir, for putting your trust in me," he replied.

"Yeah, I thought the ID was appropriate in your circumstances," Castello said, smiling.

"There are already some five files received on this program, all with the same name and consecutive numbering. I will update you with the latest daily. Take your time and we can discuss what's going on here when you're ready," he suggested.

"Yes, of course," Justin replied, standing up to leave.

"I'll add some of our basic training videos later, in case any of the juniors ask what you're doing," he added as Justin left his cabin, not sure what to think of this development.

Justin went straight back to the wardroom, where he found a screen and keyboard sitting on a small desk in the corner with a single chair. When he switched on the power, it revealed a Submarine Force Atlantic welcome page that required a login and on entering his ID, a new page opened with just three files named: ICE CAMP WHALE.

On opening the first file dated March 2024, he found a description of how the camp on the Arctic ice sheet was set up with personnel from the US Navy, Royal Canadian Navy, French Navy, UK Royal Navy, and the Royal Australian Navy.

He guessed that was where they were probably heading right now. The next two reports from the joint base in Alaska were about the *"ICE camp really is one of our squadron's bread and butter exercises."* It was clear that the military of five nations had done this before. Justin kept himself busy for the next five days, watching training videos, much to the amusement of some junior officers in the wardroom.

Then on opening a new file from the end of April 2024, everything changed. This was not from the Submarine Force, but from NOAA about space weather. NASA's Solar Dynamic Observatory noting solar flares spawning from two active, large and complex flares that had appeared on the solar disk. Maybe this was why the captain was asking for his opinion. He logged off and walked forwards along a long corridor that led to the control room, where he met the COB standing in his way.

"Stop, you're not allowed in here," the chief insisted.

"Well, I need to speak to the captain," he replied, catching his eye at the far end of the room. The captain beckoned to the chief to let him pass to talk to him.

"So, you read the latest file?" he asked.

"Yes, we're going to the ice station," he replied.

"We are transiting the Davis Strait as we speak. That leads to the North West passage and then we'll be under the ice," he replied.

"And we're going to break through the ice?" Justin asked.

"Of course, that was on our primary mission objective; the crew are most excited. Perhaps we were selected because of you."

"Really, why's that?" Justin asked.

"We received intel today asking if you are still onboard. Obviously, I can't reply to that, but someone at Camp Whale wants to meet you as soon as we arrive," he replied.

"Anyone you know?" Justin whispered.

"Not personally. I hear she's a lieutenant like you. Been doing AUV research, so must be bright."

"But will we arrive before this aurora storm starts?"

"Maybe, but geomagnetic storms don't affect these regions close to the North Pole. If it starts, we'll drop you off and submerge. Then come back and pick you up again when the storm is over," he explained.

"Understood, I'm really looking forward to this," Justin replied, knowing he was completely out of his depth on almost everything they had discussed.

9 – THE DISH

Meanwhile, back on the island of Montserrat, it was also a Monday morning at the end of April.

Susan showered and dressed in her old clothes of blue jeans and a work shirt to return to her work at the observatory. Then she went to find a coffee, where she found Bee sitting at the kitchen bar, already dressed in shorts and a t-shirt.

"You're up early, everything alright?" Susan asked.

"Yeah great, just wanted to make sure you have the mobile phone and know how to turn on record," Bee said.

"Yes, all powered up and ready to go," she replied, handing the phone to Bee and filling a mug with coffee.

"You know, I've been thinking about the installation of this dish, and it sounds most suspicious to me. We know the UK is all fucked up with political chaos and the king is suffering from cancer, but why can't this be done by the British Government?" Bee asked.

"You mean it's more likely to have been agreed with the US and paid for by NASA or one of their space black operations," Susan replied.

"Yes, we need to hear who you meet and how this project is promoted to you," said Bee, handing the phone back to Susan.

"Wow, this coffee is good, much better than we had before! Look, it's almost 8 a.m. I gotta run and take the short drive to the observatory," said Susan, picking up her small backpack and walking to the entrance door, followed by Bee.

"Love you and don't take any crap from the Yanks," Bee shouted at her, as Susan waved, got into the Moke, and drove off. She passed Olveston House and up the hill to the observatory.

On her arrival, there was just one large open truck with a big wooden crate on the back. Two men in khaki clothing were preparing to open the crate as Susan parked close to the other cars, carefully took out her mobile, and pressed record. Then she placed the phone in the top pocket of her work shirt and walked across towards the truck.

"Good morning, you're here to install the new dish?" she asked, when after a short pause, one of the men jumped down off the back and came to greet her.

"Well now, you must be the prof in charge of this project," he asked in a clear American drawl with a big grin.

"Yes, I'm Susan West and recently arrived on the island," she said, which she immediately regretted. The men were young, had no insignia on their khaki work clothes, and were definitely not British.

"Well, howdy, ma'am, my name's Ollie. We're all the way from Tennessee, here to set this contraption up for you. Up the mast, we were told," he replied, pointing to the radio mast above the observatory.

"Yes, of course, as high up as possible," she replied.

"No, ma'am, it's got to go on that platform there to get the satellite connection," he replied, pointing to a place in the sky.

"Right, so it's got to be carefully aligned to what exactly?"

"Well, I guess it's to the top of the volcano, but we can't see that today with all those clouds," he said, sounding confused.

"Well, maybe it's not the summit of the volcano, but I can align that in my office later," she replied, realising they were not going to tell her more and wanting to go back inside. Then she hesitated and asked, "You did bring the alignment instructions, didn't you?"

Just as the front of the wooden box burst open, they saw something that surprised her. It was not a dish, just a large metal pole.

"Yes, of course, will bring it to you as soon as we get the receiver up on the mast," he replied and walked away to help his partner.

Susan was feeling the heat from the morning sun, so walked towards the entrance of the observatory and went inside. First, she removed the iPhone from her top pocket and, pressing the stop record button, walked up the stairs to the offices on the top floor. On entering, the two observers looked up and Daniel ran over to welcome her.

"Good morning, Susan, did you talk to the men outside? Did they tell you what they want to do?" he asked.

"Yes, they're from the States and I have no idea what's going on," she replied.

"Okay, let me show you to your new office and maybe I can get you a coffee," he said.

Susan went inside to find a modern L-shaped desk, newly painted, with all the old files removed. She sat down on a high-back chair, placing her backpack on the floor, and looked to see there was a 26-inch screen on the desk, with a black box beside it, when Daniel entered.

"There you go, your coffee for today," he said, smiling.

"Ah, I brought back the data records that I took to study over the weekend. Can you put them back in the room downstairs?" she asked, taking them out of her backpack.

"Yes, of course, I'll take them down now," he replied.

After he left, she looked at the screen and, reaching for the button, switched it on. When it came alive, there was a welcome message on the screen to Susan West with her photo, but nothing more. She pushed some of the keys on the board, but there were no other connections. When Daniel returned to her office, he looked puzzled.

"When I returned the records to the basement, I saw that all the missing records had been replaced. So, I looked at the next one and it was all blank and the next one… they were all blank?"

"Yes, Daniel, I think some people are trying to cover their tracks, but don't worry about that now," Susan replied, drinking her coffee.

"Can you keep an eye from the observation platform and tell me when the dish has been installed," she asked, feeling more concerned about what was happening outside.

Susan spent the next hour on her phone, looking at observatories around the world and with no news, went to look outside. She found both observers on the platform, looking back towards the radio mast.

"Looks like it's finally installed," shouted Daniel's assistant, but when she looked up, it was just a tall pole mounted on the platform. Feeling bored with the lack of progress, she went back inside to look at the observation screen with the camera on the volcano summit. Everything looked normal, some smoke or perhaps cloud, but nothing unusual until Daniel shouted out to her.

"Susan, you need to come and look at this now." She ran outside and looked up, only to see the dish had opened and looked similar to the James Webb receiver millions of miles away in space.

Taking her phone out again, she took a couple of photos of the small imitation and went back inside. She sent one copy of the image to Janet with a short comment – WTF. Going back to her office, she sat down and was going to look for the specs of the JW telescope when her screen came alive with a photo and details of the telescope outside.

This replica has a 2.5m-diameter gold-coated primary mirror made up of 6 separate hexagonal mirrors. The mirrors have gold coating to provide infrared reflectivity and covered by a thin layer of glass for durability. This telescope can also observe objects in the Solar System at an angle of more than 85° from the Sun. This includes Mars, Jupiter, Saturn, Uranus, Neptune, Pluto, their satellites, and comets, asteroids, and minor planets at or beyond the orbit of Mars. In addition, it can observe dangerous and unplanned targets within 48 hours of a warning to do so, such as comets and gamma ray bursts.

Susan sat in front of her PC, taking screenshots of all the telescope details provided. She took her mobile out of her pocket and pressing record she said out loud, "*comets, asteroids and minor planets at or beyond the orbit of Mars, might this be a program to track the BB comet...*" when she was interrupted by Ollie at the door of her office. Placing the iPhone next to the PC, she left it on record.

"Good to see you got online already. It's impressive, huh? Well, not quite as impressive as the real JW, but a nice smaller replica. Now I need to align it to the coordinates we've been given," he said.

"Yes, I had no idea this was being developed somewhere in the US. Have you installed this on other islands?"

"Yes, this is as far east as we've gone. I have a schedule we need you to follow," he said, pulling a card from his back pocket. Ignoring his comment, she pressed him for more information.

"So, which other islands have you installed this miniature telescope on?" Susan asked.

"Well, *errr*... Barbados and St Lucia, but that's confidential."

"And what is this triangle of telescopes actually looking for?"

"That's confidential as well," he replied.

"Really, if I don't know what the target is, how can I help you track it?" she reasoned.

"Look, all I need you to do is keep a watch on the screen here from 8 a.m. until noon and again from 8 p.m. to midnight. More instructions will be sent when it's operational," he said.

"Well, that's a lot of observation time for one person. Can't I share this with one of the observers here?" Susan asked.

"No, these observations can only be done by you. You've been designated as the person responsible for this project on Montserrat," he replied.

"I signed up to install and monitor this project and you signed up for your position here. That's unless you want to leave the island," he said, trying to make her position quite clear to her.

"Alright, Mr Ollie. I'm a trained astrophysicist who understands how astronomical telescopes work. I've completed observations on some of the largest telescopes on the planet and this fake receiver can't track anything in deep space. At this low altitude, it can't see through the atmosphere with all the cloud and dust from the volcano. All I need to know is the name of the person or company who built the replica, and perhaps we can work together," Susan replied.

"Well, putting it that way, perhaps there is something we can work together. Me and my partner were looking at your pictures when you first arrived on the island, and we got thinking. What's two attractive women doing on this island… without any men," he said and paused.

"Yes, do go on."

"Okay, so here's the deal. If you get more friendly with us, come down and have a few beers at our house down in Woodlands, we can perhaps answer some of your questions," he proposed.

"Well, that's quite an unusual idea, and I need to check with the other woman if she would agree to such a get together."

"No, it has to be both of you, and I would like to start this coming weekend. Perhaps we can meet down on that beach close to where you live; would that be more convenient for you?" he asked.

"Yes, that's a good idea. Now, it's past noon so my duties here are over. I'm going to leave you here to set up the alignment, or whatever it is that you need to do," Susan replied. Picking up her phone and the backpack beside her desk, she left the office as fast as she could.

When Susan got outside, she was shaking and took the water bottle out for a drink to help her calm down. She had stepped out into the full heat of the morning sun. Her skin flushed as the backs of her knees started to sweat. Then she stopped the recording on her phone, put it back in the top pocket of her shirt, and looked around. The truck that had brought the dish was gone and she started to walk back towards the Moke. She stopped to take a shot of the dish on the radio mast and, turning around, saw a man sitting in the shade under a tree. She recognised him as he waved and walked towards her.

"James, whatever are you doing here?"

"Hello, Susan, I think you're going to need my help," was all he said as he climbed into the Moke beside her. Susan reversed the mini, crashed through the gears, and drove off at speed down the hill.

"Tell me, James, what the hell's going on on this island?" Susan shouted at him, as hot air rushed past them in the open car.

"Pull into the car park at Olveston's and I'll explain," James replied, pointing at the driveway to the big house. Susan turned off the road and parked in the shade under a tree, and they faced each other.

"Look, I chose to bring you back in 2024, because that's when the comet enters the outer solar system. I thought this would give us time to understand what went wrong with NASA's calculations. Sadly, this planet today has turned out to be much more unstable than I expected," James said.

"And you thought that with Janet's plane we could find a solution, by doing what? Going into space to intercept a fifteen-mile-long comet? You must be mad," Susan replied, glaring at him.

"Alright, it's going to be more difficult than I thought, but what happened today that upset you so much?" he asked.

"Two American dudes came here today. You know the type that hit on young women looking for sex. He said they saw our photo when we arrived and thought we might want some male company!"

"He said that in your office?"

"Yes, he insists on meeting us on that beach below the house on Saturday. James, he must know about us coming back. I mean, it doesn't take a lot to work that out. Maybe he found out that Janet's plane is at the airport from that technician we saw. Then we appear the next day and they put two and two together. He also threatened that if we didn't comply, we would need to leave the island."

"Great, so what did you answer?"

"Obviously, I agreed, said something about asking Bee. Then they want me to look at a screen for eight hours a day, inside a hot, airless room. You know, James, we should never have come back," Susan said, with tears in her eyes, handing her phone over to James.

"Listen to the tape. I recorded everything from the moment we met this morning. He said they have installed the same receivers on three islands, in a triangular formation, but at this altitude they won't see much past the moon. So, what's this all about, James?" she pleaded.

"Really! But if that's true, they're not looking to monitor anything in deep space, but something 120 miles above our heads!"

"You mean what? The ISS?" Susan asked.

"Yes, the International Space Station, and this has become much more dangerous than I imagined," James said, handing her phone back.

"I'm going to have to leave you, Susan. I have to go back and see what's being done inside the observatory. Drive straight back home now and tell everything to Janet and Jana," he said.

James got out of the Moke and disappeared behind a tree. When she looked again, he was gone in a puff of dust. Susan rubbed her eyes and smiled at last. She had heard about James and his teleportation, but never seen it before. Starting the engine again, she drove slowly back towards the house on the Old Bluff.

10 – ON THE ICE

We join Justin on his nuclear-powered submarine now in May 2024.

"Waiting for permission to vertical surface. We are perfectly hovering at zero speed. All personnel must no longer walk around the boat. Stationary surface NOW, Stationary surface NOW."

The order is repeated around the ship, as Justin, with the captain, wait in the control room for the submarine to break through the ice.

"We should have a helicopter up there. The space is only about 300 yards wide and runs a mile straight north and south. This is the only place where the ice is thin enough to surface through," Costello advised Justin.

"The tower is strong enough to break through the ice."

"Yes, but it must be a perfect hover. We use ballast with seawater, or the boat would tip over," he replied, as the confirmation was made on loudspeaker: *"ON SURFACE NOW, ON SURFACE NOW."* Justin looked at the captain as he explained the procedure.

"I'll be the first to go up to the bridge so we both need to go and get dressed. Follow me and we'll get you some Arctic protection from the cold outside. Better if you wear some of our submariners' clothes underneath," he continued. Justin followed the captain back to his cabin where a man was waiting with Arctic trousers, a fur lined jacket, and with boots and gloves.

"It might be negative twenty to thirty degrees when we get up there. I'll go on ahead to clear the ice off the top of the sail and raise our mast. You go with this man and get changed like me," he said, pulling on his warm Arctic pants. Justin followed the sailor. He was given an officer's blue uniform and told to change in the wardroom.

"I'll come back with your Arctic kit shortly," he said, eyeing up Justin's size to ensure a good fit. Once Justin had changed, he was checked by another officer to make sure his protection was good.

Wearing his hooded jacket and with goggles on his face, he was declared good to go. Justin was led forward towards the control room that gave access to the hatch up to the bridge. As he climbed up the ladder, he was hit by the cold Arctic air coming down from outside and gasped at the change of temperature. On reaching the top, he pulled himself up onto the deck plate of the bridge and looked around. All he could see was the huge expanse of a flat ice field and the orange tents of the Whale Camp in the distance. Meanwhile, the captain, with the COB, was pushing blocks of ice off the sail, down onto the hull.

"You'll have to wait some more while they fix a rope ladder so we can climb down onto the ice. Pretty impressive, eh!" Costello shouted, waving at the people below. More crew arrived to fix two short access ladders on the submarine. The first down from the sail onto the hull and the second down onto the ice.

"Watch your step as I go down first, then follow me," Costello ordered. Justin watched as he climbed down and then followed him to join the captain, who had been greeted by a small group from the camp.

"Justin, come and meet Mathew Jones, who's the Commander of Ice Camp Whale for 2024. He's going to be your main contact during your time here," Costello said, as Justin and Mathew gave each other a high five with their Arctic gloves.

"Come and walk with me back to the camp and tell us what it's like living on a nuclear submarine," Mathew asked.

"Different, very different from anything I've done in the Marines," Justin replied, as they walked back through the snow towards the camp, leaving the captain behind.

"Yes, I forgot you're a serving officer in the Royal Marines. You must have trained on those big UK assault ships, very different from the cramped conditions inside a nuclear submarine," he replied, but Justin wanted to know more about the forecast aurora storms.

"Tell me, have the geomagnetic storms started here?"

"Why yes, they started a few days ago, on the seventh of May. We expect them to peak on the tenth, with the strongest auroras for a century," he replied. Justin was confused. When he looked up at the sky, he saw nothing, and Mathew just laughed.

"We don't usually see the lights here; we're too close to the pole. In May it only gets dark for an hour and a half, so you may not see the lights at all, I'm afraid," he replied. When they arrived at a large tent used as their control centre, Justin turned around to take one last look at the ice floe, and no longer saw his home, the *USS Albany*.

"What happened to the submarine?" he asked, pointing across the ice to where they had just surfaced.

"Oh! He didn't tell you. Your captain had to submerge again, to protect his ship from the coming magnetic storm. Don't worry, we have two nuclear submarines out there, all on standby, just in case anything happens," he explained.

"What do you mean in case something happens?"

"Let's not get ahead of ourselves, shall we. That's in case the ice floe should break up. It hasn't happened in the past four years, but we have enough boats to take all sixty of the personnel to safety at any time! Let's go inside," Mathew replied.

On opening the canvas, Justin stepped inside to find a much warmer temperature and a round of applause from a group of people sitting at a table inside. A young fresh-faced woman got up and advanced to shake his hand. Justin pulled his gloves and face mask off to outstretch his hand.

"You must be Lieutenant Benbow, I presume? The pirate from the nuclear submarine," she said, shaking his hand to much laughter.

"And you must be the lieutenant with the AUV," he replied.

"Yes, Lieutenant Mercedes at your service. Welcome to Camp Whale. Please come and get a hot drink," she replied, as the rest of the people came to congratulate him.

Justin was handed a mug of something hot that had been spiced with fruit and rum. He took one gulp and thought this had to be better for the next few days. Looking around, he saw banks of electronic equipment, communication equipment with lights flashing, and lying on the floor was a hydrogen balloon. Justin sat down in a daze with all the chatter until Mercedes came and sat beside him.

"We know it's tough living on one of those boats. You just missed one of your exes who left this morning. She told us to talk to you," Mercedes said.

"You don't mean Officer R.N. Elizabeth, do you?"

"No, she's a captain in the US army. Flew in yesterday on a Canadian flight and flew out today on the twin otter aircraft that supports the ice camp," she replied.

"Really; so what did she want?" he asked.

"She told us what you did on the island with the hydrogen balloon and surprisingly, she told me a lot more," she replied, pointing to the balloon on the floor.

"Alright, now you have my attention."

"No, not here. Come and visit my AUV tent later when you've settled in and I'll tell you her story. Sorry, but I need to go now," she said and, standing up, went to talk to Mathew.

After that, Justin was taken on a short tour of some of the experiments at the camp, everywhere except the AUV experiment, and finally to more basic sleeping quarters for the men. He found he had left his kit behind on the submarine, so he asked if they could provide him with a toilet bag for his stay. Then he found a small canteen where a meal was being served. When he sat down with his plate, he was joined by Mercedes, who came and sat beside him.

"Wow, surprise, we meet again, so what do you think of the camp? If you're ready to come and see my AUV equipment, follow me out of the door when I leave and I will explain," she said.

Justin waited until they finished and followed her to a large tent that was also heated. It was a tent like he had never seen before, with solid plastic flooring and a long hole cut in the ice and a crane above where the AUV was resting. Grey billows of insulation hung down from above and facing them on the wall was a sign that said: "Laboratory for Auto Marine Sensing System."

"Come on in, no one else is here. We finished the test an hour ago and everyone went home or went to eat like you. Good thinking, Benbow," she said, smiling at him.

"So, what did Elizabeth K say to you?" he asked.

"God, you're so bloody direct, you Brits. She said no one would believe her about what happened with the cylinder, so she went over to the US military. Can you believe that?" Mercedes asked.

"Yes, that's quite possible. Our government has no interest in such things unless they land on the grass outside the Houses of Parliament," he replied.

"And then she said she saw stars when the force field came down. So, you did fuck her, pirate, didn't you?"

"OMG. If she saw stars, she saw stars. But I didn't, does that answer your question," he exclaimed.

"Alright, here's the deal. She told me that another object will land close to the ice station during the height of the magnetic storm in one or two days' time," she said.

"What! Can you confirm that?" Justin asked.

"Partly yes. I looked online at ATLAS. That's the Asteroid Terrestrial-impact Alert System website. They have an early warning for small objects that might enter the Earth's atmosphere. It reported this object was of no concern; pieces might land anywhere on the ice miles from the camp. You believe that?" Mercedes asked.

"So, Elizabeth came to warn us," he replied.

"Yes, and I told the Camp Commander and was told to say nothing to anyone about this. Did you see how your sub left in such a hurry after they dropped you off? They know but can't say the truth. All about the fear of creating a panic," she replied.

"Okay, so what do you have here to destroy a force field?"

"We have three hydrogen balloons at the camp. One up to two thousand feet, another up to a thousand feet, and the last at about five hundred. What does the best job?" she asked.

"Honestly, I'm not certain, but I don't think this field goes up very high. We attached a box of tin foil to our balloon, that created a huge storm in the tropics. That might create days of snow here and make matters worse," he replied.

"Yeah, we can adjust the balloons to only go up from 500 to 1,000 feet with no cloud seeding. Why do you think the force field will come down around the camp?" she replied.

"It may be some kind of short protection to allow time for it to land, without being aggressed by the locals. If the subs remain under the ice, there's not much they can do, right. But if it lands close to the camp, what would Mathew and his team do?" he asked.

"God only knows. But we do have this AUV that we programme to investigate seawater at different depths. It could be made to look at something on or under the ice up to a mile away. Maybe look even further if it should submerge. What do you think, pirate?" she replied, smiling.

"Probably against research regulations, but good thinking. Not much else we can do tonight, so let's see what happens," he said, getting up to leave.

"Yeah, thanks for dropping by. See you in the morning for brekkie? Around eight, if you're not busy," she replied, with a wave as he left the laboratory. When he walked outside it was twilight, and the sky was full of green auroras that looked quite ominous. When he reached the men's tent, there was a group of people outside with mobile phones taking pictures of the green lights in the sky.

He quickly ducked inside the heated tent to make his way to his assigned camp bed, only to find a toilet bag by the pillow with a note. He put the note in an inside pocket as he couldn't read it in the dim lighting.

Settling down on his bed, he fell asleep, waking up just before local time at 7 a.m. and made his way to the toilets and washroom to shave. Justin walked to the tent for breakfast with Mercedes. He saw her sitting alone at a table at the back and taking a mug of coffee and hot porridge with honey, went to join her.

"Hi, how did you sleep?" she asked, smiling at him.

"Good, slept better than I ever did on the *Albany*," he replied, looking at her in daylight for the first time. She was young, with straight orange hair, rosy cheeks, small mouth, and a dimple. Definitely a science geek, he thought.

"After you left, I went to our control room to check out some videos about your mission four years ago," she said.

"What do you mean? Anyone in the navy can find this stuff online?"

"No, of course not. Only persons with a high-grade research pass and even then, it was hard to find," she replied.

"Anything that included me?" Justin asked.

"No, it was a shot of a man running down the beach into the force field and being thrown back. Remember that?" she asked.

"Yes, only too well. Showed exactly what we were up against. Why's that important?" he replied.

"Because he died of cancer two years later," she said.

"By chance or coincidence?"

"No, a massive dose of radiation that he never recovered from. If the field comes here, we need everyone inside and in lockdown," she replied.

"So now you can see how dangerous these visitations would be," he said.

"Got it! So how did you get ashore in the first place, with the balloon and bottles of hydrogen?" she asked.

"We swam ashore underwater down a channel, pulling a flotation bag behind us," he explained.

"Clever Pirate, but then you couldn't get out again."

"Correct. It was like that hotel in California. You can check in, but never check out. Anything else?" he asked, smiling at her.

"Yes, I saw a photo of hundreds of people sitting on a beach; what happened to them?" she asked.

"The governor reported them as migrants. Arrived on a boat and all left in a week. Another great British cover-up."

"Okay, and the cylinder that crashed into the sea?"

"Oh! That was real. I dived down to check it out, almost as big as a cruise ship. Then it got moved up onto the beach and the people woke up from their sleep pods," he replied.

"What do you mean by sleep pods?" she asked.

"Oh! It's just an idea that on long journeys through space, travellers would be put to sleep in cryogenic chambers. We called them sleep pods and saw hundreds of them," Justin replied.

"You don't expect me to believe that, do you?"

"No, you don't have to. You can check out my story with Sam, the navy seal who was with us on the mission," he replied.

"Do you have a number to reach him?" she asked.

"Yes, of course. He's my contact on the island in charge of security at Osborne Airport. I have his number on my phone, but it's with my kit on the submarine," he replied.

"Even if I believed you, we can't start calling international numbers from here, it would look suspicious," she said.

"Very well, I understand. Also, I had a note from Mathew to meet him at nine, so it's time I should leave," he said.

"Thanks, Lieutenant, for telling me your story. It's been most interesting," she replied, as he put his jacket on and left the tent.

Justin walked over to the control centre as fast as he could, as he was already ten minutes late. He entered through the double doors to find a group sitting around the table and guessed the meeting had already started. He pulled off his jacket and sat down on the only vacant seat at the table.

"Welcome, Justin, I'm sure you have been active with your own private discussions; would you like to share them with us?" Mathew asked, as everyone turned to look at him.

"Right, okay. Do you want to know what I think is really going to happen in the next two days?" he asked everyone.

"Some of you at the camp may have researched the ATLAS website of any objects that might hit the ice during the solar maximum that will peak in two days' time," he replied.

"Yes, we all know that, but we lost all satellite communication after the storm last night. We want to hear your advice," Mathew interrupted.

"Alright, talking to the AUV people, it is possible that if this thing lands close, there may be some kind of force field placed around the camp. So, if this happens, and only if this happens, we need everyone to remain in their tents," said Justin.

"Okay, but what's this got to do with the AUV? I mean, apart from the pilot being an attractive woman," someone asked.

"No, listen, this underwater vehicle may have the ability to force this object to submerge and allow the subs to destroy it," he replied.

"The AUV can do nothing hostile. The subs maybe, but that's only possible if it's under the ice. Don't you see that, mister?" someone else shouted at him.

"Sorry, you seem to know about this. Alright, let's talk about balloons, shall we?" Justin asked in desperation.

"Yes, we have three. If the force field comes, we'll go with a low-energy solution that may be the best way to earth the power and destroy it," replied Mathew. As the meeting started to break up and everyone went to drink their special coffee, a member approached him.

"Look, mister, I know you came from that boat to try to help us, but that AUV woman needs your help! She's been without a man for three months, so as a Marine, some think it's your duty to help her," he told Justin, winking at him.

Justin realised that in such a small community, people watch each other all the time and replied, "Wasn't there another visitor? A US army officer who left the day I arrived? Was she any help to any of you?"

"Oh her! She only went to talk to the AUV team and left the next day. We have no idea why she even came," he replied and quickly moved away, so Justin went over to speak to Mathew.

"Later, Justin… I need your help to check on the network of beacons surrounding the camp. Might do you good to get out of here for a few hours," he suggested.

"Yes, great, that would be good to see the orientation of the camp from its perimeter," he replied.

"Okay, get your boots and gloves on and meet me outside in five. You can join me on of our electric snowmobiles. It's a distance of three miles around the camp," he said.

When outside, they walked towards the parking space for the snowmobiles.

Once the machine started, Justin climbed on the back and hung on as the machine sped away east across the ice. They travelled along a partial snow road that bounced in places on the uneven ice until they reached the first GPS beacon planted in the ice.

"We've upgraded the old beacons with new RTK-GPS units that provide data accurate to the centimetre level rather than metres. These new beacons measure small-scale deformation before they become cracks and trigger an alarm in the command tent," Mathew explained. After checking the power in the beacon, he stopped and looked at Justin.

"I heard you talking about the visit we had with a past colleague of yours, after our meeting. She upset Mercedes with the idea of an alien visitation here. You don't think it's true, do you?" he asked.

"Honestly, I think it's unlikely. Why would an alien want to land on this freezing wilderness?" Justin replied, pointing to the bare ice and cold.

"Thank you, that's what I thought as well. Although we have seen some unusual craft around here," Mathew replied.

"Really, and what kind of craft might these be?"

"Just the usual circular flying saucer. What they call UAPs today, but we know they are all ours," he replied.

"They have mastered anti-gravity and all that?"

"Must have, the base here is powered by just a box. Provides electricity, hot water, heating for the tents, everything for the camp, and no radiation," he told Justin. "Right, let's move on to the next beacon."

Justin wanted to ask more but decided to wait until they finished. When they returned to the snowmobile park, he asked, "Do you know where these craft are based to visit the camp?"

"Not officially, but we think they fly out of Prudhoe. Nowhere else close that's US territory and a great place to train pilots over the ice," he replied.

"Really, so this camp has several functions, does it?"

"Yes, several covert functions! Come on, let's get back and find some lunch," Mathew said, smiling at him. They walked back to the canteen tent together and ate lunch. Justin then made an excuse as he wanted to talk to Mercedes again about his latest discovery. On entering her AUV tent, he found it was full of people doing a scientific experiment, so he sat at the back and waited for them to finish.

Justin listened to the conversations about salinity and a GPS system until they all finally left, and Mercedes came to talk to him.

"Well, hello, if it isn't Admiral Benbow again. I looked at your forbearers online and found an interesting person of action in the Caribbean," she said, smiling at him.

"Ah yes, and the first chapter of Treasure Island with the 'black spot'," he replied, grinning back at her.

"So, what's new, Justin? You look worried."

"Went outside to check the beacons with Mathew, who told me there are UAPs flying around here that belong to us," he said.

"Oh that. Yes, I've heard rumours, but never seen one myself. What's your problem with that?" she replied.

"Nothing really. Will they come if the aliens land outside?"

"My intel doesn't include everything from our National Intelligence services, but I'm told they may come tonight," she replied.

"What! You can't possibly know that unless... Elizabeth?"

"Yes, she texted me. We have our balloons at the ready."

"Right then, so the whole camp must know by now," he said.

"Probably, as everyone's running around today," she replied.

"And you've programmed the AUV to investigate?"

"Yes, as best I can. But only if it lands within a couple of miles from us," she said.

"Right, I'll go and get some rest then, ready for tonight."

"Or you can stay here at the laboratory to keep me company," she asked him suddenly.

"I'm not sure if that's such a good idea, but where?" he asked, looking around the cramped contents of the room.

"I have a pullout bed in the corner over there. Honestly, Justin, I'm frightened," she replied, as her phone came to life.

"OMG it's landed! I've just got this text," she exclaimed, and held it up to for Justin to see, as alarms sounded all over the camp.

"Ah! A message for you from Mathew. You're to report to the control tent immediately," she said.

"Alright then, sorry but I have to leave," he replied and, grabbing his gloves and face mask, he left the tent and ran towards the control centre.

When he looked up and around, there was no sign of any force field and he felt that something didn't feel right, so slowed to a fast walk instead. On entering the tent, he came face to face with Mathew. No one else was there.

"I've just received confirmation that an object has landed over a mile from the camp. We need to leave straight away," he insisted.

"Right, yes, I heard the sirens, but what exactly has landed?" Justin asked.

"Well, that's what we have to find out. Are you coming with me or not?" he said and, putting on his gloves and mask, he rushed towards the door, followed by Justin. They both ran over to the snowmobile park and he started the same machine they used earlier.

"But where's the backup? Where are all the people?" Justin shouted above the sound of the motor.

"The sirens tell people to stay locked down in their tents until we sound the all clear. We don't want them to get trapped outside by a force field, do we? Climb on the back, we must leave as fast as possible," he insisted and a few moments later, they were flying across the ice, past where his submarine had surfaced.

Justin hung on as the two-man snow scooter bounced over the ice gullies, while Justin on the back could see little. Finally, Mathew stopped and pointed at a small round object lying in the snow a few hundred yards in front of them.

"There, that must be where the object landed," Mathew said, pointing and looking at the coordinates on a handheld device. Then he took a video of the scene, ending with a submarine in the distance.

"Well, it looks like your boat is back. Let's get closer, it appears to be more like an egg."

Mathew opened the throttle again to get closer and stopped less than ten feet away. What Justin saw was metallic and oval in shape, the colour of gold, some twenty feet long, ten feet across and about six feet high. *Not big enough to be extraterrestrial,* Justin thought.

Mathew jumped off the snow scooter and went to touch the object with his gloves.

Justin watched as the object lit up and started to vibrate on the ice. He then saw that the outer casing of the egg was sinking into the ice, pulling Mathew with it.

"Help me, I'm being sucked downwards! I can't get off this thing! Can you do something?" Mathew shouted urgently, as the tracker flew out his hand and landed on the ice.

Justin climbed into the driver's seat, lined up the scooter and, opening the throttle to the maximum, hit the side of the object that finally released Mathew. The last thing he remembered was being thrown in the air, as the skis of the snowmobile now became stuck on the side of the egg object. Justin landed on the ice close to Mathew. Then he saw a flash, and everything went dark, and he knew he was no longer in the same place or time.

11 – ICE CAMP WHALE

Lieutenant Mercedes Bradley held onto a metal support while watching on a screen for the impact of the object on the ice field outside. When nothing moved on any of the sensors outside, she felt there was something very wrong with being cheated.

Cheated at losing almost a month of scientific data if the landing occurred close to the camp as her team members started to arrive in the tent. Mercedes was dressed in black clothing, as her assistant arrived first, out of breath from running in the cold air outside. She was dressed in orange overalls, still wearing her white Arctic pants and looking scared.

"Are you sure about this, Mercedes? You're sure the thing has landed on the ice?" she asked, looking down at the grey plastic covering the floor, unsure of what was happening. Emergency sirens had sounded all around the camp to tell everyone to remain inside their tents that had been waived for the AUV team.

"No, I'm sure it landed. If it was a rock from space, it should have crashed on the ice. I was sent these landing coordinates, so I think we must see if the AUV can find anything under the ice," she replied.

Boxes of equipment were all around on the plastic floor, where a large hole had been cut in the ice. Above was the crane that supported the yellow Auto Underwater Vehicle now on the surface. Grey billows of insulating hung down from above as another two members of her team arrived to set up the AUV for the test run. She handed the phone to her tech guy to input the coordinates into the AUV to prepare for the launch.

"Hey, I saw Mathew and that Marine guy just roar off on a snowmobile, so they appear to know where it landed," he remarked.

"Ah, that's just wishful thinking. I bet they come back empty-handed in half an hour," another remarked, laughing.

"Come on, guys, concentrate on the job," replied Mercedes, feeling nervous if anything went wrong and the AUV failed to return to them at the camp. What they had programmed was way outside normal protocol and she was the person responsible as she read out the launch checklist.

"Battery charged on full power?" she asked, until someone shouted check.

"Maximum range two miles, agreed?"

"That's a lot more than normal," her assistant replied, as everyone turned to look at Mercedes.

"I know, but we agreed this range is necessary in case it's outside the usual mile limit," she replied.

"Well, there'll be one hell of an inquiry if you lose the bloody thing," her assistant replied.

"Look, there is at least one of our subs outside under the ice that has no idea what's happening up here. That boat has a crew of a hundred and fifty persons and there's no way to contact them. I'm taking that decision to ascertain if there's any possible danger outside," Mercedes replied coolly.

"Alright, the coordinates are loaded, with an auto return here. We are good to launch," the tech guy replied, with a thumbs up, as the motor of the AUV was started and released in the water.

They all watched on a screen as the mini sub descended to a programmed depth of fifty feet below the ice and moved in a northerly direction away from the camp.

Everything went well for the first ten minutes. When they lost contact with the AUV, Mercedes started to get worried. It had happened before, and the mini sub had returned, but this time it looked different. Mercedes went to the back of the tent to put on her outdoor Arctic pants and her white jacket and slowly returned to see if contact with the AUV had been recovered.

She remembered how only a month earlier she had seen the start of the building of Ice Camp Whale, in the Beaufort Sea. It was inside the Arctic Circle, and the arrival of two US Navy fast attack submarines forced her to make a decision.

"Listen up, everyone. I'm going to go out there to try to contact the AUV with one of our handheld trackers. Remember, it's only fifty down below the ice. Keep watching the screen and see if you can regain contact while I'm gone," she ordered. Standing up, she put on her gloves and goggles and left the tent.

"Wow, that was the fastest underwater failure I've ever seen," said the tech guy.

"Can you do anything at all from here?" an assistant asked.

"No, of course not, it's all an auto vehicle. It might have hit an underwater iceberg, or there was a sudden change in salinity that's confused the computer and sent it down lower. That happened before, but this time it's not that deep, so we just don't know," he replied.

When Mercedes got outside, all she could see was the huge expanse of the flat ice field and the orange tents of the camp. She ran around to the snowmobile park, only to find all of the snowmobiles had been disconnected from charge. She was left looking at a big caterpillar tractor with a trailer used to transport stores. In desperation, she climbed onboard and, starting the motor, engaged drive, and lurched out onto the snow.

At a top speed of almost fifteen miles an hour, she had time to check her course to the landing coordinates on the tracker device. Ten minutes later, there was a big explosion in the ice field as a submarine surfaced from under the ice. Having never seen a submarine surface through the ice before, it was both exciting and frightening, as the nuclear submarine rose through the ice. She watched as huge blocks of ice fell off the black tower rising higher and higher above the ice sheet. She cut the engine, knowing what would come next.

First the sound of the ice cracking, then fine snow and a pressure wave that lifted the tractor as the ice below her moved. Holding her breath for a moment she thought *What the hell; they've come back to pick up this man...* and then continued to the landing place.

Ten minutes later when she arrived, there were two bodies lying in the snow and an upturned snowmobile lying on the ice sheet. She stopped, jumped down from the tractor, and ran across to see if they were still alive. The first body she recognised as Mathew. He was dead, frozen stiff. The second body was the man from the submarine Marine Benbow, who was still alive. Using all her strength, she hauled his body up to the trailer and then lifted him up onto the flatbed. Taking a final check around the site, she saw a black tracker device in the snow.

Carefully picking it up, she placed it in Justin's jacket pocket, who was still unconscious on the trailer. Then she drove as fast as the tractor would go back towards the submarine.

On her arrival, two sailors were fixing the rope ladders down onto the ice and she stopped to talk to them.

"You're from the *USS Albany*?" she asked.

"Yes, we are, and you are?" one of the men replied.

"I'm Lieutenant Bradley from the ice camp over there. We've had an accident, and it involved this man from your boat," she explained. As soon as she confirmed her name, the enlisted men saluted her. Mercedes saluted them back and continued.

"This man was brought here on your boat two days ago and should be taken back on board as quickly as possible if you want him to survive," she ordered. One of the men went to lift Justin out of the trailer and, finding he was coming awake, propped him up against the rope ladder on the hull. Mercedes jumped down from the tractor to talk to him.

"Justin, what happened out there with Mathew?" she asked. Justin's eyes recognised her and he was trying to speak.

"It came alive…" was all she heard as he drifted in and out of consciousness and she started to slap his face to learn more. When they lifted him up onto the hull of the submarine, Mercedes followed.

"Now listen to me. You must lift him back onboard and tell the captain not to leave this boat. Understood?" she said.

"Yes, ma'am, we have a hoist for that. What about you and the people at the camp? Don't you want to come with us?" he asked.

"No, we are already closing it down and hope to leave by plane shortly. Something that landed on the ice must have hit their snowmobile and may be dangerous, so don't go out here. None of you should leave this boat," she insisted.

Mercedes watched as they placed Justin in a harness that lifted him up to the top of the tower and then pulled him inside. When the men at the top gave her a thumbs up, she climbed down onto the ice. Placing the goggles back on her face, she continued her journey to the camp on the tractor.

***

Back on the submarine, they carefully lowered Justin down into the control room, where the Chief of the Boat was waiting for them to explain what happened.

"My God; looks as if this man was in a bar fight! Well, that's our Marine Benbow, where did you find him?" he demanded as the two men held Justin up.

"The navy lieutenant from the camp brought him over on one of their caterpillar tractors. Said his snowmobile was hit by something out on the ice. The other man she found was already dead," the man reported.

"Right, anything else?"

"Yes, she told us to tell the captain not to leave the boat," the second man said.

"Right, I'll pass that on to the captain. Now you can go back up the sail and put up the radio mast. There must be some new comms that we are not aware of. Don't say any of this to anyone on board until we receive orders regarding the situation here," the chief replied.

"What do you want us to do with this man?" one asked.

"I'll get others in the crew to take care of him. Best if we put him in the officer's wardroom with a hot drink. Now you two look lively," he said, ordering two other men to take Justin away to recover.

***

Mercedes finally reached the ice camp and saw her assistant standing by the snowmobile park, waiting for her return. She parked the tractor and jumped down to run across to her, almost in tears. Looking at the state of her boss, her assistant knew something bad must have happened out on the ice, but tried to sound positive.

"Our AUV came back, and with new data. The object looks to be stuck in the ice sheet but we don't know where it came from…" she started to say as Mercedes burst into tears.

"I found both Mathew and Justin lying on the ice," she said.

"Really, so where are they now?"

"Mathew was already frozen dead, and I took the Marine back to the submarine that just broke through the ice," she replied, pointing to the boat not that far away.

"What! You must be joking? Mathew was one of the most experienced persons at the camp. You don't think that when the sub broke through it moved some of the ice sheet and the mobile fell into a new crevasse?" she replied.

"No! I was able to speak to Justin briefly and he said the thing was 'alive'. Is that what our research data is showing?"

"Well, we don't know yet for sure yet, but that's where it's pointing. You do realise that when you drove into the camp, you went through the force field," she replied, handing her a pair of X-ray glasses.

"What? Already? When did that happen," Mercedes asked.

"Not sure exactly, but soon after you left. That means nobody can leave the camp for now."

Mercedes took one look and sighed at yet another problem.

"Come on, let's walk over to the control tent and see if we can help fill a hydrogen balloon. There's no way we can recover Mathew's body now; at least not until they remove the field," Mercedes replied.

12 – FALL OUT

Back on the island of Montserrat, Susan drove into the driveway, parked outside Janet's house, and ran inside. There, she found Jana and Bee playing a word game with the two girls.

"Ah! You're back," Bee shouted, jumping up to give her a hug.

"How did it go with those two young men? We heard a report on the local news," she continued.

"Really, what did it say?" Susan asked, sounding concerned.

"Nothing much; something about protecting the island from the volcano, I think. I hope they were helpful, Susan," Bee asked.

"Yes, err, yes of course. In fact, they have invited us to a beach party on Saturday," Susan replied, as Jana came to hear the news and asked if Susan wanted to eat lunch.

"Come with me to the kitchen and I'll find you something cold to eat. We've eaten with the girls already, but I guess you must be starving," Jana said as she led Susan towards the next room and waited for an explanation.

"Jana, I think I need a glass of wine."

"Of course, coming right up. Take a deep breath and all the time you need," Jana replied as she watched Susan collapse onto a bar stool, her hands over her face, as her backpack fell onto the floor.

"Jana, they know all about us," she blurted out, grabbing the wine glass and drinking it all down in one. Slowly Jana moved around the bar and, taking Susan's head in her hands, started to read her mind. After a long minute, Jana released her and shook her head.

"My God, and you told all this to James as well."

"Yes, he's gone back to find out more. These men are willing to use blackmail to get us to comply or have us removed from the island." Suddenly, Janet appeared in the room.

"Who said anything about removing you from the island?" Janet asked.

"Oh! Susan's meeting with the men who were installing the dish at the observatory didn't go well," Jana replied, when Susan's mobile phone rang. Taking it out of her pocket, Susan saw the call was from the governor and answered it.

"Sarah, how can I help you?" Susan asked and then continued, "Yes, of course, same place as last time. Yes, 4 p.m., I'll be there," as the line went dead.

"Well, Susan, you had better explain to me what's going on, before you leave the house," Janet said.

"Oh! I can do better than that. Here, listen to the conversation I had with this man Ollie, because I recorded it on my phone. Take it and listen to the tape," Susan replied.

"Very well, but I want to see you in my office before you leave to meet Sarah, do you understand?" Janet demanded, and, taking the phone, left the room and went back downstairs, leaving Jana and Susan looking bewildered.

"I think I'm going to join you with a glass of wine," Jana said, taking the bottle and a glass in her hand. She smiled at Susan.

"If you feel up to it, can you come with me to my bedroom? We still have plenty of time, so let's see if we can find out more about this man Ollie on the remote viewer," Jana asked.

"Yes, of course, anything to understand more before meeting Sarah," she replied, and followed Jana downstairs.

The bedroom was dim with the curtains drawn as she realised the baby was sleeping in a cot close to the double bed. Jana cleared a space on a side table and brought another chair so they could face each other. She placed the bottle and their glasses at on the side of the table with a black tablet in the centre.

"I remember doing this with James all that time ago in the future, but have you done this since we arrived?" Susan asked.

"Yes, of course, and I did it with Bee before you left the airbase if that's any help," Jana replied, pouring them both a glass of wine.

"Now I want you to relax, drink from glass, and breathe in and out slowly. When you are ready, I want you to think of this man Ollie in your mind to see if you can connect to him again. Then I will turn the tablet on and see if his face appears on the screen. The image may be very faint, but if you can concentrate on how he hurt you the most, I can take over from you to find out more."

"Alright, I'll try, but never done anything like this before." Susan drank some more, closed her eyes, and tried to relax, until Jana activated the tablet, but nothing appeared on the screen.

"Susan, think what this man said to you. He wants to take you to his place to do something you most fear? Find his face when he spoke to you," Jana asked, as slowly a blurred face appeared on the screen as they held hands together on the table.

"Alright, I've got him," Jana said as Susan slumped back in her chair as if in a trance.

"Right, let's see when he arrived on the island. Ah! Looks like a military helicopter; now he's down at a dock somewhere on the island. We need to go back to see where he came from in the US… if I can look into his past?" Jana said, when suddenly the screen went dark with a message in big black letters – G3P and switched off.

"Damn it! We've been thrown out by something much bigger."

"But what does G3P mean?" asked Susan.

"Oh, that's the Global Public-Private Partnership we've been following, but you've probably never heard of it. It's a global corporate elite group that includes Central Banks and the UN. It's just a pity that no one has asked the rest of us if we want to join such a partnership," Jana explained.

"You mean it's a power grab to control the planet's global subjects by unelected representatives? Why haven't any of the people fought back and objected?"

"Oh! They tried and then some private NGOs gave the planet the COVID virus that locked them down for over a year."

"No, Jana! This sounds more like science fiction to me! The planet can't have gone this mad since we left less than ten years ago," Susan replied.

"Well, Janet and I have been tracking this since we came back and it only gets worse," Jana said, reaching down to a file on the floor and placing it on the table.

"I think I need another glass," replied Susan.

"Take the file and read it in your room, if your daughter is having an afternoon rest. Don't say anything to the governor at your meeting.

Stick to the scientific facts about the dish and leave her to question why it's been installed here. That's her job," Jana said.

"But can you get back on the viewer and find out more about this man Ollie before Saturday?" Susan asked.

"I'll try, but I think James will find much more about him than I can today," said Jana, as they hugged, and Susan left the room. Once outside, she met Janet in the corridor.

"Well, I never, I see you have got our file on these events," said Janet who indicated to follow her to her office.

"Susan, I've listened to your recordings and there's nothing except when you first met in the morning. I agree he sounds like a young American, from Tennessee if I remember, not cooperative but not threatening in any way. After that, the only sound I heard was you drinking from a water bottle, I think."

"You think he used some blocking device for our conversation in the office?" Susan asked.

"Probably, these people are clever and don't want anything negative used against them. Now, for your meeting with Sarah this afternoon, I want you to stick to the scientific facts about this so-called JW dish that has been installed at the observatory, understood?"

"Yes, ma'am. It can't look into deep space at this altitude, so what's its purpose?" she asked.

"Did you learn any more from this man Ollie who did the installation?" Janet asked.

"Confidentially, he told me he had installed the same dish on two other islands. Bahamas in the north and St Lucia in the west. Do you want me to tell her that?" said Susan.

"Susan, you never stop amazing me! Yes, of course, you should say that very confidentially. That's exactly what these people want to continue after the pandemic. Also, it will give Sarah a reason to call her British numbers on these islands to see if the intel is correct," Janet said, smiling.

"Right then, I'll start reading the file Jana gave me."

"Indeed you should, but make no mention of the contents at your meeting and please take your phone back. Remember, recording anyone without their consent is illegal under UK law, so don't show her you may have done it today," Janet replied, handing the phone back.

Susan walked back to her room to find it empty, so her daughter must be napping with Bee. She started to think of the questions that Sarah might ask, and spent time researching the observatory on the island of Maui. Surprised to find it's situated at an altitude of over 10,000 feet and not open to the public, she realised she would have to be more creative if she was to pass any close questioning. Feeling sleepy from the wine, she lay down on her bed, until Bee knocked on the door to wake her.

"Susan, it's quarter to four. I think you had better get moving."

"Oh, my goodness, is that the time? Thanks for the call, I have to get going," she replied, jumping up off the bed. Susan pushed the phone into her back pocket and ran upstairs to be in time for the meeting. She arrived at Olveston House just after four and found the receptionist waiting for her on the steps.

"Susan, you're late and the governor doesn't like waiting." With that, she followed the girl out onto the terrace, to a table at the far end, like last time. Sarah acknowledged her arrival and motioned her to sit as she was talking on her phone. While waiting for her to finish, she poured herself a cup of tea, adding the milk and sugar after.

"You know, Susan, you really shouldn't do that," Sarah said, looking at her closely.

"Putting the milk after the tea is not good for the taste," she replied laughing, that broke the tension between them.

"So, Susan, what have you been doing up at the observatory? I hear you've been busy since we last met."

"Yes, you could say that. Two Americans arrived this morning to install a new dish..." she explained.

"Yes, yes, and you weren't impressed. Can you explain why?"

"Well, I'm an astrophysicist, not a professional astronomer, but I know that for any ground-based telescope to look into deep space, it needs to be at a higher elevation than the observatory on this island," she replied.

"Yes, and you had one of the highest on that Hawaiian island Maui, wasn't it," asked Sarah.

"Yes, that's the Haleakala Observatory at over 10,000 feet, so I think you should question why this dish has been installed here."

"Really, that's quite a denial for a project we were told might warn us of a future volcanic eruption," Sarah replied, pouring herself a cup of tea.

"So, tell me about your astronomy research in the Pacific, because my people did some investigations and were unable to find your name listed at any of the telescopes on the Maui High-Altitude Site. That's strange, isn't it?"

"No, not really. There's a lot of competition for even an hour's viewing time at these big telescopes. It's necessary to register with a credited organisation like Oxford University to stand any chance of being awarded a slot and I'm not a professional," Susan said.

"So, what did you do?"

"I found a job as a filing clerk at the Atlas telescope that's run by NASA. It wasn't anything like filing; in fact, the US job description was as a 'fact checker.' We had to read all the asteroid terrestrial-impact reports to check if the warnings were correct. A one day's warning for a 30-kiloton 'town killer,' a week's warning for a 5-megaton 'city killer,' and three weeks for a 100-megaton 'country killer,'" Susan replied.

"But what were you really looking for, Susan?"

"I was looking for something much bigger. A 'planet extinction' event, like what happened to the dinosaurs."

"You thought that might exist in our solar system?"

"Yes, there was a report tracking the biggest comet ever discovered. It was found by two astronomers Berardinelli and Bernstein and came out of the Oort cloud in 2014, moving slowly through the solar system," Susan explained.

"So where is it now?" Sarah asked.

"Don't worry, it's been renamed as C/2014 and is being tracked by dozens of astronomers. NASA now estimates the closest approach to Earth will be around April 2031 at a distance of a billion miles," Susan explained, smiling at Sarah.

"Phew! That's good to know, so what's this got to do with our little observatory here?"

"Absolutely nothing, except..."

"Yes, except what?"

"Did you see the photo of the two young Americans installing the dish on the mast at the observatory?"

"Yes, of course, that's why we're here."

"By the time I arrived in my office, there was a new screen on my desk. When I switched it on, there was a welcome message to Susan West. It was like you see at a hotel when you first check in."

"Alright, go on."

"Once the telescope was online and opened, the screen started to receive messages about the size and abilities of the JW receiver. These specifications were impossible for a telescope that's almost at sea level, so I took some screenshots. Would you like me to download copies to your phone?"

"Alright, if you think it's important."

"Here, I've highlighted six of these screen messages and a couple of the shots of the receiver on the mast."

"Well done, I've got them. What does this thing do if it can't look into deep space? We were told it's monitoring the volcano."

"This is where it gets interesting. Both the men who arrived were dressed in military uniform but no insignia. The only installer I spoke to was an American, name of Ollie from Tennessee. I need your help to find out the name of the lab in the US that manufactured the receiver because he said that's confidential."

"Hmm. Yes, that's strange, and no company logos on any of the images you just sent to me?"

"No nothing. No logo on the computer screen to confirm the manufacturer. Someone must have a record of who this company is and who's funding it, because it all looks expensive and top of the range."

"Alright, leave it with me; do you have time for a quick drink?" she asked and seeing the receptionist on the terrace, she waved.

"Please can we have two large G&Ts," she asked and then turning to me admitted, "I rarely drink at my meetings, but you have given me a lot to think about, and anyway I'm not officially here," then looked up as the drinks arrived on a silver tray with a small ice bucket.

"Well, cheers, and well done with your concerns," she said as they raised their glasses to their continued good health.

"You have to understand, Susan, that even as the governor, I'm not aware of everything that happens on this island. From memory, I think this project was proposed by the island PM, about the same time your project was proposed here. He said it was donated by one of his contacts in the States," she said as she added more ice to her glass.

"Does G3P have anything to do with this?" Susan asked.

"Oh! My God. Don't get me started on this; it's a nightmare. Nothing is confidential anymore; it's just our new G3P policy. Leaving me to work out which new policy they are referring to."

"Really? As bad as that?"

"Yes, there are so many Policy Makers, many Policy Distributors and even more so-called Policy Enforcers. Fortunately, we are too small and off the grid to care much about this," Sarah complained and changed the subject.

"Enough of this. Tell me, how's everything worked out at Janet's house? Two ten-year-old girls running about and a baby, it must be quite exhausting," she asked.

"Yes, it's been busy, but Janet keeps order in the house, and it's working well."

"And the other woman Bee, still working on her plants?"

"Oh yes and taking care of the girls when I'm up at the observatory," Susan replied, finishing her drink. They shook hands and when Susan got up to leave, she whispered in Sarah's ear.

"Confidentially, Ollie told me they had installed the same receivers on two other islands: Bahamas and St Lucia. Might be worth checking out if that's true," Susan said and giving her a pat on the shoulder, moved back along the terrace to leave the house. As Susan walked back to the entrance, the receptionist caught her eye and called out to her.

"Wow, drinks with the governor, that's never happened before. You must be someone special," she said.

"Yes, but the governor is not officially here today. It's a private visit and you should keep it that way," she said, and continued walking out down the stairs, to drive back to Janet's house.

13 – LATER

Meanwhile, James had jumped forward in time to his previous hiding place below the tree in the observatory car park. Seeing the workers' truck was still parked outside, with one of the staff cars, he advanced his medallion a couple of hours and reappeared just after 7 p.m., as the light was starting to fade fast. When he saw no one was around, he walked slowly up towards the observatory.

Arriving at the door to the entrance, he activated his medallion again and walked inside, then climbed the stairs to the offices above and began looking around. He checked that the two recording devices were online and then sought out the office used by Susan. It was a small room with a window closed with drop down shutters and a new metallic door. It looked to have been recently installed, as the old wooden door had been cast aside and left up against an outer wall.

So far, so good, he thought to himself as he saw the new door had been installed with a biometric viewing device. It was situated at eye level, but he quickly decided not to interfere with it just yet. Instead, he walked over to the small window. Activating his medallion again, he walked into the small room and sat down in the chair in front of the desk. Hearing no alarms from the outside, he switched on a small desk light and sat looking at the screen and a black box placed on the desk beside it.

Feeling more comfortable, he searched the back of the screen for the button to switch it on. The screen opened with the message 'Welcome Susan West' and he flipped through a few pages of the description of the receiver's details Susan had mentioned. James was about to give up, having found nothing of interest, when suddenly the screen flickered for a moment and then went online to a place that was only too familiar to him. The inside of what looked like the International Space Station, with a number of astronauts floating around in the background!

What the hell? James thought as he remembered that the orbit of the ISS takes it down the centre of the Atlantic. It must be almost over the island of Montserrat for him to receive these live pictures on the screen. In fact, he realised it would be 200 miles above his head, but with an average speed of 17,000 mph, the dish outside wouldn't be in contact for long. The next few images scared the hell out of him as a close-up of a female astronaut, who appeared to look like Elizabeth, was working on a small cylinder. She was the spook who went over to work for the US army and he listened to her voice on an intercom to the ground.

"Everything lined up for a maximum geomagnetic pulse on our next orbit," he heard her say as the screen started to lose contact and a message appeared: 'Contact Lost.' James sat back in his chair, dumbfounded at what he had just seen and switched off the screen. He remembered that the orbital time of the ISS was around ninety minutes, so nothing would happen for another hour and a half.

Jana had guessed that Elizabeth was onboard the ISS, but what was this maximum geomagnetic pulse she was talking about to ground control? If they planned to hit the volcano outside with such a magnetic pulse, it would most certainly cause seismic alarms to sound all over the island.

James thought of going to warn Susan, but there was nothing anyone could do to stop this from happening anyway. Except there was one option that might be possible, if he acted quickly, but it would mean going back outside again and he was going to need some workman's tools…

***

When Susan arrived back at the house after her meeting with Sarah, she went straight down to her room and lay down to rest, not wanting to talk to anyone about what had been discussed. After about an hour, she heard the children coming down for a bath and Janet tapped on her door, carrying a tray of soup and bread.

"I thought you might want something of substance after your meeting with Sarah. She called me to say how impressed she was with your progress but was somewhat worried about the new dish," Janet said.

"Thanks, I spun her a story about the Impact Alert System on that Hawaiian island; just hope I didn't overdo it," replied Susan, dipping the bread into the soup.

"Well. She most certainly will get someone to check up on your story. Whether NASA will admit to any of this comet story is another matter."

"There's something interesting about this comet's approach to our planet that's been discovered. Using the Hubble telescope, they found the orbit will pass perpendicular through the outer solar system," Susan explained.

"Is that important?" Janet asked.

"No, and the orbit can change as a result of planetary perturbations, so these results can be misleading," replied Susan.

"Anything else I should know about your meeting?"

"Yes, I did tell Sarah confidentially these men had installed similar receivers on two other islands – Bahamas and St Lucia," Susan replied.

"That's something that will certainly be followed up on and in the meantime…" Janet replied.

"In the meantime, James has gone back to the observatory to see what he can find," said Susan.

"Very good; let me know when he gets back. I'm sure he will uncover a lot more than we can. Let's hope we can all get a good night's rest," Janet said, leaving the room.

***

Using his medallion again, James walked back into the office, where all appeared quiet. Then he went back down the stairs to find the tools he would need in the basement. After going down a second flight of stairs, he found rows and rows of shelves containing all the rolls of seismic recordings and other files and records. At the end of a long corridor, he saw an outer door that was held ajar by a piece of wood.

Going inside, he turned on the light and found he was in a small storeroom at the base of the radio mast. On the wall was a large metal handle with some faded instructions that looked more promising. Reading the instructions, he became aware that it might be possible to turn the platform above using the metal handle. There was a series of metal rods and gears leading upwards that had not been used in years.

Inserting the handle into the base, James tried to turn the gears, but found they were locked in place, whichever way he tried to turn the handle. On reading the instructions again, he found there was a locking mechanism that needed to be released by simply removing a locking pin. Once the pin was taken out, James could move the platform to the left or right, but which way to turn the platform away from the Soufrière hills and the volcano above? Trying to visualise the landscape outside from a basement was not easy. He knew he had to turn the platform towards the coast in the west, as that was a part of the exclusion zone and uninhabited. This would reduce the full force of any geomagnetic burst away from the volcano, so he turned the handle to the maximum, reinserted the pin, and hoped this would reduce most of the damage.

Replacing the handle, James looked up to see some new black cables that had been installed for the connection to the screen in Susan's office, when he heard noises upstairs. He quickly turned off the light as he heard more urgent voices.

"Go and see if anyone has interfered with our installation down in the basement while I check the office upstairs. Keep in touch on your phone, will you," he heard the man say with a clear American accent.

"Look, calm down! Control says that the screen in the office was activated tonight. I'll go down and check the cables, but that may have been from a power surge from the island's grid, nothing more," he replied. Meanwhile, James had already left the room and moved down the corridor to find a hiding place under the stairs.

"We need to be sure the dish will work perfectly for the pulse in under ten minutes' time, so keep your phone open and let me know what you find," was all he heard, until he heard footsteps coming down the stairs, towards him. The man was using the light on his phone, but if he turned on the main light, James would certainly be seen. James waited to see if his work would be discovered, as the man saw the door to the room was open.

"Ollie, I'm sure someone has been down here," he heard and then a scream as a cat screeched and hissed at him.

"OMG! Ollie, there's a bloody cat down here! Didn't see that before, but there's a bowl on the floor and some food. Those observation students must be dipso to keep an animal down here."

"Check the wiring; has anything been disturbed?" Ollie asked.

"No nothing, it's the same as before."

"Alright, come back, there's no one up here and the door was still locked, so come back up…" His voice faded as he walked back upstairs.

James breathed a sigh of relief and, looking at his watch, saw that the ISS should be over the island in the next few minutes and decided it was time to leave. Walking quietly upstairs, he found the main door open, so he walked across the car park to sit and watch from his place under the tree. His gaze lifted, staring up at a star-studded sky. It was beautiful, and yet it felt too big. Like if he looked too long it would swallow him up.

Nothing happened for the next few minutes until there was a beam of light from the dish so bright that it wasn't possible to see where the flash was directed. It most certainly wasn't towards the southwest and not the Soufrière hills. After a few minutes more, a second beam was emitted that lasted for several minutes. When it stopped, James could see geomagnetic lights all along the western coastline with a curtain of pink, purple, and green colours, like the northern lights.

James stopped to think what might have happened if the beam had hit or was close to the volcano and decided that it was time to return home. Setting his medallion to inside Janet's house, he pushed the button and found he was standing alone in his bedroom. *Good*, he thought, *everyone must be outside watching the lights,* and feeling tired, collapsed onto the bed and fell fast asleep.

*****

It was shortly after Bee put the girls to bed that she noticed some bright lights outside above the shore and ran to tell Jana to come and look outside. They shouted at Susan to come and then ran outside and down the driveway to see the colours of the geomagnetic storm.

"Looks like it starts somewhere over Richmond Hill, but what's caused this tonight?" Bee asked.

"I bet it's something to do with that dish they installed at the observatory and perhaps James has been involved," Jana replied.

Janet and Susan watched the light show from the front door of the house. A few moments later, Janet's phone rang, where she saw it was Sarah calling her.

"Janet, I've declared a National Emergency on the island. You and Mrs West must meet me at the observatory," she demanded, and the line went dead.

"What did she say?"

"Sarah's declared a National Emergency. She wants to meet us both up at the observatory."

"Well, at least we know what damage this dish can do," replied Susan, who ran inside to find her phone and her rucksack before leaving the house.

PART THREE
PICK ME UP –
April 2024

14 – AURORAS

As Janet drove down the drive, she stopped at the gates to talk to Jana and Bee, still looking at the lights.

"Jana, you will find a government warning on your phone. It asks for people to stay indoors at their house until further notice. Please do as they say, as we don't know what may happen next," Janet insisted.

"Okay, so where are you both going?"

"Susan's been summoned back to the observatory, so we may be gone for a few hours," said Janet.

"I'm sorry, didn't see that on my phone," Jana replied, as the car drove off into the night, leaving them both looking at the government advice.

"Alright, Jana, let's go back inside, I want to check that the girls are both asleep in bed," Bee said, and they ran back inside the house.

***

As Janet drove towards Salem, she started to ask more questions about how such a small dish could create a geomagnetic storm.

"The Webb receiver they installed has six adjustable mirrors that can focus a pulse of high energy, like a laser, onto a small surface," replied Susan.

"Yes, yes, I understand that but where does this pulse come from?" Janet asked.

"Well, that's what I've been trying to figure out with James. He thinks it's connected to the ISS that orbits the planet sixteen times a day. Each orbit passes either directly or close above the island roughly every ninety minutes," Susan replied.

"What! You mean it's coming around to pass over us again in about an hour?"

"Actually, in less than sixty minutes."

"No seriously, Susan, this must be a joke. I hope you didn't tell Sarah any of this."

"No, of course not. I wasn't sure at our meeting."

"And now you think it's possible? I can't believe the International Space Station could be involved in such an attack on an island in the Atlantic. Do they want to start a war?"

"No, it might not be the ISS that sends the pulse. It could be a military satellite or even something privately owned that wants to start an international crisis. We have so many wars raging at the moment in Ukraine, Palestine, Yemen. You know, to name just a few." As the car passed Olveston House, they saw a truck driving towards them in the dark.

"Watch out, that truck's going to hit us," shouted Susan as she helped swing the wheel to avoid a head-on collision, and Janet braked violently to bring the car to a stop beside the road.

"What the hell just happened? That truck deliberately tried to hit us," Janet exclaimed, shaking with fear from the near miss.

"Yes, and I saw it was being driven by Ollie; that's the American who installed the dish. Now he's found that his little plot has failed, he's trying to run to escape."

"You mean he wanted to kill us?"

"No, I think the people behind this wanted to start a volcanic eruption to depopulate the island. Come on, let me drive the rest of the way to the observatory. We have less than thirty minutes before the ISS returns above us," Susan insisted, getting out of the car to drive, as they continued onwards up the hill.

When they reached the observatory, there were several government cars parked outside, with the large Toyota truck that was familiar to Susan. On either side of the entrance stood armed Monserrat police officers. They both got out and were greeted by the governor standing at the entrance door.

"Good evening, Susan. By the calculations of my advisers, this space station will return above us shortly. Please lead the way to your office upstairs to see if we can stop a repeat of the events earlier."

"Yes, of course. But I think it's better if the police check that the building is empty first."

"We already did that; it's all clear," replied Sam.

"Alright then, but just the governor and Sam can follow me. The police should control this group outside until we are sure it's safe," Susan replied, and led the way upstairs. The lights were on when they reached her office, and Susan immediately saw that a security door had been installed with a biometric device that perplexed her.

"Sam, can you deactivate the device and get the door open without blowing us all up?"

"Yes, ma'am, that's what we're here for," Sam replied, taking a US army revolver from his holster.

"Wait, Sam, are you sure this is safe?" Sarah asked.

"We are at nine minutes and counting…" replied Susan, and Sarah nodded.

Sam's first shot took out the biometric device, and no explosion followed. Then he told everyone to stand back, as he shot at the hinges holding the door in place. Finally, the door came away from the doorframe and Sam reached up and pulled it to the floor. At that point, Susan rushed forward into the office, sat down in her chair, and switched on the computer, to see her welcome on the screen once again, but nothing more.

Now Susan was desperate to find a solution, as she looked at her watch that showed just five minutes to when the space station would be in range again. At that moment, Daniel walked into the office, holding a cat in his arms, and spoke to her.

"I know how he did it," he said to her.

"Daniel, what are you talking about?"

"A man came in and turned the platform twenty degrees to the west to hit Richmond Hill. That's what he must have done." By which time Sarah and Sam had entered to listen to the conversation.

"Thanks, Daniel, but do you know how to stop it happening again?" Susan asked in panic.

"Yes, I think you should disconnect the wires to that box leading to your screen. It might help," he said to Susan. She removed both wires leading to the box and looked at him again.

"Well, I'm not sure, but I brought some wire cutters and think someone should go down to the basement and cut the new wires they installed coming down from the radio tower."

Susan looked at her watch again, which showed two minutes, and passed the wire cutters to Sam. He ran out of the room and down the stairs to the basement.

"Susan, are you sure about this?" asked the governor.

"No, but now we wait. They must know from their military satellites there's a big crowd outside the observatory. They may decide with their cover blown to stop sending the pulse again," Susan replied, and moved the black box off her desk and slid it onto the floor, to put it into her backpack later.

When nothing further happened, everyone relaxed, and Sarah went out onto the observation platform to look at the curtain of lights that had appeared on the western coastline.

"Susan, come and look at these lights. Are you sure this was caused by the dish they installed?"

"Most certainly. If you look at the graphs on the seismic machines, there are two sudden spikes," she replied.

When Sam returned to the offices, he started to question Daniel about how he knew about turning the platform by hand.

"This was installed during the volcanic bombardment over ten years ago, with a camera under the platform."

"So, when the platform is turned, it turns not only the camera, but the dish above as well?" Susan asked.

"Exactly. The observers wanted to see the damage being done to Plymouth on the eastern side of the volcano, and again on the western side," he explained.

"And how many people knew about this?" Sam asked.

"Well, all of the observers at that time, but most have left the island or retired," Daniel replied.

"Come and look at the screen here; the camera is pointing at Richmond Hill in the southwest, not trained on the volcano at all." Everyone looked at the screen of the aurora from the light storm.

Sarah was getting impatient with this discussion when a new figure appeared in the office and approached the governor.

"Ah! Professor Ferguson, what a pleasure to see you. What brings you to the observatory at this time of night?" asked Sarah.

"Good to see you, Governor. Well, it was those lights, and I have a theory about where they have come from," he replied, smiling at everyone.

"Very well, let me introduce you to Susan West, who has come to us from the Atlas Observatory on a Hawaiian island. I hope the two of you are able to work together on a solution," Sarah explained, in anticipation of some better news.

"Thank you, but I need to get some seismic records from the basement in order to confirm my ideas," he said and, turning around, walked over to the stairs, and disappeared from sight. Sarah then spoke to Susan aside to explain who the man was.

"Professor Ferguson was the director here during the volcanic bombardment, and since his retirement is still the official Director of the Observatory. However, after the events tonight, we really need someone younger and I want to propose you as the new director, if you would accept the position," she asked.

"Yes, I would be honoured," Susan replied.

"Very well then. Tomorrow, we'll be holding a press conference outside the observatory to reassure the people about the auroras, as the press will be all over it by then. We will announce your appointment at the same time, if you can prepare a short statement in reply. Nothing about the dish. Stick to something new about volcanoes," she said. As the evening was clearly winding down, she started to prepare to leave.

"Thanks, Sam, for your accurate shooting tonight. Let me know when you catch the pair who installed the dish, won't you," Sarah said, and went down to find her car still parked outside.

Susan then went back into her office, sat down at the desk, and carefully placed the black box into her backpack, then she went downstairs to find Janet.

"My God, Susan, whatever happened in there?" Janet asked.

"No time to tell you it all now. I've been appointed as the Director of the Observatory, so have to go back inside to do more work on the seismic data with an ageing professor."

"You mean Professor Ferguson? He's been on the island for years and a good man. Listen to what he has to say," Janet replied.

"Okay, but you don't need to stay here all night. Please can you give my bag to Jana when you get back and I'll call her to explain," she replied, handing the bag over and giving Janet a hug.

"So how are you going to get back?"

"Oh! I'll get Sam to drop me off when we're done. Don't worry, I'll be okay. Good night," Susan said, walking back towards the entrance door, where the local press were already being held back by the police and shouting questions at her.

"Can you give us a statement, love?" and "Are we being invaded?" she heard before the outer door closed again and she thought: *This job is going to be fun.*

When she got back to her office, it had already been taken over by the professor. On the desk were the same seismic printouts from January 2020 she had been looking at. They showed two distinct spikes of energy. He looked up when she entered.

"*Err…* can you make us some coffee as we need to wait until midnight to compare the two graphs?" he asked.

"Yes, of course. What exactly are you looking for?"

"Well, you see here the energy spikes had no aftershocks. That shows this was not caused by a volcanic disturbance. I want to wait until midnight to compare tonight's data with that from 2020. Let's see if it's the same," he replied.

"So where does this energy come from if it's not volcanic?"

"Ah! Well, that's where I need your advice. If you were working up at the Asteroid Impact Alert System in the Pacific, you might be able to help me," he replied.

"Right, let me go and get the coffee," Susan replied, wondering if she should tell him the truth.

"You told Sarah you were working on the BB comet theory or C/2014 as it's called now. But since then, it's proved to be on a perpendicular orbit that's less of a problem," he said, as Susan realised he was right up to date on this subject.

"But, coming in perpendicular to Saturn with so many moons that it's become a graveyard," she replied, drinking her coffee.

"A head-on collision might solve the problem, while a near miss could change the orbit entirely. But you're not an astronomer are you, more astro physics if I remember. So why are you so sure it will hit our planet in 2030?" he asked, looking at his coffee.

"Just an educated guess. What if it did?"

"Or have you been to 2030 already?" he said, smiling.

"Ah well, I may have dreams from the future."

"And what's it like, if I may be so bold to ask?"

"How much do you know about the space movements over this island today? The governor knew the ISS was coming overhead; how's that possible?" Susan replied.

"Well, the radio tower was wired up to GCHQ during the eruptions. I assume Sarah asked for support, and they heard these goons talking about a transmission to the ISS. Most likely, isn't it?" he replied.

"Alright, and what about the person who changed the direction of the platform?" she asked.

"A silent intruder who can walk through doors sounds like the most logical answer," he replied.

"Do you really believe that?" Susan asked.

"Yes, you hold a device against a solid wall and you can pass through. It's called 'material interference' if you want to look it up."

"I've never seen that," Susan replied, looking at the clock and wondering how much longer they would have to wait.

"So exactly what are you looking for with this comparison?"

"Simple isn't it. If the two line up as I expect, then it's not an attack on the island's volcano, but more likely a signal sent out into space," he replied.

"Oh! So, it's an 'ET call home' event is it now?" Susan replied, looking confused.

"Yes, my dear, I'm sure you have no idea what happened in January 2020 if you read the diplomatic reports from the previous governor. He said that a ship hit the beach with over 500 illegal migrants who were subsequently sent back to South America. Do you believe that?" he asked.

"No, I can't comment, because I wasn't on the island in 2020."

"So where were you in 2020?"

"I was on the island of Maui until the fire. Working at the Atlas Observatory, as we already discussed. Another coffee, Professor?" Susan teased him, but she was getting valuable information about what had happened on the island in the past. When the clock reached midnight, the professor got up and walked over to the first machine. He tore off the seismic report and came back to Susan, smiling.

"Alright, let's see if they match," he said, as he placed the new graph onto the old and it was almost a perfect match.

"See the same burst of energy twice, and no aftershocks on either. This is a message being sent out to space for whatever reason only you can explain," he said. Susan looked at the data and had to agree it was almost a perfect match.

"Professor, I haven't been completely honest with you tonight. I need to call someone who perhaps can come and help us with this."

"Alright, I can wait, if you can make me another coffee in the meantime," he asked. Then Susan thought it would be better to call Jana from outside rather than in the office.

Susan made more coffee and, handing a mug to the professor, announced she was going downstairs to get some air. Once outside, she opened her phone and called Jana.

"Jana, did Janet give you the black box from my backpack?"

"Yes, I found it, but what does it do because I can't open it or do anything with it," Jana replied.

"Do you still know how to drive the Moke? Because I need you to bring it back to the observatory as soon as possible."

"Alright, I can do that, although you know I hate driving that old car in the dark. Can you quickly tell me what's going on?"

"There's an old professor here who has shown me that the energy burst tonight was the same as the two energy spikes back in January

2020. So, whoever is behind this is not trying to activate the volcano, but send a message into space."

"Wow, that's interesting, so what does this box do?"

"I have no idea, but it was the interface between the screen on the desk and the dish outside. I think we should try to connect to the ISS on its next pass over the island. Anything else new at the house?"

"Yes! James is back and still sleeping from all his teleporting. I was able to read his mind, and he definitely saw Elizabeth on the space station, so I'll bring the remote viewer as well," replied Jana.

"Great, I'm sitting outside the observatory, and will wait here for you here to arrive; drive carefully!" Susan replied, closing the line. She drank her coffee, watching the colours in the sky, when the professor came and sat down on the step beside her.

"Do you mind if I join you?"

"No, not at all. I called my colleague who should arrive in about fifteen minutes. In the meantime, I wanted to talk to you about what really happened at that event on the beach in 2020," she asked.

"Oh! I think you already know the answer to that," he replied, as they both sat and waited for Jana to arrive.

15 – CONTACT

In fact, only ten minutes later, the lights of a car approached as the ageing Moke ground to a halt at the entrance to the observatory. Jana jumped out holding the backpack and handing it to Susan, gave her a hug and started by asking a question.

"Where's this professor guy you told me about?"

"That would be me. Professor Archibald Ferguson at your service, ma'am," he replied with a bow as he emerged from the shadow of the front door.

"And you are?"

"Oh! I'm Jana from Czechia, Janet's assistant, and can sometimes read other people's minds," she replied, making a fake curtsey back to him that made Susan smile.

"Well, I'll try not to think of anything naughty then. Now if you would be so good as to follow me up to my office, we can begin," he said as Jana ran on ahead and followed him up the stairs. Jana sat straight down at the desk, while Susan went to get another chair for the professor to sit on close by.

"Ah! Thank you, Susan. Can you go to the other side of the desk and open the screen again," he asked.

"Now, Jana, as Susan probably explained, these are the seismic graphs. The one below is the record from 2020 and the other on top is the latest from tonight. If you can tell me what you think?" he asked.

"Yes, interesting and looks pretty much the same recording, but not much use as a paper record, is it?"

"Why not, young lady?"

"Because we need something audible. Susan, I think, wants to send it as an audio message back to the space station tonight, right?"

"And how are we going to do that?"

"First I need to take an image of the graph on my phone to generate a jpg image and then open a graph reader app to set up all the values," Jana said, standing up above the latest seismic graph to take a photo.

"Then we open this online tool to select the bitmap and the axis scaling from the low and high points in the image for the Y-axis. Now can you help me, Professor, with the time on the X-axis. The bursts of energy were short and very high, if you can give the figure in seconds to set the time," Jana asked, as the professor measured the first burst as 90 seconds and the second as 270 seconds.

"Nearly done, Professor. There we are, now we have a bitmap image that can be converted to almost any audio file we want with an online image to audio converter."

"You really think we can make these seismic readings into sounds that you can play back on your phone?"

"Yes, never done it before and it may not be perfect. For conversion to an MP3 file, we have to choose the audio frequency ranging from 8,000 Hz to 48,000 Hz. Let's try each of these and listen to the audio noise," said Jana.

"What do you think, Susan?"

"Well, radio waves transmit at around 10,000 Hz and microwaves up to 300,000 Hz, so your frequency numbers are very low."

"Right, let me and the prof look at that."

"Even then, how do we transmit this recording you've made up to the ISS? I've reconnected the box and opened the screen, but it only acts as a receiver," replied Susan.

"Why not try to reconnect the box the other way around?" suggested Jana.

"I hope it doesn't blow us all up," replied Susan, turning off the screen and reversing the connections to the box.

"All right, everyone, let's see if this makes a difference." The professor looked on with alarm at Susan, but nothing happened until she turned the screen on again.

"Wow, I've got a full interactive screen at last! Yes, yes, yes, there's even an icon on the taskbar to send a file," Susan said, as Jana moved over to look at the new screen.

"I must say you two are anything but dull," exclaimed the professor, as Jana thought to herself that there were people watching their every move.

Looking up, she said in a loud voice, "We still need a VHF file if anyone can hear us."

"Jana, who are you talking to?" asked Susan.

"Dunno, but let's see if they answer!"

Susan looked at the professor and smiled at him.

"I'm sorry. Jana does this when she thinks she's being watched," said Susan, looking at the time.

"She's probably right," replied the professor.

"The next fly past of the ISS is in about ten minutes, and I can't stand this wait anymore. I need to go to the toilet. If anyone else needs to follow, it's down in the basement," Susan announced.

"Right, I'll watch your screen," replied Jana, as they waited.

Five minutes later, Jana saw the screen had downloaded a file and was wondering what to do next.

"Don't do anything with that download, Jana, before we check it out," Susan barked at her. She indicated to Jana to stand up and move aside and then sat down in the chair.

Susan placed her finger on the download to see if it would open, but nothing happened. Looking at her watch again, the space station would be in contact again in the next two minutes, so she waited. Meanwhile, Jana moved onto the floor to open the backpack and take out her remote viewer, as Susan looked down to speak to her.

"Jana, stay down there and don't show your face, alright. Do whatever you have to protect us," was all she said as Jana nodded in agreement. When the professor heard this, he wheeled his chair back to the observation desk and sat down in front of a screen.

Susan wondered if her role in this small office was to secretly bring the aliens back with their biometric device. So, they had been watching her all the time, she thought. When the screen opened again, she found she was looking at a woman on the ISS. Meanwhile, Susan calmly looked at the screen and waited for her to speak.

"Mrs Susan West, or should I mention your maiden name? Well, how nice to make your acquaintance and you're with Jana, the Czech girl, so I'm told." As Jana was frantically searching for her image on the viewer, she noticed some wire cutters on the floor. She picked them up in case she needed to cut the conversation.

"Yes, I'm told you're Elizabeth who was on the island in 2020. I'm assuming that from your red hair on the screen," Susan replied.

"That's most observant, so you are working with James Pollack then?" she asked.

"Yes, so what is it you want?"

"If you don't open the link we sent you before we lose communication, then both of you will be removed from your dimension."

"Or you mean you will kill us anyway!" replied Susan.

Jana was reading Elizabeth's mind and seeing it was not just a threat, she cut the cable to the box and the screen went blank.

"What the hell did you just do, Jana? I hope you have a good reason for doing that."

"Yes, she's not on the ISS, but a small capsule following its orbit. That's why there was a delay for her to start the conversation," Jana replied. Standing up again, she placed the box and her tablet into the backpack.

"Come on, Susan, we need to get out of here; this place gives me the creeps. I'll explain the rest in the car," she replied. When they came out of the office, the professor was waiting outside.

"I hope you didn't hear any of that conversation, did you?"

"No, I was monitoring the volcano; was it important?"

"Well, I would be grateful if you don't mention it to Sarah."

"Of course, there are some things that the governor should not be told about on this island, aren't there?" he replied, smiling.

"Exactly. Sarah is planning a conference for the press tomorrow outside the observatory. I hope you might be able to explain the aurora to the media then," Susan said.

"Yes, but will you be there as well?"

"Of course! I still want to work here at the observatory, but under your guidance as the director. I don't want to get involved in the politics on the island. You know so much more than me," Susan replied.

"Very well, I understand. And now?"

"We're going home, if you wouldn't mind locking up?"

"Yes, of course, no problem. Did you ever manage to speak to anyone on the ISS?" he asked.

"No, we never spoke to anyone on the ISS, did we, Jana?" she replied, and Jana shook her head as well.

"Good night, Professor, expect to see you again in the morning," Susan said, and they both walked down the stairs and outside to the car.

***

"Give me the keys if you want me to drive," she said to Jana, who willingly handed over the keys and they both got into the Moke.

"All right, tell me what you really saw that so frightened you," Susan asked.

"When I finally got into her mind, I saw us sitting in a commercial jet that was about to crash. I saw all the yellow face masks falling down on the plane, when she said we were going to be removed. Do you remember that?"

"Yes, of course, but we weren't flying on a plane at the time, so might this be an event we will face in the future?"

"No idea. There were some videos James showed me for that plane MH370; do you remember that?" said Jana.

"The one that crashed into the sea in the Indian Ocean?"

"Yes, but it never crashed, it was taken down by drones and moved into another dimension."

"Do you believe that?"

"Well, it was clearly a military video and the US serviceman who released it got jail time, so it's probably true," Jana replied.

"Still, at least you remembered to take their box. That may enable us to figure out what was on the file they sent us."

"Look, we're back at the house already so can you stop and let me out? Think it's better we close the gates tonight," Jana said.

"Really? You think the press will come up to Janet's house in the morning?" replied Susan.

"Well, that's where you live, isn't it! Go on ahead and I'll walk back," she shouted.

Janet was up when she went into the house, sitting on the settee in the children's play space, talking to Susan.

"That was quite an event tonight wasn't it, Susan," Janet said.

"Yes, I was saved by Jana coming to pick me up. Come on, I think it's time we all go to bed," Susan said. Jana took the backpack and went to find James to tell him the story.

16 – MEDIA

Susan was up early helping the girls get dressed while Bee went to make them breakfast. After that, she took a shower and was thinking about what to wear for the press conference when the governor rang.

"Good morning, Sarah, how can I help you?" she asked.

"Well, I'm not happy. I just heard from Ferguson that you don't want his job after all. He showed you some seismic data from the past and now you can't accept this position."

"Yes, if you put it like that. I think he's a better man for the island, as I wasn't here in early 2020," Susan replied.

"So, what do you want to do?"

"Carry on working at the observatory as his assistant and still come to the press conference today, if you agree?"

"Alright then but come with Janet in her car and I'll reserve you a place in the car park. Will you stand on the platform with the rest of us and answer any questions about the science? Susan, this has turned into an International Press event with crews flying in from Antigua and even the USA."

"I understand, but the auroras should disappear by tonight."

"Good. Oh! One more thing. Sam has located the two men who installed the dish. Both have US diplomatic passports so no point in questioning them. They have already removed the dish, and the metal door, but say there's a box missing. You know anything about that?"

"Yes, don't you remember it was thrown into the forest after the door was shot open?"

"Susan, my dear, you have spent too much time in the US!"

"Alright, we have it. With your permission, can we keep it until we meet again in private on Friday?"

"Alright, same place, same time."

"What time does the conference start today?"

"It's been delayed until noon to allow for the TV cameras to be installed, so wear something smart," she said, and the line went dead.

"I did it!" shouted Susan at the top of her voice, punching her fist in the air that brought Janet knocking on the door and entering.

"Everything alright, Susan? You appear excited this morning."

"Yes, I just convinced Sarah as to why I don't want the job and we're invited to a press conference at noon, if we can take your car."

"Why the press conference, if nothing happened," Janet asked, when Jana stuck her head around the door and said there were TV camera crews at the gate of the house already.

"Alright, I'm going to call Sam and ask for an escort," Janet replied, and left the room looking confused. Jana stayed and gave her a hug and then asked if she could help her get ready.

"First, we have to find you something that looks professional."

"All I have are the clothes we bought at Mary's clothing store. What am I going to do?"

"Don't panic. Janet sometimes gives me her castoffs when I go with her to conferences. What would you like to wear?"

"Oh! I don't know. A dark blouse and black pants would be fine with me. Nothing flashy," Susan replied.

"Okay, let me see what I can find," Jana replied and left the room as Susan started on some makeup for the first time in weeks. Jana returned with an arm full of Janet's old clothes.

"My God, Jana, you found all this. Sorry, I'm at least two sizes bigger than Janet so none of that will fit me."

"Well Janet's running around in circles now after she spoke to Sam and she's talking with James about the box. She's also asked Lucy to come and help with the girls, as you'll be away most of the day."

"That's good, Bee must be exhausted. Look, thanks for your help, Jana, but I'll wear something clean from Mary's that will look as if I work here. Please take all these clothes away now," Susan asked. Shortly after she left, there was a knock on the door, and she saw Lucy standing outside.

"Come on in, Lucy, it's good to see you," Susan said.

"Well, I don't want to bother you if you're not dressed," she began, seeing Susan doing her makeup in only her underwear.

"That's not a problem; how can I help you?" Susan replied as she realised that Lucy must have been on the island during the events in 2020. "I was talking to Professor Ferguson last night about the past and don't really understand what happened."

However, Lucy looked her in the eyes with a reply that really shocked her.

"You were on the ship with Kiya, weren't you?" Lucy said.

"Yes, Lucy, of course I was. Then we found her again on another planet, far away in the future. But I'm back here now, working at the observatory, trying to understand what caused the lights in the sky," Susan replied.

"Well, she's coming back later today, and I thought you should know," Lucy replied with tears in her eyes.

"But how do you know that?" Susan asked. Lucy turned away and ran out of the room and Susan called after her.

"Wait, Lucy, can you tell me some more?" Susan shouted.

By 11 a.m., Susan was dressed and ready and went to find the children and a coffee before they left, where she found Janet sitting at the bar in the kitchen.

"Good, you kept to the island style after all," Janet said, looking at Susan's brown shirt and black jeans. "I have to admit I decided to do the same, with similar colours. It is, after all, a science conference not a fashion show, isn't it."

"The media wants to hear answers and that's what James has been doing with that box you brought back," Janet continued.

"Made any progress so far?" asked Susan.

"Yes, he's been talking to one of my clients in Silicon Valley and has identified it as something experimental produced by Lockheed Martin recently," Janet said looking at Susan. "Is something worrying you?"

"Yes, Lucy came to see me and said something about our past that upset me," Susan replied, looking down into her coffee cup.

"I see, so are you going to speak at the conference?"

"Not unless I'm asked questions about the science."

"Well, as an outsider, you almost certainly will be asked." Janet slid a paper across the table to Susan.

"What's this? A new paper predicting volcanic eruptions?"

"Yes, a study from researchers at Imperial College, London, might help to liven up the discussion a bit," replied Janet, smiling.

"Read it in the car. Our escort arrives at eleven thirty, if you can meet me at the front door in fifteen minutes," Janet continued, and finishing her coffee, she left the kitchen.

Susan carefully folded the paper and putting it in her back pocket, went to find her daughter who she guessed would be playing by the pool.

"Hi, girls, what are you doing today?" she asked as she saw they were being looked after by Lucy.

"You're going to a conference and we're going to watch you on the television," Mary replied.

"Very good," Susan replied clapping her hands.

"My mummy's gone to sleep," said little Nut.

"Well, you're in good hands with Lucy aren't you," Susan continued as Janet appeared, smiling at everyone as they waited for the transport to arrive. When the doorbell rang, Janet opened the door, and found a local police officer waiting for her, next to a white van.

"Mrs Rumford, we were instructed to take you in our van, as there's not enough parking space at the observatory," he said. "There's a lot of press waiting for you at the gate and the boss thought it safer if you travel with us."

"Very well, of course. We'll be right out in just a minute," Janet replied, going back inside to fetch a clutch bag and her phone.

"No backpack today then, Susan. If you've got your phone, we'll be on our way." Susan kissed the girls goodbye and left them with Lucy. As they walked out towards the van and climbed into the back, there were shouts from the press waiting at the gates.

"If you don't want to be photographed, you had better lie down in the back," the sergeant said as he turned the vehicle.

"Well, we don't have anything to hide and they came a long way so let's just wave, shall we, Susan," Janet replied. Another police officer held the gates open as they drove on their way to the observatory.

When they reached Olveston House, there was a police roadblock, with a local crowd, and they were let through immediately.

When the van drew up outside the observatory, they saw it had been transformed into a media centre, with a raised platform for the speakers and rows of chairs for the media and government officials. Sam helped Janet out of the van, while Susan was whisked away towards the platform where Sarah was waiting for her again.

"Good, you made it at last," she said, shaking Susan's hand as a bevy of photographers seated on the ground rose to take their picture.

"Susan, I still don't understand why this aurora has made so much of a news frenzy when these lights were seen in Florida only a few weeks ago?" Sarah asked.

"Florida is much further north, and the whole northern hemisphere experienced a geomagnetic storm. Montserrat is closer to the equator when there were no storms and no other island saw these auroras," Susan replied, but her words were lost as she came face to face with Professor Ferguson again.

"Ah, Susan West, I presume!" he said, shaking her hand and smiling as the press took more photos of them.

"Did you prepare some notes, as I found something you might want to consider," she said, reaching into her back pocket and handing him the copy of the research paper.

"Oh! That's most kind because I overslept and didn't have any time to prepare much," he replied, taking his glasses out and then disappeared to read the latest ideas.

Slowly, the podium was being filled up with other government officials and Susan was pleased when she was told her seat was at the end next to a young British Secretary who warmly welcomed her.

Sarah brought the meeting to order and made a short speech of welcome to people watching from around the world, the press, and other distinguished guests. As Susan looked down, she could see the mobile television vans from the US, all with their satellite dishes pointing to the sky. Next, she called on the prime minister to make an address of reassurance to the people of Montserrat that was short and sincere. Then she called on the Director of the Observatory to advise on his work at the observatory and the state of the volcano.

After a short problem with his microphone, he pulled out a piece of paper and told everyone the new research that had been done predicted no large-scale volcanic eruptions, making sure to mention Imperial College, London, and the University of Bristol in the UK.

Susan realised that after half an hour of speeches, no one had said anything about a geomagnetic storm or the auroras that everyone had seen on the island and was dreading the questions to come. Slowly, all the foreign reporters started to move towards her end of the table as the governor announced the time for questions from the press. The young secretary stepped down from the platform and collected a hand microphone to pass to the members of the press. Immediately, a show of hands was raised and Sarah pointed to a tall American from the ABC news channel to start. At first, he complimented the governor on arranging such a large conference for such a small island and then asked if there was anyone with experience to explain the auroras seen on the island. No one on the panel moved until the governor said that Susan West would be only too happy to enlighten him.

It was then that Susan noticed another woman with headphones had moved to sit beside her with a microphone stand and a stack of cards. She placed the first one down on the table that gave all the details of the person asking the question. Susan blinked and thought, *This is going to be fun*, as she answered by reading off the card.

"Thank you for your question, Matt, and I must say I enjoyed reading your book *No Time to Panic*, so that's what we are doing here today," Susan replied as the audience laughed. Sarah asked for the next question from CBS news, from a blonde woman Debora with a South African accent, as a new card appeared in front of her.

"This question is also for Mrs West, who I understand trained as an astrophysicist from the CV circulated. Is she able to comment seriously on the appearance of the auroras on just one island in the Caribbean?"

"Yes, I can try but I'm not a meteorologist." Susan paused to clear her throat and continued.

"Remember the geomagnetic storm two weeks ago that was seen as far south as Florida? Many people watching today in the US confirmed that. Monserrat is further south, not a lot, but our geomagnetic poles have wandered south in the northern hemisphere and north in the southern hemisphere. Does that answer your question?"

"Not entirely. So, when do these movements stop or might accelerate?" she asked.

"The straight answer is we don't know."

"Thank you for your question, Debora, now the last question is from Ken," Sarah announced. "He's the well-known BBC correspondent in our region. Over to you, Ken," she finished as a new card was put down in front of Susan.

"Another question for Susan West. When I saw you had moved from Maui in the Pacific to this beautiful island in the Caribbean, I thought you must know something that none of us know. Can you tell us in a few words why you came here?"

"Yes, I needed a job. We lost everything from the fire in Lahaina. We were lucky to find a local to sponsor us on this island thanks to Janet Romford," Susan replied, wiping a tear from her eye and Janet stood up to applause from the crowd.

"Thank you, everyone, that's the end of the conference and thank you for coming," Sarah said. Shaking hands with the prime minister and the professor, she smiled at Susan and gave her a thumbs up. While Susan wondered what was coming next for the island. When she looked around, the woman with the cards had disappeared and the young secretary returned.

"That was a brilliant piece of questioning; do you enjoy your work here?" the secretary asked.

"Yes, it's very different from before and much better. What is it that you do?"

"Oh! I'm on secondment at Brades, helping Sarah with the admin mostly, so a day out today is bliss for me," she said.

"Okay, would you like to see inside the observatory? I can sneak you in for a short visit if you like," asked Susan.

"Well, I don't know if I should. Sarah may need something."

"Don't worry, I'll take the blame if you get caught. What's your name, by the way?"

"I'm Carol, originally from Manchester, just like you."

"Come on this way. You will see what our government is paying for." Taking her hand, they ran up to the entrance and went to go upstairs, only to hear the voice of the PM coming.

"Quick this way, to the basement. We don't want to get caught, do we?" said Susan as they waited for the voices to disappear. Then Susan went back first and beckoned her to follow. Once at the top, Susan pulled her into the small office and told her to sit while she checked outside. Finding only Daniel there, Susan went back to find Carol looking at the screen on the desk.

"Why does it say, 'Welcome Susan West – Please Reconnect,' on your screen," she asked.

"Oh! My goodness, I must have forgotten to switch it off," she replied. "Come on, let me introduce you to Daniel, one of the observers on the volcano." Susan took her outside to the observation desk, introduced her, and ran back to her office to call Jana.

"Jana, I need to speak to James urgently. Is he there?"

"Yes, but he's on a call to Cali with some tech nerd. You have a problem?" Jana asked.

"I don't know. I just checked into my office here and the screen's asking me to reconnect. Has James found a purpose for the box, because I'm certain I turned the screen off last night?"

"Yes, they think it's something to move things from one dimension to another. If you can't turn the screen off, then cut the connection wires." Susan looked at the screen and tried turning it off again, only to see confused lines on the screen, when Daniel appeared.

"Susan, I think you should come and see what's happening outside," he said, and she followed him to the screen with the camera trained on a hill of barren volcanic ash.

"Some kind of craft has just landed on Richmond Hill," he said.

"Can you increase the magnification, Daniel?" she asked and turned to Carol, but she shook her head.

"That's the maximum we can get on this camera," Daniel said.

"Alright, do we have binoculars to get a better view, and where are the wire cutters that were in my office? Please can you find them."

"Yes, Susan, here are the wire cutters."

"Carol, I can't turn off my screen, so can you take these and go into the office and cut the cable to my screen, while I go and look outside to get a closer view."

"Yes, Susan, but that's government property. Are we allowed to damage that here?" Carol asked.

"Yes, we are at this observatory," Susan demanded and, taking the binoculars, she went outside with Daniel. There was no longer any craft on the hill, but there was clearly a body lying in the ash. Susan immediately thought of what Lucy said about Kiya, but it had to be reported whoever it was up there, so she called Sam.

"Sam, I'm up at the observatory and have to report there appears to be a body on Richmond Hill."

"Yes, that's already been reported, and I've asked for a helicopter to fly up and recover the body. I'm on my way to you and will be there in five," he said, as Susan realised that Carol had not returned. When she went back to the office, she found it empty and sat down with her hands in her face. When she looked down, the wires had not been cut and the screen was simply unplugged, so she called Jana again.

"Jana, did James activate the dimension icon because we have just lost one of the workers up here," Susan began, when James took the phone.

"Yes, Susan, we activated for just one second. What's happened with you?" James asked.

"James, are you mad? You just moved the governor's private secretary to another dimension. Now you get her back!"

"Wow, it does work. Okay, you turn the screen on, and I'll open the icon like last time and she should reappear, I think," he said.

"Alright, but I'm not sitting in the office to disappear, so give me ten seconds from now, as I'm plugging the screen in again." Susan ran out to join Daniel on the observation deck. The next they heard was Sam, who had just arrived, shouting that a young girl was lying on the floor of her office. When they went to look, there was Carol lying on the floor, and Susan breathed a sigh of relief.

"Oh! My goodness, that's Sarah's secretary who first saw the body on the hill outside. Is she alright, Sam?" Susan asked.

"Yes, I think so. If you bring her some water, I'll sit her down in this chair," he said as Carol slowly regained consciousness.

"How do you feel, Carol? Should I call you an ambulance?" asked Susan.

"No, no. I was sitting in this chair and must have fainted from the heat. There's a woman called Kiya on the mountain outside who needs to be rescued; can you do that?" Carol asked.

"Yes of course, there's a helicopter on its way now," replied Sam who looked at Susan and asked if they could talk outside.

"Susan, what the hell's going on here? How does she know the body is a woman named Kiya?" he asked.

"Because another local girl told me that this person Kiya would be returning today."

"And how do they all know her name?"

"She was on the island in January 2020, before the pandemic. I talked to the professor last night and he confirmed what happened."

"Is that why you turned down the job as director here?"

"Partly, and I don't want to get involved in island politics."

"Alright then, where do you want them to land with the body, because you know we don't have a hospital on the island."

"Can you ask the pilot to land on the Old Bluff, just outside Janet's house and I'll call them to meet the chopper there."

"Well, I hope you know what you're doing because the governor is going to ask questions, isn't she."

"You can refer her to me, as we have a good relationship."

"What about the girl outside? What do we say about her?"

"Well, Sam, nothing happened. I'll make us all a coffee and you can take us all back to Olveston House. Now can I call the house and tell them when the helicopter will arrive?" Susan asked.

"Very well, I'll call the airport now and let you know an ETA shortly," Sam agreed, and Susan went to ask how many people wanted a coffee. As she waited for the water to boil, Susan sent a text to Jana to say all was well at the observatory and to expect a chopper to land outside shortly. She got a two-word reply: "Lucy knows," and she smiled at all these telepathic people.

After coffee, Sam drove them back to Olveston House where the lunchtime buffet was finishing, and they picked Janet up again.

Sam insisted on driving them back to Janet's house, where the pilots were just leaving after carrying the body of a woman inside. Sam thanked the pilot and crew, who were not certain if she could be revived. To repay him for his services, Susan invited Sam inside, just in time for him to watch a naked body being lowered into the pool by a local teenage girl he recognised.

***

The next morning, Janet found that Kiya had regained consciousness, having been revived by the water. Lucy asked Janet to drive them both to her house in Woodlands to let her recover there for a few days. Meanwhile, Susan was getting ready to return to her work at the observatory. The only question Susan had was why Kiya had come back now and what it would mean for their future on the island.

17 – OBSERVATORY

The next morning, Bee was relieved to learn that Janet had taken Kiya to Lucy's house to sleep. She was sitting with Susan and Jana around the breakfast bar, drinking coffee.

"Does anyone know why Kiya has come back to the island?" Bee asked.

"No, but as they carried her out to Janet's car, I was able to touch her head and she was warning about something still up on the hill," replied Jana. Susan noted that before standing up to leave.

"Or maybe she was trying to escape from someone on Richmond Hill. Look, I'm back to work at the observatory this morning and will take another look from up there," she replied, and went downstairs to get her backpack. When she returned, both the girls were eating breakfast, and she stopped to give a big hug to her daughter and then spoke to Jana again.

"Can you have a look on your remote tablet to see who may have brought her back here yesterday?" she asked.

"Okay, I'll try, but I think we should wait until she's ready to explain what happened. Have a good day at the observatory," Jana replied, and Susan left for the short drive to her work.

Susan parked outside as usual and seeing dark rain clouds above her, fitted a cover on the Moke and went inside, where Daniel was waiting for her, with the wire cutters in his hands.

"Good morning, Susan. Do we still need these or can I put them back in the storeroom?" he asked.

"I think we're done with those for now, as well as the screen on my desk. Can I come down with you to see if there is a spare screen I could use instead?" she replied.

"Of course, it's down in the basement, if you follow me." Susan picked up the screen that the men had brought in her arms and went downstairs with Daniel. When he unlocked the door, she saw it was a large room with old electrical equipment from twenty years ago.

"My goodness, this really is a junk room! Whoever saved all this stuff?" Susan asked.

"This was the professor's private storeroom; not many people know it even exists," he said, taking the screen from Susan and placing it at the back of the room.

"Now, you're looking for something to plug in on your desk to look at the volcano?" he asked.

"Yes, but is the camera still turned on Richmond Hill?"

"It is, *err*. I think the prof used this large screen in the past and may have a better definition than the screens we have. I'll carry it upstairs for you," Daniel replied, handing her the key to lock the door, whereupon they went back upstairs to her office.

"Why don't you make yourself a coffee while I connect the screen to the camera feed for you?" he suggested.

When Susan looked at the weather outside, she saw it was raining "cats and dogs" from a heavy storm outside. She made herself a mug of coffee and went and sat in Daniel's chair next to his assistant. As they watched the rain pouring down on the observation deck outside, the assistant turned and asked about the body they had seen yesterday.

"Do you know if the person was rescued?" he asked, which brought her back to reality.

"Yes, a body was found and brought down by one of the helicopters. It may have been a tourist who got lost now that we have more visitors to the island. It's a dangerous part of the exclusion zone," replied Susan, who realised more questions were going to be asked about this. When Daniel returned, he saw the rain.

"Wow, that's quite a tropical storm. I've connected the screen in your office. There's nothing much on visual until the rain stops, but that screen has an infrared filter, if you would like to come and see," he remarked and Susan went back to her office to check it out.

"Look, I didn't want to say much in front of that UK student, and don't want to start more gossip again. I'm sure Ferguson has told you about the events that happened in 2020."

"Yes, he hinted, and said the official reports were a cover-up."

"Right, well he knew, because the government had this screen installed to watch those events in infrared. At that time, the platform was made to turn 360 degrees to monitor all the island."

"Yes, yes, Daniel, but that was four years ago, so what's new?" Susan asked, looking at the screen that showed only mist and cloud.

"Are you ready? I'm going to switch over to infrared now," said Daniel and she could see at least three blurry figures moving around on the side of Richmond Hill.

"What the fuck! You mean they're back?" Susan asked.

"Keep your voice down," replied Daniel, as suddenly Ollie appeared dripping wet at the door and Daniel cut the image.

"Howdy, Mrs West, you're right, I'm back. I've come to collect the screen and the box we left behind," he said, as Susan looked at Daniel in panic and he answered.

"Ah, yes, the screen. We have it locked away in the storeroom downstairs. If you wait, I'll go and fetch it for you," Daniel replied.

"And the box, we want that back as well," he shouted at him.

"I'm sorry, but we had a problem with that yesterday. It affected one of the governor's staff badly after the press conference."

"What do you mean by affected?" he asked.

"She lost consciousness in my office. Now, if you follow me, I'll show you what we did with that," Susan replied, getting up and leading the way out onto the observation deck.

"My assistant here was so concerned that it was dangerous that he threw it into the forest, as far away as possible," she said.

"You Brits are mad, you know. That's US government property and we want it back," he shouted at her.

"Well, I think it hit that tree over there and then bounced down into that gully. I'm sure you can find it; perhaps better when the rain stops," she replied and walked back inside, where she found Daniel holding the screen in his arms. Ollie grabbed the screen and, turning at the entrance, shouted something about reporting her to the governor and left.

"What an impatient young man," Susan replied, as Daniel smiled with a sigh of relief, while Susan went back to her office to look at her screen again.

***

Meanwhile, back at the house, James and Jana were discussing why Kiya was having bad thoughts up on Richmond Hill. Jana had tried to connect to her with the remote viewer but without any success.

"Do you remember the ship that hit the bridge in Baltimore some weeks ago?" Jana asked James.

"Yes, of course. It was first claimed by some to be a conspiracy theory. So, you don't think it was an accident?" asked James.

"Well, it may look like an accident, but it's still not clear what caused the ship to lose propulsion. They recovered the ship's data recorder a month ago, and nothing's been reported since. Normally in these cases, an inquiry is announced, but the president agreed to renew the bridge with Federal funds… just one day after the collision with no explanation of why he was responsible," replied Jana.

"Except Baltimore is a democratic state, isn't it?"

"Yes, but there were none of the usual maritime insurance investigations and that raised alarm bells in my head."

"Jana, what are you getting at here?" asked James.

"Look, we know what the box can do as a 'dimension displacer.' What if they scale it up and direct so much energy that the whole ship is moved ever so briefly to another dimension? That's what you did with Carol and we saw it with the MH plane," replied Jana.

"Well, it's possible to hack a ship's GPS, but we're talking about an enormous container ship. The pilots could see the bridge and yet, were still unable to turn or stop the ship in time."

"Exactly, that's my point. Someone needed to control the time dimension to make certain that the ship slammed into the bridge."

"So, if this was an assisted accident, who was responsible for it and for what purpose?" asked James.

"No one knows, just like the aurora lights we saw here," Jana replied as her mobile rang with a call from Susan.

"Jana, are you with James, because there are some strange things going on up at Richmond Hill," Susan asked.

"Alright, I'll put you on the speaker. Go ahead now."

"I'm up at the observatory and found a better screen to look with the camera outside. It can see the hill with infrared vision."

"Okay, what have you seen, Susan?"

"Well, we had a big rainstorm here and during the rain I could see nothing except the mist on the hill. When I switched over to infrared, I saw at least three figures moving around high up on the hill," she said.

"Are you sure? Because that's a part of the exclusion zone. No one lives up there anymore, Susan," Jana replied.

"I know, and Daniel, my assistant, saw it as well. You know what, as soon as the rain stopped, all the figures disappeared," replied Susan.

"Alright, don't tell anyone else about this. I need to check this out with Sam. I don't think his helicopters would fly in a heavy deluge like that, would they?"

"No, and I think Sam, or one of us, should go up to this hill to check it out," replied Susan.

"Alright, let's talk about this when you come back for lunch." When Susan closed the call, Jana posed a question, more in fear.

"So, James, it sounds like the aliens are back," she said.

"Probably. Can you call Sam to check about a helicopter? Then ask him to meet me at the old houses on the Cork Hill road, just before the exclusion zone," he replied.

"You've been there before?" Jana asked.

"No, just looked on Google Maps. We'll probably have to start at the bottom and walk up," James explained, smiling.

18 – RICHMOND HILL

When Susan returned to the house, she went straight down to Jana's bedroom to talk to James. Only she found Jana alone feeding her baby and excused herself for barging in.

"Oh! I'm sorry, Jana, do you know where James is?"

"*Err*... James, yes, he left a short while ago. He went out on the terrace to teleport from there to meet up with Sam after you called. They're meeting somewhere down below Richmond Hill," she replied, holding her son up to let him burp.

"Jana, this is serious. If the people I saw moving around up there are aliens, we, all of us, are in great danger."

"Yes, I know. If they are back, we will have to move." Janet appeared, having overheard the conversation, as the door was open.

"Who said anything about moving, Susan?" Janet asked.

"Well, *err*..."

"Yes, I heard you saw something up at the observatory, but now we appear to have another problem. The governor called me and requested that I bring you to Government House at 2 p.m. this afternoon. Can you explain why?" Janet asked.

"That American Ollie, turned up during a rainstorm wanting his screen and the black box they installed back," Susan replied.

"Really, and you gave them back to him?"

"The screen, yes, but the box is here with James."

"Well, the American said you were rude and it had been thrown into the forest. Is that true?" she said.

"No, *err*. Yes, I said that because I wanted to get rid of him. I already told Sarah I would give it back to her at our meeting on Friday. That was to give James time to check it out."

"Alright, I understand. So where is the box now, Jana?"

"James took it with him when he left to meet Sam, below Richmond Hill," Jana replied.

"What! And I heard James activated it yesterday. So, what exactly does this box do?" Janet asked.

"Apparently, it almost killed Sarah's PA. The poor girl was terrified," Jana said.

"She was sitting in front of the screen one minute and disappeared the next. Then Sam found her lying on the floor. Don't you understand that box is dangerous? It can kill people," Susan replied.

"So how did you get her to come back?" asked Janet.

"I told James to reverse the settings on the box and re-activate it again," replied Jana.

"Don't any of you have any respect for the science being developed today? Sarah told me this is the latest AI box to come out of the US. It was developed to 'Save the planet,'" Janet replied.

"More likely to destroy the planet. They refused to tell us what the dish was for, who manufactured it, and all they wanted to do was move people off the island," Susan replied.

"You should know, James found out from a contact in Silicon Valley that the box was a 'dimension displacer'. Why's that being tested on this island without any scientific approval? Nor any supervision from the UK. Janet, it doesn't make sense," explained Jana.

"Alright, now I understand. Go and get some lunch, as we need to leave a quarter before two."

"You think I've started a political incident then?"

"I really don't know, but I have a bad feeling about this diplomatically. You had better bring your British passport," Janet replied, and Susan left to find her daughter and grab something to eat.

****

When James appeared at his destination, he was next to a wooden telegraph pole without any wires. In the distance, he saw the damaged houses on the Cork Hill road and Sam's all-terrain truck parked there already. Sam waved and James walked towards him with a small knapsack on his back.

"James, I got your message and came as fast as I could. I brought you some kit and boots if you want to climb that hill above us," he said, pointing at the hill partly covered in mist.

"No, I don't need any more kit, but can't you drive up any closer, because it's much too far to walk," replied James.

"Yes, the road used to continue further up. We can try that if you prefer," Sam replied. James climbed into his truck and Sam drove up a rutted road that had almost disappeared in places.

"Here we are at the turning point, I can't drive any further," said Sam, and as he turned the vehicle for a fast descent, they both got out and looked up at the hill again.

"Look, we're less than halfway up, so as a military man, how do we look at the enemy from here?" James asked.

"Wait, let's take a look at the target through binoculars and see," Sam replied.

"Anything?" asked James.

"Yes, there's a bloody great pillar of light coming down on this side of the hill. Here, you take a look," he said, passing the binoculars to James.

"Correct. That looks like some sort of communication to a mother ship probably above us in the clouds," James replied.

"Well, I brought a 12-bore shotgun in case we had a 'close encounter', but that won't reach that far. I also brought one of the drones we use to check on security at the airport," he replied.

"Now that sounds promising, Sam. Can you let me see?" replied James as they went to look at the drone in the back of the truck. "Okay, and can this drone also carry any sort of weight?"

"Possibly, what do you have in mind," replied Sam.

James then took the black box out of his knapsack and showed it to Sam.

"We know this was the box that moved the girl you found up at the observatory. Let's see if we can move things up there as well," James said, pointing up at the hill.

"Okay, yes, it's not that heavy. Let me see how to attach it under the drone," Sam agreed, searching for some wire to hold it in place. When he finished, he gave a thumbs up to James.

"We only get one crack at this. Can you fly the drone straight into the pillar of light and let's see what happens?"

Sam took out a control panel from the back of his truck and switched on the power. Immediately, the drone came to life and rose above the truck, with Sam guiding it towards the top of the hill. James, meanwhile, watched through the binoculars.

"Can you go a bit higher?" shouted James. "More to the left and higher," he said, as the drone was caught by the light and disappeared from sight.

"What the hell did you do, because I have to account for having lost one of our drones," Sam complained, but James had turned around to hear a massive explosion coming from the direction of the volcano.

"Sam, I think it worked. The beam of light has gone. Look at this through the binoculars," James cried, handing them to Sam.

"Yes, James, but I think you have caused the sulphur fields to erupt over there. There's a flood of gas, mud, and water cascading down the hills," replied Sam, pointing over to the Soufrière volcano. "Come on, we need to get the hell out of here," he insisted as they both climbed back into his truck. Sam started the engine and drove as fast as he could down the hill again.

19 – EXTRADITION

Janet and Susan arrived at the Government House in Woodlands, shortly before 2 p.m. on 6 June 2024, and parked next to several other cars outside. Susan got out and remarked to Janet as they walked towards the pink entrance doors.

"Is this it? Looks more like an old people's home!"

"*Ssh*, Susan, keep your voice down. This is the back with the admin offices; the official entrance is more impressive," Janet replied, and led the way up to the governor's office on the first floor.

"Wow, a photo of King Charles, so he really does rule over the island then?" asked Susan.

"Yes, of course he does, and this is his official residence," replied Janet, as a secretary approached and ushered them into a large meeting room.

Sarah was sitting at the head of the table, wearing a green dress in the island colours. Janet was more comfortable in a grey dress and Susan, dressed in jeans and a work shirt, was feeling most outclassed. No one shook hands as Janet realised this was going to be more than an official dressing down.

"I've called you here today as our American partners have made some serious allegations against Mrs West and I can't ignore them. Can I see your UK passport please," she asked, as Susan slid her British passport across the table, and said nothing.

"The photograph looks good, but you were never born in Liverpool in 1970, were you? The real Mrs West died five years ago, so why have you presented this passport to me?" Sarah demanded.

Janet looked at Susan, who shook her head and indicated for her to say nothing.

"Governor, what exactly are you accusing this British subject of doing? She supported your project at the observatory and brought credit to the island during a press conference you arranged," Janet said.

"Yes, I'm aware of all that, but the US government has withdrawn their support for her to work on the island."

"Is that all because of an AI box they installed at the observatory, with your knowledge and permission?" Janet replied.

"Look, my hands are tied, I spoke to the Foreign Secretary, and he agrees we must hand this person over to the US authorities," Sarah replied. That really upset Janet as she went on the attack.

"Hand her over to who? She's a British subject, whatever you may say about her identity papers. There is no Foreign Secretary at present, parliament is dissolved, and the present government is heading for its biggest defeat in over a hundred years," Janet replied.

"I'm sorry; it's been decided she will be handed over to the US authorities at Little Bay, as soon as their boat arrives."

"And you spoke to which Foreign Secretary? Because he's been trying to sell Gibraltar back to the Spanish. You know what will happen with this new socialist government. They want to get closer to the EU. Perhaps they will hand this island back to the EU and ask France to make it part of their overseas region. Then you will need to speak French!" Janet replied, when a new secretary entered the room to say the governor had an urgent call from Professor Ferguson.

"Alright, I'll take it here as we have the science experts in front of me," Sarah said, and a speakerphone appeared on the table and the call was transferred.

"Ferguson, what's the problem?"

"It's the bloody volcano, it's erupted again," they all heard in shock.

"A mass of rocks and slurry. There's poisonous gas rolling down the hill towards us. I think we're going to evacuate, never seen anything like this…" As the line cut out, everyone looked at each other in horror.

"You think this box did all this?" said Susan.

"What exactly does this AI box do? You must know something about this, Janet?" asked the governor.

"Yes, your head of security at the airport went to check out Richmond Hill where they recovered a body yesterday. He met with one of my team who had the box and I'm guessing that may have caused the volcano to erupt," Janet replied.

"So, this box has immense power that may have caused danger to all the people on the island."

"Yes, and it can displace persons as well, as we saw with your assistant, who no longer appears to be here," asked Janet.

"No, we have sent her back to the UK for treatment after that experience. What is it that you will do, Mrs Romford, in this situation?"

"In one word, we will leave. All of us, tonight," she replied as Susan gasped at her comment.

"Really, and how do you intend to do that after the last flight left for Antigua already this afternoon?"

"I have my own plane that will pick my people up this evening and return to England. Then we will wait for the US to proceed with these extradition charges in the UK," Janet threatened.

"I see. In that case, I will have to consult with the PM here on this delicate matter. Please excuse me for a few minutes," she replied, stood up, and left the room.

Janet smiled at Susan and they gave each other a big hug, then seeing bottles of water on a side table, she took two bottles with glasses and returned to the table.

"Well, Susan, what do you want to do, go back to London, or be handed over to the US authorities?"

"But can we really leave by tonight?"

"Yes, I gave Sam a call. NASA or whoever I rented the plane from haven't come up with their repayment of over a billion. I'm needed at a board meeting in London next week, to explain how we can put pressure to get their investment back," she explained as she called Sam on her phone and Susan listened in.

"Sam, it's Janet. Yes, we heard there was an eruption, but listen. We're at Government House and have a diplomatic problem with your US people. Can you take James to the airport and say we want to take the craft out for a little spin?" she asked, but Susan didn't hear his reply.

"I understand it may take a few hours to prepare the plane. That's okay as we don't need it until this evening. Can you do that for us? We need to return to England tonight," Janet insisted, and then cut the call.

"My God, Janet, this isn't just about the volcano on the island but something much bigger," replied Susan.

"Yes, I'm afraid so. It goes right to the top! Can you put the TV on in the room. I just had an alert on my phone that our king is speaking on the D-Day landings that took place some eighty years ago," she asked, and Susan got up and opened the screen to the BBC World Service live report from Portsmouth.

"Here we are, two Brits watching our king in the Government House on Montserrat, can't get more British than that," she said as the governor came back into the conference room and sat down, waiting for King Charles to finish his speech.

"Janet, Susan, why don't we all have a cup of tea to resolve this matter," the governor said, smiling at everyone, as an assistant brought in a tray with a teapot, milk, sugar, and three cups with saucers.

"Now then, Janet, let's have a discussion off the record, shall we? First, I understand you have a payment problem with the US authorities after returning their craft to the island," the governor opened.

"Yes, it was all done according to a legal contract. Payment within a month of return, and I've heard nothing more. So, without any payment, I'm entitled to take the craft out for a spin, don't you think?" Janet replied, passing a cup of tea to Susan.

"I have no idea of your business arrangements, but exactly how many people do you want to leave with tonight?" she asked.

"The first flight will leave with me, my company secretary Jana, and the two children on the island. I brought these children here and believe I'm responsible for their safety."

"What about the others you sponsored?" she asked.

"And after that, it's up to the others to decide to stay or leave. If Susan and Bee want to stay and face being deported to the US, that's their decision, and I will respect that," Janet replied.

"Very well, and when will you be ready to do this?"

"As soon as the craft has been prepared to fly again. I think the pilot would like to leave before dusk. If I can have your permission to leave from the airport, it would be better. That would help to avoid more gossip from the locals," Janet asked.

"Yes, that can be arranged, and your transport, that will be done privately?" Sarah replied.

"Of course, that will leave you to deal with more auroras, an erupting volcano, and possible aliens. You know, Sarah, the situation here is better than a Sci Fi book. I promise to come back once you've got it all sorted," said Janet, helping herself to another cup of tea.

Sarah turned up the volume again and everyone went back to watching the D-Day celebrations on the TV, while Janet waited for an update on the plane's readiness from Sam. After a few minutes, Sarah got up and announced she would bring her staff to the room and left.

Almost immediately, a local man entered and went to sit next to Susan, who she recognised from the press conference as the island's prime minister. He started to talk in earnest to her.

"I was impressed with your Q&A at the conference and think it would be a mistake if you left the island now," he said in a low voice.

"Well, I don't want to be handed over to the CIA, so what choice do I have?" Susan replied, as the television was showing a speech by the Prince of Wales on the screen.

"Look, Sarah doesn't know what to do. All the British leaders are away today and on some day trip to Normandy tomorrow. She's only getting advice from the spooks in London, who can't rock the boat," he replied.

"So, it's US Intelligence who is putting all the pressure, isn't it," she replied, covering her voice.

"I was here during the 2020 event that was covered up by everyone, including her predecessor. There was no way 500 people can land on a boat and then simply disappear," he said.

"What did you see at that time," Susan replied.

"Did you speak to Ferguson? He spent days up at the observatory watching their movements at night. He thought they were building something. But we're not allowed to ask any questions," he replied, and stopped as Sarah entered the room again.

Sarah returned, followed by her assistant carrying a tray of sandwiches, and trailed by several of her local admin workforce. They must have been invited as they came and sat at the table opposite Susan to watch the D-Day commemorations of the Normandy landings.

The PM passed plates around and they both took a few sandwiches. Then he motioned to her to leave to continue their conversation in the corridor outside, and they left the room.

"What do you mean building something? He never told me that," she asked.

"There's a place just below the exclusion zone called Windy Hill, where he saw hundreds gathered each night. He thought they were working on something. We never found out what, as they made warning signs that say 'entry is strictly prohibited' in this zone. Since then, none of us locals have been allowed up there," he said, eating some sandwiches at the same time.

"But you must know more; what's happened since then?"

"Yes, at the start of the pandemic, when we were all locked down, they sent some army engineers up there. They built a couple of wind turbines, with no cables coming out. Said it was done to 'save the planet' and all that green bullshit," he replied.

"So, the electricity generated is being used by something or somebody in a restricted area," Susan asked.

"That's the question we all would like to know. Will you stay to help us find out?" he asked, when Sarah appeared with an empty tray in her hand.

"I hope you are able to convince her to change her mind," she said, and disappeared down the corridor.

"Whatever did she mean by that?" Susan asked.

"Oh! She's probably going to get new instructions from whoever is advising her. Look, they're in complete panic if any of this should be made public. I heard more news that someone called Justin Benbow is being sent to the island. He will be the new head of police. Do you know anything about who he is?" the PM asked.

"Yes, I know Janet was proposing someone when I first arrived. An army guy, I think, as head of police, that's interesting."

"Yes, and I think he was on the team they sent out when the event first started in 2020. Strange that, isn't it," he replied, when Sarah returned and told them to come back into the conference room for an announcement. Susan looked at the PM and smiled.

"Here we go again," she said and followed him back inside, taking her seat next to Janet again.

Sarah remained standing and, switching off the TV, asked all members of her staff to leave the room. Susan took the break to send a text to Janet that read 'Justin is coming back', to which she received a reply, 'Yes, it was on the local news,' as Sarah sat down to talk directly to both Janet and Susan.

"I've been in contact with our US partners, and we have agreed on a solution to the present situation on the island," she said.

"In view of the recent media exposure, Susan and her colleague can continue their work on the island, under my strict control and no further contact with the media," she announced, that brought a wide smile of support from the PM.

"Turning to Mrs Romford's affairs, I understand that you have business in London that also needs to be resolved. You have my permission to take your private jet and leave from Osborne Airport tonight," Sarah confirmed and without even a glance at Janet, she left the room.

"Wow, that's quite a climb down. I wonder what made her change her mind," asked Susan.

"Well, I sent Sarah a copy of the company agenda that proposes a vote at the meeting to hand the plane to Space X if NASA still refuses to pay," Janet replied.

"So, she passed it on, and they gave way. But does this SpaceX have that kind of money?" asked Susan.

"Oh yes! Musk will receive a $50 billion bonus when it's approved at his shareholders meeting next week. That's a great deal more to cover what we're owed," she replied. Susan was stunned at how technology and the space race had developed since they were away.

"Come, Susan, I think we can leave and return to the house. I have some calls to make and packing to do before the flight tonight," Janet said.

Standing up, she turned to shake the PM's hand for his support and they all left the room.

Once back in the car, Susan started to worry about how this decision would impact her life at the house.

"Janet, who's going to run the house while you're away?"

"You are, my dear. I have every confidence in you after all these recent events," she replied.

"Yes, but I don't have the local power that you do."

"Well, I've offered to provide lodgings to Justin at the house. Then you will have the Chief of Police staying to protect you. You do remember him don't you, from your time at the RAF base."

"Yes, of course. But that was only for a month before we left the base," replied Susan.

"He doesn't know anything about his future, but you need to ask him about his past on the island," replied Susan, as the car reached the drive on the Old Bluff. When they entered the house, Bee and the two girls were already waiting inside to hear the news.

"Good news today, your mothers will be continuing their work on the island and I'm taking a short trip to London," Janet announced, as Susan nodded at Bee, who looked on surprised. Meanwhile, Jana appeared in the shadows, looking more concerned, and went back to her room to start packing. Janet soon came to talk to her.

"Jana, I know this isn't perfect, but really, I think your baby would be better in a cooler climate. We can hire a full-time nurse to look after him," Janet offered, to calm her down.

"Alright, I understand, and maybe this was the best you could do to stop Susan from being deported. But you know there's a risk of these aliens again and Susan may need my help."

"Yes, that's why Justin will be back as Chief of Police, and I've invited him to live with us here. To give support and…"

"Yes, yes, I heard that on the news and he's a good man who James can work with. But where is James now as I can't find him on the island after the Richmond Hill incident?"

"Sam told me they were down at the airport preparing the plane. We need to leave before 6 p.m. if you can start packing a few essential items," Janet asked, looking at her watch that showed it was just after five.

"Right then, see you at the door in half an hour to say goodbye to everyone," Janet said.

"Yes, of course, I'll be there," Jana replied, and went to explain the situation to Susan and Bee.

"How long do you think you will be away?" Susan asked.

"It's going to be at least a week, as the board meeting is scheduled for next Wednesday. Our return will depend on what's decided. Whether we return the plane here, or hand it over to another company in the US called SpaceX," Jana replied.

"What are you going to do with the plane until then?"

"Bee, I don't know; that's up to James. Listen, I must go and pack things for him and find him somewhere to stay. Come and say goodbye at the entrance with your girls, before five thirty," Jana asked and left their room.

Right on time, Janet appeared with a small case and Jana followed with a smaller pink carry-on bag, holding her baby wrapped in a shawl. After goodbye hugs, Janet handed the keys of her car to Susan and asked her to drive them to the airport.

PART FOUR
YOU NEED TO KNOW –
MAY 2024

20 – SURFACE

When Justin awoke, he was lying on the floor of the wardroom on the *Albany* submarine, still dressed in his Arctic jacket, boots, gloves, and a mask. Not being sure what was happening, he pulled himself up onto the bench seating that ran around by the door, pulled open his torn Velcro fastening on the jacket, and threw his gloves and mask on the table. He was thinking about what had happened and where Mathew was, when a sailor arrived, arms full of another jacket.

"Here you are, I've found you a larger size that should fit better," he said, helping to pull his old jacket off his shoulders and replace it with another. "Yes, that looks better; is there anything else I can get you?"

"The face mask. Do you have something that can see X-rays?" Justin asked, thinking of what may happen next outside.

"Well, they're only for the captain and the COB," he replied.

"Of course, but I'm expecting to see X-rays," he said.

"Alright, I'll go and see if we have a spare," he replied, and left. As Justin waited, he saw a coffee jug on the table and stopped to fill a mug with the hot drink. Sitting down again, he was starting to feel much better when an officer arrived to check his clothing. Seeing liquid on the floor, he asked him what happened.

"Sorry, must have spilt it from my coffee," he explained, as Justin realised it was melted ice from when he first arrived.

The officer ignored him, tightening up all the fastenings on his jacket and gloves.

"So, where's your mask?" he asked, when the sailor returned with a new mask at last and Justin was declared ready to go outside.

He was led along the corridor back to the control room and, remembering the access ladder to the top of the sail, gave a thumbs up sign and climbed up to the top. As he pulled himself up onto the deck plating, he saw Captain Costello and the COB pushing blocks of ice off the sail, like before. That confirmed to Justin that somehow, he had got back on board as he started to remember that he had been on the ice with Mathew, the Camp Commander. On seeing Justin stand up on the sail, Costello used the same words as last time.

"The crew have already fixed the rope ladders so we can descend onto the ice," he explained, but Justin was looking at Ice Camp Whale. With his X-ray mask, he could clearly see a force field active all around the camp, but decided to say nothing for now. As they waited, no one came out of the camp to welcome them this time.

Two more crew members arrived and confirmed the radio mast was fixed on the tower and the chief went back down inside. He was now worried what new messages might be received. After that, Costello looked at Justin and announced, "I'll go first to meet the Camp Commander."

"No, Captain, there is no Camp Commander to meet. Allow me to go down first," he replied.

"What the hell's got into you, Lieutenant Benbow! The captain always goes down first," he replied.

"Not this time; it's too dangerous. Let me see if it's safe for you to leave your submarine," he replied and started to climb down the ladders. When they both reached the ice, Costello stared at what he saw as insubordination. Justin took off his mask and handed it to the captain, who put it on in disbelief.

"What the hell happened here? How did you know there was this force field around the camp?" he asked, as they both walked towards the force field surrounding the camp.

"I told you. The same that happened to us in the Caribbean," Justin said calmly.

"Well, come on, we have to get inside. There may be sick or injured persons inside there," he shouted at Justin, trying to push his way past until he fell down on the ice.

"Look, maybe I didn't make myself clear. This field is a force of high radiation. If you go inside, you can't get out again to resume command. If you try to walk out, you will receive a massive dose of radiation that will eventually kill you," he shouted back at the captain, who lay on the ice just in front of the field. Then they saw the COB shouting and running across the ice towards them.

"Captain, stop! Captain, we've received some previous orders not to surface here. This place is a trap. Something landed here they think may be a nuclear bomb! We must submerge and leave as soon as possible," he explained. Justin put his arm out and helped Costello to his feet and they all jogged back towards the submarine. When they reached the ladders, Costello turned to Justin and ordered: "You don't repeat anything the COB said! We found a force field around the camp, were unable to enter, and now we are taking you and all of us out of here. Is that clear, Lieutenant?"

"Yes, sir. Understood," Justin replied, as the crew shouted up to the sail, "Captain coming on board," that was repeated up the line. Costello leapt up the ladders, shouting to his men: "Prepare the Comms; Prepare the Comms," until he disappeared down the hatch and was gone. The COB turned to Justin and remarked, "What happens to the people at the camp? How did you know about the force field?"

"We saw that on an island in the past," Justin replied.

"No, here at the camp. You've been here before, haven't you?" he asked, looking at him suspiciously.

"I don't know what you mean," Justin replied, and they both climbed back up the ladders to get back on board.

Once Justin climbed down into the control room, Costello was waiting for him, and Justin asked, "Are there other subs underwater around here?" taking off his jacket, mask, and gloves.

"Yes, there are two. We've sent an urgent code by sonar, and they are already on their way out of here," he replied.

"So, we are the last boat at the ice camp," Justin replied.

"Yes, this was the latest report we received. It sounds like the camp was being evacuated when the force field came into operation," he said, handing him the paper to read.

"Begs the question of who sent the object to land on the ice in the first place," he replied. Then they heard the lower hatch being closed and the COB arrived in the control room.

"All closed up and ready to dive," he reported to the captain.

"Right, let's go to diving stations, Chief, and submerge," he replied, as an announcement went out from the officer in charge of diving the submarine.

"All personnel on board, we are ready to dive. We are GO for an Arctic full blow, with a sounding of 1,490 fathoms beneath the ship. We will make a stationary dive to 180 feet. DIVE, DIVE, stationary dive the ship to 180 feet," he ordered, as two blasts were heard on the diving alarm.

Costello turned to Justin and explained as the crew started to fill the ballast tanks with seawater.

"We bring the water in so we can control the angle as we go down. The diving and officer of the watch are controlling our angle of pitch and roll if you look at the gauges over there. Right now, we have 63 down angle and negative acceleration," he explained, as Justin hung on as the submarine was going down at a steep angle.

"When we do a static dive, we don't have any forward momentum of the boat, or the bow planes to help us. We must adjust the pitch and roll with ballast, using just seawater," Costello said, as the Chief of the Watch shouted more orders.

"Test turn plates and rudder, extend bow planes, start positive acceleration," he ordered and then he heard:

"Course 060, zero-degree bubble," that the captain acknowledged. They were finally underway and leaving the ice camp as fast as they could.

"We're going northeast in a cardinal direction, doing twenty turns of the screw – that's revolutions a minute. We're sailing across the Arctic Ocean towards the North Western Passages. That will lead us out into the North Atlantic Ocean eventually," Costello confirmed.

"So how long to our next destination?" he asked.

"That depends on our speed. It's about 5,500 nautical miles to our next objective in the Caribbean. At an average speed of twenty knots, that would give an ETA of around eleven days at sea. But first you need to write a report of what happened at the camp," he replied.

"Of course. I can do that in the wardroom," Justin said.

"Alright, bring me your draft to my cabin by tomorrow," he insisted as Justin realised he was being dismissed and left the room. Justin was feeling both tired and sick after so many challenges that day and went straight to his officer's rack to sleep.

***

Justin was up early the next morning, or whenever he woke, as time appeared to be always the same on a submerged submarine.

Taking a notepad, he went to the wardroom and wrote two pages of a report that he pushed under the door of the captain's cabin. Then, feeling better, he went to the galley to find some coffee and breakfast. Here he got a lot of smiles from the crew, and on returning to the wardroom, was asked to meet the captain.

"Lieutenant, I read your drafts but how did you know there were more subs under the ice, apart from us?" he asked.

"Well, Mercedes told me," he replied.

"Ah yes! The lieutenant who controls the UAV lab you wrote about here," Costello replied, slamming the first page on his desk.

"Look here, we can only include reports that can be verified by other crew members of the ship. Everything else is not evidence and goes in the bin, understood?" he insisted.

"Yes, sir. Understood," he replied.

"Alright. The second page of your report is fairly accurate. Although your heading of a 'Second Surfacing' will have to be removed," he said. Justin looked at an Arctic jacket hanging on a chair with a huge tear down the front that he pointed out to the captain.

"That's the jacket I arrived back with on your ship," Justin said.

"Yes, I know, but none of that can go in my report," he insisted.

"I understand. So what happens to me now?" he asked.

"We're going to take you down to the US naval base on Antigua. It's going to be a fast covert operation where we surface at night and you go ashore in an inflatable with our liaison officer. We've done that many times before. Then you make your way alone across to the island of Montserrat for your new posting," he replied, smiling.

"So, no one has any idea of where I've been for the past two months?" he replied.

"Yes, something like that… and we need to keep it like that. Understood?" he replied.

Justin went back to the wardroom to sit at his desk and think. Impulsively, he opened the screen and entered his password, where a new message appeared in a military code. The only part he could understand was the time of 15.00 hrs. When he looked up at the clock in the wardroom, it showed almost twelve. Thinking that it must be twelve noon, he walked down to the officer's mess to check and found the lunch meal was being served. Sitting with the junior officers, he casually asked if they knew the ship's position and was told they were out of the North West Passage and moving into Baffin Bay. Only then was he sure they were safe from any explosion, and he returned to sleep.

When the explosion came, the shock waves ran through the water and the ship. Alarm bells rang and lights flashed on and off that quickly woke him. When he looked at his watch, it was exactly 3 p.m. He walked down the corridor to see if the captain was in his cabin, and finding it empty, he went inside. When he saw his torn Arctic jacket was still over a chair, he looked inside the pockets, only to find the tracking device that had been used by the Camp Commander.

Putting it inside his pocket, he returned to the wardroom and waited for the captain to return. Slowly, as the officers returned from their emergency stations and knowing he had been on the ice with the captain, they started to question him.

"When you saw the force field, how did you know that it was dangerous to go inside?" one of the officers asked him. Justin just replied that he had seen it before.

"I was the Officer of Watch up on the sail after you left and one of the lookouts reported seeing a body and a snowmobile lying on the ice not far off in the distance. Can you explain what caused that to happen?" he asked.

"Sorry, I don't know. My best guess would be an interaction with the object that was reported to have landed earlier," he replied.

"And what kind of interaction might that have been?" he asked but was interrupted by the COB, who pointed at Justin.

"Captain wants you in his cabin now," he ordered. Justin, feeling most relieved, got up and left the room.

"Come in and sit down; everything alright?" Costello asked.

"Fine. Sorry, but your officers appear to be a bit jumpy after the blast today," he replied.

"I'm afraid our voyage south is going to be delayed. We've been ordered back to our submarine base at New London, in Connecticut. This sometimes happens with a logistic stop for crew rotation, but this time it sounds different," he advised.

"Alright, so how long might we be delayed?" Justin asked.

"Can't say. This time they want to change the whole crew on the *Albany* and replace with a new crew. That takes longer," he replied.

"Any reason given for this decision?" he asked.

"You know our officers and crew are spooked by the experience in the Arctic. After any crisis on a nuclear submarine, the crew may be changed. That's to limit any damage to the operation of the whole fleet," he explained.

"And what about the captain?"

"I expect to be relieved of my command as soon as we dock," the captain said, looking pained.

"What! That's not possible; you were following agreed objectives weren't you?" he asked.

"Yes, but those were countermanded. We only received new instructions after we surfaced," he explained.

"So, it's a cover-up, like they did in the UK. I was arrested, made to write a report, and interrogated by MI5 and the Ministry of Defence. Then was told to take leave on full pay, so I wouldn't appear at any inquiry. Stick to the real events that took place and don't talk to anyone, and not the press," Justin said.

"You really think so? Will you sign the final report with me?" Costello asked as he passed the report across his desk. Justin took one look and, taking the pen, signed in the space next to his name.

"You're not going to read it?" asked Costello.

"No, why bother? We're both guilty as charged," he replied.

"But there's nothing else we can do," he said, signing the report as the Captain of the *Albany*.

"Yes, there's a lot you can do, very discreetly. You need to contact Mercedes, the young lieutenant who was running the AUV project at the ice camp. Explain what's happened to you after we arrive. Any inquiry may not just be about your submarine, but also about what happened at the camp," he explained.

"But I never met her," he replied.

"Doesn't matter. Ask her if she remembers meeting me. Remind her she found a video online of a man running into the force field, and told me he later died from radiation," Justin said.

"Alright, I'll think about it. What are you planning to do to meet your objective in the Caribbean now?" he asked.

"I think I need to change my mode of transport, as I'm on a tight schedule as well. How long before we arrive at this New London base?" he asked.

"About another two days at sea," Costello replied.

"Very good. It's been a pleasure serving with you on your boat. I wish you all the best with this transition," he said, standing up. They shook hands and Justin left, wondering what he was going to do next.

***

Two days later, he was woken by the officers coming back from breakfast with their new postings. He lay in his bunk listening to the conversations.

"What you'd get, Harry?"

"Back on the old *Toledo*, for a second tour," he heard in reply.

"I'm posting to the *Arizona*, not due back for another month."

"Lucky you, a month's leave is all I can dream of," he heard.

Then he watched as the officers changed into their khaki service uniform to leave the boat. Ten minutes later, they had packed their kitbags and had left by the after hatch. Cool, fresh air was blowing down inside the boat that made Justin shiver. He climbed out of his bunk, found his carry-on bag, and changed into his civvies clothes as fast as he could. Never was he so happy to leave a boat.

Wearing the same woollen pullover and jacket he had worn in Scotland, he walked to the hatch, and freedom outside. Pushing his bag up in front of him, he climbed the ladder into bright sunshine and emerged on the after deck of the submarine. Here he found a seaman on guard duty, with a lady's green suitcase on the deck.

"I wanted to say goodbye to Captain Costello. Do you know if he's still onboard, or where I can find him?" he asked.

"No, he left hours ago. He'll be in the Blue Duck bar if you want to find him," he replied.

"Thanks. Oh! We have a woman officer joining the boat?" he asked, pointing at the suitcase.

"No, she's a redhead asking about you. She went up to the forward hatch, if you want to catch her," he said. Justin dropped his bag and ran forward to find her standing at the main hatch. He shouted and waved until she saw him and walked back.

"Hello there; what are you doing on this boat?" he asked.

"I came to find Costello. He called me earlier and sounded in a bad way. Do you know where he is?" she asked.

"Yes, but he's not onboard anymore," he replied.

"Well, good to see you, pirate. You made it back to dry land," she replied, smiling at him.

"I'm also leaving this boat now, so we can go ashore together to find him, if you want," he proposed.

"Okay, agreed," she said, as they walked back across the gangway to the quay.

"Is that your car waiting over there?" he asked.

"Yes, I told him to wait in case… where are we going?" she asked.

"The Blue Duck bar in New London, the guard told me earlier. Don't think it can be far," he replied, as they got into the car and drove off. They crossed over the river and drew up outside a red brick building with a Blue Duck sign in less than ten minutes.

"Can you give me a few minutes alone with him? After that, he's all yours," Justin asked.

"Sure. Where are you going after that?" she asked.

"After the change of captain and crew, I thought I'd continue my journey by plane. I've got some time, maybe do some sightseeing in NYC," he explained.

"You got a phone? Turned it on yet?" she asked.

"No, it won't work without a US chip, will it?" he asked.

"Give it to me and let's take a walk," she replied; opening her door and taking his phone, they left the cab.

"Justin, if you turn your phone on here, the FBI will arrive to arrest you in less than thirty minutes. Do I make myself clear? You don't have an entry visa, do you? Standing out here you're an illegal migrant who can never leave on a plane without an ESTA," she explained.

"So, what can I do?" Justin asked.

"Here, take your phone and don't activate it here. Let's go and find Costello in this bar," she replied, opening the door to let him enter first. Justin walked inside, looking around the bar, then walked to the booths at the far end where he found the captain.

"Well, well! If it isn't Lieutenant Benbow come to say goodbye," Costello said, not looking surprised. Justin realised the captain had been drinking since losing his command.

"I've come to give you something that's US government property. I found this in my Arctic jacket on the boat," he replied, placing a black tracker device on the table. Costello looked at it, smiling at first, then he laughed. Laughed out loud in the empty bar.

"You think that's going to get my command back," he said, finally picking up the device in his hand. Somehow, he activated a signal that appeared on a TV screen in front of them.

"What the fuck is that thing?" he shouted, as Justin turned around to see the images on the screen. It was the recording made by the Camp Commander and showed an egg-shaped object in the distance on the ice, and then a shot of Justin and the submarine on the surface of the ice. Mercedes ran forward and stopped the transmission from the device.

"What the hell were you two doing up there on the ice? How did you get hold of this tracker, Justin?" she demanded.

"Well now, who the hell you are you, lady? This is starting to get more interesting. Girlfriend of yours, Justin?" Costello asked, looking at the angry face of the young woman.

"You two have no idea what you've done. If that tape leaks out, it won't just be the CIA arresting us, it will be our National Intelligence agency as well," she quietly told them.

"Alright, ma'am, calm down. You've got my full attention now. But I was never on the ice with that object. Let's ask Benbow to explain what happened," he said calmly to everyone.

"Yes, but it's not so easy to explain. You see, I went on the ice after leaving the *Albany*, not once but twice!" Justin started to explain.

"Hold on, kiddo. Stop right there, because I have his report for you to read first," he said. Costello pulled out a small plastic file from his leather jacket that contained the handwritten report.

"I assume you're the AUV lieutenant mentioned in the report. Please open and read. I didn't include it in my navy report as it's mostly science fiction to me," he said and then asked the barman to bring them coffee for three persons.

After she finished reading the report, Mercedes turned to question Justin again.

"Yes, I understand now. You went with Mathew to check out this egg-shaped object we just saw on the screen. He got into difficulties, and you used the scooter to try and push him off. I'm sorry but I put his tracker into your Arctic jacket," she explained.

"What exactly were you doing on the ice?"

"We lost contact with our AUV and I tried to follow it on a tractor. When your sub broke through the ice right in front of me, I was really scared. Then I continued and found two people in the snow and an upturned snowmobile," Mercedes admitted.

"Well now, that's quite a story," Costello replied.

"Yes, I'm sorry; should have told you before. I found Mathew already frozen dead but managed to bring Justin back to your boat. You were unconscious most of the time, so two members of the crew had to winch him back onboard," she said, looking at Justin.

"The chief never mentioned any of this to me," said the captain.

"And now, neither the captain nor the crew can confirm surfacing on the ice to pick me up at Camp Whale. They can't admit it, as they got orders not to surface," Justin replied.

"But the video we saw shows the boat did surface on the ice again, with your face on one frame, so they will have to admit it," Mercedes exclaimed as the coffee arrived on the table and the barman announced to them all: "I've closed up the bar until you guys are finished here. Costello is a good man and if you can do anything to help, that would be appreciated."

Justin looked at Mercedes and continued.

"Just answer me one question. Did your AUV determine if this was an alien object?" he asked.

"OMG, Benbow, I can't confirm something like that!? But *err...* We think it was not made on this planet," she said.

"This is crazy. I think we're done here. Time for you guys to leave," Costello said, smiling at everyone.

"Wait, let's finish the coffee first. You've lost your command, but I've lost most of my research. They've even sent me back to school at MIT to study quantum physics," Mercedes said.

"What are you suggesting?" he asked.

"If you sit here and do nothing, they will only come to arrest you. Together, we might make a better team to survive the official inquiry that's coming," she replied.

"And what about Justin?"

"We've already resolved that. We drop him off at the *Albany* on our way back to Boston. He's not going anywhere else for now," she said, putting the tracking device in her jacket. Everyone started to get up as Justin was led out to the front door, where the barman was waiting.

"Looks clear outside. I'll summon the car to come and pick you up," he said. Costello sat in the front with Justin and Mercedes in the back until they reached the port and, once past security, they drove down to the *Albany*. When Justin got out, he took his bag from the trunk and found Mercedes waiting for him.

"I'll walk with you down to your boat. I need to tell you something," she said, which surprised Justin.

"I couldn't say anything in front of the captain, and we still don't know the source of the object that landed. Space debris crashes onto this planet, but this egg-shaped object landed close in some thick ice. Our AUV was unable to confirm its origin," she said.

"And the force field?" Justin asked.

"Oh! That was done by us to try to protect the camp in the event of detonation. We left a door open so we could continue to dismantle and evacuate the remaining personnel from the airstrip at the back of the camp," she explained, as they arrived at the gangway onto the boat.

"Really, but why didn't it detonate on landing?"

"It submerged, and then got stuck in thick ice. That may explain why it didn't detonate. We think it was programmed to go under the ice to destroy our boats," she replied.

"Who did the detonation?" Justin asked.

"The US army did that, once your boat was safely out of harm's way," she replied.

"And why the *Albany*? That boat was used in a voyage of deception," he asked, pointing at the huge sail towering above them.

"I don't know. She's one of an older class, and perhaps they thought the boat was dispensable. Justin, we were all used in this deception. You, me, and all the people at the camp to counter the Russians, or whoever was responsible. They think the Arctic is their home patch; we needed to show them that it's part of a free ocean," she replied.

"Understood. So what are you going to do now?" he asked.

"If you agree, I'm going to release the video to the media with your image at the end. That should stop a formal inquiry and perhaps get Costello reinstated," she said, taking the black tracker out of her pocket and showing it to him again.

"Yes, go ahead and press the button. I'm going off the grid anyway, so it can't get any worse," Justin replied, smiling at her.

"Thank you, pirate, that's done," Mercedes said, smiling.

"Now, take the tracker with you. It has a global satellite phone linked to my private number. Call me if you need assistance; once you arrive on the island, of course," she said, handing the device to Justin, who put it in his jacket.

"Will I see any of you again?" he asked as Mercedes turned to say goodbye.

"Well, you have my number, and I'll come to visit your island when this has blown over. Good luck, you'll be back in the tropics in a couple of days," she said, giving him a kiss on the cheek and walked away to the waiting car. Justin picked up his bag and, crossing the gangway again, found the same guard still on duty.

"Good to see you again. That's one attractive lady you've got there. The new captain wants to see you and we sail at midnight," he advised. Justin walked to the after hatch, threw his bag down, and climbed back down inside.

Back in the officer's quarters, he looked at the ship's clock and saw it was already past lunchtime, but the ship appeared deserted. He changed into his submarine clothes, and walked forward to the wardroom, but found no other officers onboard. Then he walked to the captain's door and listened to the discussion taking place inside.

"The ship's objectives are quite clear. We have to sail at midnight regardless of how many crew we can find. They want us out of Groton with the Benbow Marine before the press get a hold of the story and start asking questions," came through and then heard more discussions…

"What's the minimum crew number we can run the ship on the surface with…?" This was followed by a muffled reply.

"We searched the boat from top to bottom; the device is not onboard."

"Alright, so how's this submarine in the Arctic being shown on most US news channels right now?" was the reply.

"More questions are being asked on media channels about the ice camp that's now disappeared," he heard.

Until "Has anyone seen the man yet?" was asked, Justin then decided to move to the galley to find something to eat. Again, there was no one there, except a brew of coffee freshly made. He helped himself to a mug, sat down and decided to do nothing until some crew arrived. After a while, a senior navy officer entered and smiled on seeing him.

"Ah good. We need more coffee. What's your name, sailor?"

"Ah, well, I'm not a sailor," he replied.

"We need more coffee now," he demanded.

"And I want something to eat," Justin replied, smiling.

"And you are?"

"Lieutenant Justin Benbow, of His Majesties Royal Marines. I'm on your boat on passage to the British Overseas Protectorate of Montserrat," he replied.

"OMG!" the officer exclaimed, dropping the empty mugs and running back to the captain's cabin shouting, "I've found him, he's in the galley, drinking coffee!" to everyone's amazement.

21 – BENBOW

When Susan drove into Osborne Airport carpark, she saw Sam standing by his white security van waiting for them. The time was just after 6 p.m. Sam opened the sliding door of the van and Janet and Jana with her baby, left the car. This time Janet sat in the back with Jana, while Sam put their luggage in the back. Then he returned to the car to speak to Susan.

"There was a late arrival from Antigua just now that has brought someone you know to the island," he said.

"Justin?" Susan asked.

"Yes, Lieutenant Justin Benbow, an officer in the King's army and on secondment here as our new Superintendent of Police. You had better hurry to arrivals to meet him. He needs accommodation with you tonight. That is, until he officially takes up his office," he replied.

"Yes. Of course. I'll drive up there now," was all Susan said. She was excited to see Justin again, but more frightened about what they had been through in the future. Then she realised that no room had been prepared so she called Jana.

"Jana, did you know we are expecting a guest tonight?"

"No, Susan, it's Bee! Jana gave me her phone before she left. Janet called and told me to prepare James's room, as they're going away. So where are you now?" Bee replied.

"I'm at the airport going to pick Justin up now. We should be back in the next half an hour," replied Susan.

Feeling more confident, Susan parked the car and ran into the small terminal building to see if he had already arrived, when she felt a tap on her shoulder.

"Mrs West, are you waiting for me?" a voice asked behind her. Turning, she saw it was a much younger man in his khaki military uniform, with an army beret.

"*Err.* Yes, if you're Army Officer Justin. I was sent to meet you and take you to Janet's house. I mean your accommodation," she replied.

"Very well, and where is Mrs Romford tonight?"

"Oh! She had to leave on an urgent trip to London, so I'm afraid you've just missed her. Come this way and I'll drive you to her house," replied Susan, watching him carrying his green holdall.

He opened a back door of the car and threw his bag in the back and came to sit beside her in the front. Susan started the car, reversed, and drove out of the airport, not knowing what to say.

"I have been here before years ago, so what is it that you do on the island, Mrs West?" he asked.

"I work at the observatory on the island, and please call me Susan," she replied, as she realised she had taken the wrong turning and was driving towards Brades.

"Is everything alright, Susan, you do seem a bit nervous."

"Yes, well, this is Janet's car and I'm getting used to driving it while she's away. I've taken the scenic route as I thought you might want to see Government House on the way," she replied.

"But Mrs Romford does still live in a house on the Old Bluff, doesn't she?"

"Yes, of course. We're on the road going down from Brades and will arrive there once we pass Woodlands," Susan announced, as the car slowed to allow some children to cross the road.

"You know, Susan, I'm sure I have seen you before?"

"No, I don't think that's possible. We only met today."

"Ah yes, I remember. I saw you at a press conference with some US journalists. Something to do with auroras on the island, if I remember correctly."

"Yes, that's correct. You've been doing your homework on Montserrat before you arrived."

"Of course, that's my job here isn't it?"

"Well, Justin, can you tell me what you saw on the island in 2020 when you were last here," Susan asked, as she carefully drove through Woodlands.

"I assume you have been on the island long enough to know what really happened."

"Of course, but I want to hear it from someone who was actually here at that time. Can you tell me truthfully what you saw."

"Okay, as a military man, it was an invasion. Hundreds of survivors on the beach and all those sleep pods still give me nightmares," he replied.

"Thank you, Justin, for being honest with me."

"So, what exactly are you looking for now?"

"If you really want to know, its aliens or something! We think they may be back, or maybe they never left," replied Susan, as the car entered the drive to Janet's house, and they got out of the car and Susan paused.

"Listen, I live here with another women called Bee and we have two ten-year-old daughters. We cannot discuss any of this in front of the girls, is that understood?" asked Susan.

"Yes, I understand, shall we go inside now?" he replied. Susan realised he must have been well briefed about who was living at the house already.

****

Meanwhile, back at Osborne Airport, Sam drove around the airport perimeter and found the hover plane was prepared and already outside the hangar, with a ladder ready for boarding. James and the technician were engaged in deep discussion, when on seeing the van arrive with Janet, he walked over to explain the problem.

"Janet, your NASA technician tells me the plane has been modified. The time travel features have been disconnected, so we can only travel to the UK and return here in our space time of today," James explained.

"Well, that is a new development. Still, remember Jana has all the past coordinates on her remote viewing tablet. Let me go and talk to him," she replied, while Sam helped Jana load their luggage into the passenger compartment.

"Hello, it's Mr Schneider if I recall from our last meeting. I understand you have made some limitations to where the plane can fly," she asked.

"Yes, I'm just carrying out my orders, Mrs Romford. We don't want you handing the craft over to another party," he replied.

"I see, but my company has not been paid and I have to meet with a group of influential US investors to discuss how we can resolve this problem," Janet explained.

"That's not my concern here. You're only authorised to fly to London and return here with the plane undamaged."

"But the plane is in an airworthy condition to fly since I returned it?"

"*Err*, yes, I don't know what you mean?"

"So, there's no limit on the height that the plane can fly; in the Earth's atmosphere or out into space is there?"

"What do you mean?"

"Oh, but I think you do know what I mean. We've been having a communication exchange with the ISS that flies over these islands several times a day. I thought we could be of assistance, if, of course, any help was needed," Janet proposed.

"Impossible, this plane is not equipped to fly anywhere above the stratosphere. It's simple, there's no oxygen for the crew to survive," he replied.

"Thank you, Mr Schneider, you've been most helpful. Let's hope we can see each other in a week," Janet replied and left him standing alone confused.

Janet returned to board the plane and found Jana already onboard with her baby and their two cases at their feet.

"Janet, tell me, what was that discussion all about?"

"Nothing important, I just wanted to let him know that we've been in contact with someone on the ISS," she explained.

"Well, I've uploaded all the coordinates to the plane's computer if you want to talk to James," Jana said.

"Excellent. If you give me the headphones, I need to remind him that if we leave here after 6 p.m., we'll arrive at the house shortly after midnight," Janet replied, looking for the coms button.

"James, everything looking alright for us to leave?"

"Yes, Jana's given me some better coordinates for your house in Windsor, that we used in the past. They should be correct," he said.

"Okay, listen. I hired a couple to open the house and they're expecting us to arrive shortly after midnight. So, as it will be dark and maybe raining, I asked them to put lights all the way down to the river. I know you will need to wash the plane, and that shouldn't be a problem. Poor visibility and it's been raining in England for the last month!"

"Thanks for the warning, but I'm not going to hang around."

"What are you going to do with the plane in the meantime?"

"Now Jana's given me all the old coordinates, I thought to return to where all this started."

"You mean the island? What are you going to do there for a week?" Janet asked.

"Oh! You know, sit on the beach and drink beer in the sunshine."

"Listen, James, I spoke to that tech guy and asked him about flying this plane up into space."

"Really? You mentioned the strange image from the ISS?"

"Not specifically, but he said that would be impossible for our craft as there's no oxygen for the crew. So, it sounds like they may have tried this with other craft," explained Janet.

"Okay, but I have thirty minutes of oxygen. Used it for that flight to Canada, remember," James replied.

"Yes, but you don't have a helmet or a space suit, the pressure would kill you very quickly, as soon as you entered the vacuum."

"Let me think about this. We've known the US has these Orbital Test Vehicles for years. Basically, unmanned space planes that stay up in orbit for months," he replied.

"Right, and Jana tells me that the last launch in December last year used a SpaceX Falcon Heavy rocket. That would give an increased payload or a different orbit that required more power. Plenty of time to fly close to the ISS. James, what are they looking for up there," said Janet.

"We have no clue what it's doing. Just like we don't really know what's happening on the island of Montserrat."

"Okay, but don't take a closer look, and try not to damage the plane. Are you ready to leave, as I want to get off this island tonight?" she asked.

"Yes, ma'am, take care," was all she heard as the passenger door hissed closed and the craft rose silently into the sky and disappeared in a flash.

22 – ARRIVAL

Janet's house was located on the outskirts of Old Windsor in the south of England. By 2024, Old Windsor was no longer a small village but had become a large town in the county of Berkshire, bounded by the river to the east and the Windsor Great Park to the west. It was an impressive house, with grounds leading down the River Thames. That was the landing site for James on a wet night in June of 2024.

When the plane suddenly burst out from the wormhole, James knew they had arrived at their destination. Outside, he could see nothing except drizzle and mist. He slowly descended towards the ground and at about three hundred feet, he finally saw some lights and people running about on the ground pointing in a direction south.

Turning the craft, he followed the lights to a black ribbon of liquid and knowing it must be the river, he let the plane slowly descend into the water. Looking outside, he saw a huge cloud of bubbles and electricity as the plane discharged all the energy that would allow him to land safely, when he heard Janet's voice on the intercom.

"Are we back in England, James, it's been quite frightening back here," she asked.

"Yes, we're drifting downstream in the Thames. Going to jump back from here to the landing site and you'll be home," he replied. The plane rose out of the water and headed back to the house where the craft landed on the driveway. A man ran forward with a stepladder to enable the passengers to leave the plane, and Janet spoke again on the intercom.

"Thank you, James, for the safe flight. As you know you can't stay here overnight, so I'll pass you to Jana who will help you with the next part of your journey. Good night and hope to see you again in a week," Janet said, passing the headphones to Jana.

"Listen, James, I'm leaving my travel bag on the plane as it contains your survival package for the next week."

"That sounds interesting; what have you included?"

"Change of clothes, slacks, and beach shirts, and I've found you somewhere to stay for the next ten days of June. A small apartment next to the church. Remember that island off the coast of Portugal? You can hide there as a British tourist on holiday."

"Okay, ID. You got that covered?"

"Yes, but your British passport has expired. So try not to show it; hope it's not needed."

"Okay, so how do I find this Airbnb place?"

"In the morning, you can hide the plane in that disused military base. Then you walk along the beach with my travel bag towards the port. The first ferry should arrive at around 9 a.m. so try and be early. Wait until the other passengers walk off the ferry and then join them and walk towards the church. Someone will be waiting there to meet you," Jana explained.

"Sounds good. Any cash? I will need to buy food."

"A little! Janet could only find $200 in used notes but no euros. Hey, Portugal is cheap, eat fish," she said. "Oh! One last thing, Janet included a burner phone. You can make just one call to her. I already gave my phone to Bee."

"Thanks, Jana, that's a great cover for ten days! I'm more worried that some kids will find the plane, and I will have to move on again. This is the only island I know well, and my options are limited."

"I know but remember you have been there before. Look, I have to go now. Good luck and I love you," Jana replied and closed the intercom in tears. As soon as she climbed down the ladder to the ground, the passenger door hissed closed. A man ran forward to remove the ladder as the plane lit up and prepared to lift off again. James let the plane rise to the usual 300 ft and then selected the best coordinates to arrive above the water and close to the island. Pushing the activate button, the craft jumped through time space and disappeared without a sound.

When the plane burst back into space time again, James saw there was a clear night sky with the moon shining down onto the sea. He knew he was back on the coast of the Algarve, with the lighthouse of Farol flashing in the distance. Once again, he let the craft descend into the seawater and waited for the static electricity to disperse before making the next jump to the old ruin on the island.

James activated the new coordinates, and the plane rose out of the water to stop a few hundred feet above his required destination. Looking down, he could see the broken roof of what had once been a Portuguese naval base in the last war.

He could just make out a walled courtyard, where he hoped to hide the plane as soon as it was light. In the meantime, he set the plane down close to the exterior wall, turned the engine off, and went to find Jana's bag in the rear compartment. He quickly searched for a bottle of aspirin and washed some down with the bottle of water. He desperately needed to catch a few hours of sleep before sunrise and set his alarm for 5 a.m., when it would be first light.

***

James was up before daybreak, paced out the length and breadth of the plane, and went to check the size of the courtyard next to the house. He quickly saw it would be possible to park the plane there. As soon as there was enough light, he started the engine, hovered over the exterior, and slowly landed in the abandoned yard. Climbing out of the cockpit, he opened the passenger door and went to see what else Jana had included in her suitcase. There he discovered an energy bar and drank more water to help him for the walk ahead.

Finally, James changed into a holiday tee with jeans. Then, replacing everything in the case, he closed the entrance with a broken door and left the interior to walk to the beach. Looking outside, he saw no one until he reached the sea, where he saw in the distance, fishing boats returning to the island's port. *So far so good,* he thought, until he saw a man walking towards him along the beach.

James hurried to a broken wooden boat high up in the sand and sat down, hiding his pink suitcase in the boat and looked out to sea. The man walked past with just a wave and James decided to wait there until he saw the ferry boat arriving from Olhao.

On seeing the ferry, he continued walking towards the terminal. Climbing up onto a concrete path, he found an empty shelter with seats and a map of all the islands. The map showed there was a series of channels and islands known as the Ria Formosa. In fact, it was a protected nature park, he read. Then waited for the passengers to walk up from the ferry. When a small group of passengers arrived, few of them looked like tourists. Probably local homeowners or staff who worked on the island, until a group of twenty young men appeared all dressed in the same dark red uniform with 'security' written on the back.

Slowly, James got up and followed the men, pulling his suitcase behind him as just another lost tourist. It was only a hundred yards to the church where he saw a woman dressed in black waiting for someone. He guessed this was the owner of the apartment Jana had rented online and soon found that she didn't speak any English.

"Bom dia, você è o inglês que reservou apartamento aqui?" James played dumb and nodded as he recognised two words *ingles* and *apartamento* that were enough.

"Si. I'm James West, for apartamento," he replied, that brought a smile to her face.

"Muito bom, me siga," he guessed was for him to follow her to some new apartments he saw on the far side from the church.

He followed her down a small alley all painted white, to a door at the end that she unlocked and he entered the apartment.

There she handed James the key saying, *"Obrigado"* and walked out of the door, leaving left him standing alone. James was so tired he didn't really care. He saw there was a sofa, a TV that led to a kitchen, a shower, and a staircase that he hoped would lead to a bed. Upstairs, he found just one bedroom with a large bed and, throwing himself on the unmade covers, he quickly fell fast asleep.

***

Some hours later, James was woken by a knocking on the front door, and when he looked at the setting sun, realised it must be early evening.

Going down the stairs, he saw there was a woman waiting at the door, so he opened to see what she wanted.

"Hello, I hope I didn't disturb you," she said in good English.

"We're your neighbours. The owner said you didn't speak any Portuguese, so I came to see if you needed anything," she asked.

"Thank you, that's most kind," James replied.

"We are a German couple. We bought a small house here years ago in front of the church, and you must be American," she said.

"In fact, I'm British, been working in the States. It was a very long flight from New York and then London. Won't you come in?" James replied, more in the hope of some food than curiosity.

"Thank you, my name is Wilma and know most guests here have problems with the television, if I can show you," she said.

"Thank you, my names is James and I'm booked in here for over a week," he replied, as the TV came to life on a local channel in Portuguese and his heart sank.

"There are no English channels here unless you like football," Wilma said with a big smile.

"There's a big match tonight between Bayern Munich and the Portuguese team Benfica. Would you like to come and watch it and have something to eat with us?" she asked him.

"That's most kind, because I didn't have time to buy any food at the shop today. What time is the match?" he asked.

"It starts around 7 p.m. but drop by whenever you're ready. Our place is two houses down with a colourful red tree outside," she replied, and, shaking his hand, she paused at the door to let James reply.

"Thank you, I'll be there at seven," he confirmed, not believing his luck at finding some food at last.

He went straight upstairs, opened the suitcase, and took out a small washbag Jana had packed for him to shave. Going down to the shower, he then washed his old work shirt and hung it out to dry in the evening sun. He thought it better to dress down rather than appear as some rich American tourist. By the time he finished, it was nearly seven so dressed in a grey damp shirt and blue shorts, and went to walk around the church, looking for the house.

James quickly found the place opposite the church, with the tree of red flowers growing outside. Entering a small front garden, he found Wilma and her husband sitting at a table. There were more chairs, and on the table next to a TV screen was a bowl of chips, a box of wine, and a case of the local beer. James realised this wasn't going to be a dinner party, more a celebration of German football.

"Welcome, James, come and meet my husband. He had an accident on his bike in Germany and lost one leg. After that, we had to retire here on the island. It's good, except in summer, when it's too hot and too many tourists. Come and sit down and watch the match," she said, as James shook hands with the man and sat down as instructed, not knowing how to reply.

"Now, James, what would you like to drink? A local beer to start with, then we can drink the red wine if Germany wins tonight."

"Yes, that would be great. You don't have any bread to eat, do you? I haven't eaten in days," James replied in desperation.

"Bread, of course. I'll bring you some of our local cheese as well if you like," Wilma replied and disappeared inside, as her husband turned to talk to James.

"Look, the sports reporters in Lisbon think our German team is crap," he said, pointing at the screen and, taking a swig from his bottle of beer, he crashed it down on the table. James nodded in agreement and wondered how he would survive the evening.

Finally, Wilma returned with a basket of sliced bread and a plate of cheese, which James really needed.

"Sorry, James. I forgot you only arrived today and slept while the shop was open. I hope this will do until tomorrow," Wilma said, as the game started and James ate everything put in front of him. Ninety minutes later, the game was a draw and James was offered a glass of red wine that he found difficult not to accept. Her husband left to go inside, and Wilma spoke to him again.

"My son is arriving tonight from Munich. You should stay and talk to him when he arrives. He's on a project that may be of interest."

"Well, I'm in no hurry to go back, but what exactly does he do in Germany?" James asked.

"He works for a TV company, don't know much more. You need to ask him," she replied, pouring herself another glass of red wine.

"But how can he get to the island? The last ferry must have left hours ago?" James asked.

"James, you don't understand. We are local people. There are taxi boats that can bring passengers over here any time, day or night. This is how we all survive on the islands," she replied and filled up James's glass with red wine again.

James listened to the silence of the night outside and remembered how different it had been when he was here some six years in the future. He waited another twenty minutes, until a young thirty-year-old man with curly black hair appeared in the garden. He went to kiss his mother, so was obviously her son.

"James, let me introduce you to Ralph. He's unexpectedly come back, and I think you may have a lot to talk about," Wilma said and, taking her wineglass, she went back inside the house.

"Well, James, my mother told me you arrived on the island today. Except you don't look like a typical British tourist to me," he said.

"No, and I hear you work for a TV company, so what brings you so unexpectedly to the island today?" James replied.

"Oh! Very simple. They're making a film on the island and my boss wanted me to cover the story," Ralph replied.

"Really, and what kind of film are they making on an island in Portugal? Nature, global warming, or something scientific," he replied.

"Auroras! Haven't you heard? There have been auroras seen right down to the tropics. Look, I recorded this video on my phone from a press conference somewhere in the Caribbean. That's not normal, is it? Listen to what one local scientist said." When he pressed play, he was watching the recording of Susan West on Montserrat.

"Interesting, but what does that have to do with this island here?" James asked, looking him fully in the eye.

"Come on, James, you're not a tourist here, are you? What do you really do?" he asked.

"Same as you, except I'm an independent investigator, trying to figure out what's going on with our planet," James replied.

"Okay, so let's work together. Do you know there have been auroras on this island? Are you here with the film company? My boss sent me down here to find a story. He knew I had grown up on this island and expects me to come back with a scoop of what's really going on," he replied.

"Look, I had no idea about any movie production on this island before I arrived. That is until I was in the ferry terminal this morning where there were over twenty guys in uniform marked as security. Why does the island need a security contingent for a film?" he asked.

"James, I've heard a lot of rumours from the locals. Do you know about a disused building that used to be a navy base in the war? They want to cordon off the whole area until the film crews arrive next week. That's a story I want to follow up with my local contacts tomorrow," he said.

While James realised his plane might become exposed if any of them checked inside the building.

"Alright, let's work together and see what we can find out. What do you want me to do?" James asked.

"Come here around ten tomorrow and I'll take you down to the port to meet the local fishermen. If we can get onto one of their boats, they will take us to where they fish in the channel at night. That's where these lights have been seen, all along the coast," he said. James stood up to leave and replied.

"Look, I was robbed at the airport in London and need some euros. Can you exchange a twenty-dollar bill for me?" he asked.

"Yes, no problem, here you go… and you lost your wallet with all the credit cards?" he asked, placing the twenty euro note on the table.

"Yes, and my mobile phone. I'm left with only a couple of hundred for this trip," he replied.

"But you have some ID?" he asked.

"Yes, they didn't take my passport," James replied, flashing his red British passport at him, smiling. Ralph stood up and shook hands, but before James left, Ralph helped some more.

"You can find basic supplies at the island store. It's on your left just after the Janoca restaurant," he said, pointing outside. James nodded, gave him a thumbs up and left to find his way back to the apartment in the dark.

23 – JUSTIN

Meanwhile, back on the Caribbean island, Susan was introducing Justin to Bee and the two girls and explained he would be staying for the night while Janet and James were away. Bee was obviously not impressed as she announced it was suppertime for the girls and led them away to the kitchen, while Susan took Justin down to his bedroom in the basement.

"Not quite the warm welcome I expected, but I heard you have had some difficult times," he said, opening his green bag to start unpacking.

"Yes, why don't you come up to the kitchen bar once the children are put to bed and explain what persuaded you to take up this position here," Susan replied and, leaving him on his own, she went to find Bee and the children eating at a small table.

"Mummy, why can't we eat on the stools like the grownups," Mary complained, as everyone laughed, except Bee who wanted to know what happened up at Government House.

"You wouldn't believe it! Sarah wanted to hand me over to the US authorities," she replied, which only brought more questions.

"But we've never been to that place, have we?" Mary asked, so Bee quickly said she would explain this later and took the girls off to sleep in the basement.

Susan went to the fridge, took out an open bottle, and poured herself a glass of white wine, when Justin arrived in jeans, a sleeveless shirt, and holding a rolled-up newspaper.

"Long day was it, Susan?" he asked, sliding onto a bar stool.

"Yes, can I get you something to drink?" she replied.

"A cold beer would be great."

"Of course, you army guys only drink beer. Not sure if Janet keeps any of that in stock; let me take a look. Yes, there are some local cans in here, coming right up," she said as Bee returned, helping herself to a glass of wine. They sat together, both facing Justin, as Susan started her questioning.

"We can't understand why an officer in the Royal Marines would want to come back to the island as a police officer. Can you explain?" Susan asked.

"Yes, I was approached in April and offered the job in the interest of National Security and accepted a secondment," he replied.

"Justin, that was April and now it's the beginning of June. Where have you been since then?" she asked.

"It's almost as complicated as this newspaper photo of how you arrived on this island," he replied, passing the copy of the newspaper across the table.

"Yes, we both arrived here in March after working on an island in the Pacific. Sam told us you were meant to do final training in Scotland in April. So where were you?"

"Confidentially, I was on a US nuclear submarine. The only safe place you can be if they want someone to disappear," he said.

"Really, for two months? You went on some sort of world tour?" Susan asked.

"No, we went to the Arctic. Under the ice to support an International Research station that was destroyed," he replied.

"You don't mean the Whale Ice Station with that video of an object that landed close by, do you?" she asked.

"Yes, the very same. I was a passenger on that submarine."

"Justin, no one goes as a passenger on a nuclear submarine. So, what were you really doing?" she asked again.

"Look, I can't tell you all the details as it's classified, but up in the Arctic, there are bigger threats than aliens," he replied.

"That's our experience here. So, tell us again how you made it here, after leaving the Arctic," Susan insisted.

"The sub was recalled to its base and all the crew changed, pending an inquiry. When the video on the ice was released, the navy dropped all charges, and they brought me back to the US Navy base on Antigua. Took the last flight to the airport here," he explained.

"Why were you needed on the sub? For your past experience?"

"Perhaps, yes. It involved a force field again, around the camp. It wasn't destroyed by melting ice from climate change, but something almost as powerful as a nuclear explosion! I don't think you understand what's going on in the big picture in Europe with the Russians," he said, wiping his face on his shirt sleeve.

"Alright, so if this was similar to what happened when you arrived on the island in 2020, can you help us with our recent experience here?" she said, as Justin realised they were being serious.

"Look, that happened over four years ago, so what's this got to do with the island today?" he asked.

"Oh! You don't know? The island recently experienced auroras all along the north coast. While I was on duty at the observatory, we briefly experienced an online connection to the International Space Station flying overhead. I saw a woman who was recognised by others as the same R.N. officer you met in 2020. So, Justin, you must have followed up on this during your army career. Can you tell us something about this person now?" Susan asked.

"She was the head of a Special Group in the UK. Something that probably originated in the EU. They investigate the paranormal and target people who they know are time travellers," he said.

"You mean people like this man James?" Susan asked.

"Yes, that may be controlled by some elite at the UN and other extreme groups like the WEF. Their aim is being pushed as climate change, you know to *save the planet*. Except that's just a cover to control people and energy. Control energy and shut it down and the planet will return to a pre-industrial world," he replied, as Bee gasped and poured herself another glass of wine.

"Thank you, Justin, I guessed much of that. Then how and why is it possible that we may have seen her up in space?" asked Susan.

"Well, that's interesting. When I got my commission, I checked her out with the captain who conducted my interrogation at the start of the pandemic. He confirmed that she was transferred to the US military while she was on the island here."

"Yes, and tried to kill James," said Susan.

"Well, I don't know about that, but it's possible that they or NASA trained her as a space pilot over the last four years. But if you look at the many astronauts sent up to the ISS over the last two years, her name and photo have not been up there," he replied.

"Well, we're not sure she was on the ISS. When I saw her, it could have been a supply capsule that was following the space station's orbit," Susan replied.

"You mean a resupply capsule, like the Boeing Star Link craft sent up a month ago? In that case, when it docked, she could have returned on a Russian vehicle, and no one would know about her."

"No, that's too complicated. With Russia at war in Ukraine, it must be a SpaceX rocket launch and recovery."

"All right, but you must have seen something since then; what's your real concern now?" Justin asked.

"Well, we have a camera at the observatory, originally built to look at the volcano, but it can also scan the region in the infrared spectrum. During a rainstorm, I saw people moving around on Richmond Hill. It's still all covered in ash, uninhabited and high up in the exclusion zone. We would need your permission to work together on this," she asked.

"You mean without the knowledge of the governor?"

"Yes, particularly without her knowledge. You should know, she wanted me deported to the US government earlier today. That was only stopped because of Janet, who has something on the island that NASA can't disclose. That's why she left for a business trip to London just before you arrived," replied Susan.

"So, you two are 'persona non grata' at the moment then. Sounds like you've upset two governments and one of the largest US space agencies fighting over something on the island," he replied.

"Yes, and they all want to keep this covered up. We have the support of the local PM, who wants us to investigate."

"Really, you two are anything but dull, I must say."

"What you saw in Lime Kiln Bay was only the start, because we're told that much more happened after you left," Susan replied, as she stopped to pour herself a glass of wine and offered another beer to Justin.

"So how does Bee fit in to all this? What's her role here on the island?" Justin asked. Bee looked at Susan, who nodded.

"I was offered a contract here to restart growing local food on the island. This island lost a third of its land after the eruptions, and then the pandemic. Currently, we rely on imported fruits and vegetables, when it's quite possible to grow them here," Bee replied.

"But you both have a contract with Janet's UK company, don't you," Justin asked.

"Yes, and both our contracts have been approved by the PM and the local parliament," Susan replied.

"Well, that's very noble of you two. So how much progress have you made with this agricultural project so far?" Justin asked.

"It's been slow, what with all the distractions going on at the observatory. But I've been growing plants on the terrace here. We've identified two plots of land that can be returned to productive growing close to Susan's observatory, and there's a small group of locals ready to start the work," Bee replied, as Susan smiled at him.

"Really? Can I be of any help?"

"Yes, we're going to need a tractor from the municipality to help with the planting. If you can mention it to the PM that would be a great help," said Bee.

"Susan, I think that covers just about everything. I need to discuss my recommendations with the governor tomorrow. Do we have anything to eat for dinner? I'm going down to my room to make a few calls, if you can let me know when something's ready," he replied and got up to leave.

"Of course. Would you prefer pizza or curry? Both frozen, I'm afraid. Janet keeps a stock of food and wine, as you know," Susan replied with a dig at his past.

"Curry would be great," he replied leaving the room, while Susan and Bee laughed at each other and gave each other a high five.

"Going to make a few calls when he just arrived on the island? You think he has some sort of global satellite phone?" Bee asked.

"Well, do you believe his story about a US submarine?"

"Yes, it's possible and maybe better than our story of how we arrived here," Bee replied.

"Agreed, then what about your project. Where will this small group of volunteers come from?" asked Susan.

"Obviously I need help from Kiya. She's the only one who knows how this 'slash and burn' can be done," she replied, as they both laughed together. "Can you do the cooking, and I'll quickly drive down to Woodlands and see if Kiya has recovered. Let's hope she can help us."

"Alright, the keys should be in the ignition. Drive carefully," she shouted as Bee ran out of the house.

PART FIVE
DARE TO BELIEVE –
JUNE 2024

24 – CULATRA

James woke early the next morning in his apartment on the island of Culatra. He wanted to check that his plane was still undisturbed in the old ruins. What Ralph had told him about the security people cordoning off a part of the island to make a film was most disturbing.

Leaving just after 7 a.m., he walked outside to the church, past the restaurant, onto a small path made up of slabs of concrete. To his left, he could see the boats in the port as the path became narrow between houses and he passed by the island store that was still closed. On reaching a T junction, there was a sign to the Molhe Leste beach resort. He guessed this must be on the other side of the island, so he turned right and followed the path leading due south.

Continuing on this path, he admired a row of colourful small houses with flowers, and trees with red flowers, in the early morning sunshine. After walking past the island school, he came to the end of the houses and could see the ruined house in the distance on his right. There was no sign of his plane hidden inside behind the high wall; just a green tree growing above the enclosed wall. All around there was nothing but flat sand and tufts of grass. No sign of the area having been cordoned off so, being confused, he continued to walk on the path.

When he reached the large building at the end, he found it was the island's social centre. Beyond that was a wooden walkway across the sand to the beach. Now he could see that an area from the back of the centre had been cordoned off with yellow and black tape going north towards a bay on the inland side of the island. To James, that made no sense at all, so he retraced his steps back to the village.

Finding the village store now open, he purchased a can of beans, a loaf of sliced bread, and some eggs with his twenty euro note. Carrying his supplies past the restaurant, he saw Ralph sitting at a table with a group of locals outside, who waved at him to join them. He introduced James as an Americano and then pulled his chair to one side to speak to him in English.

"You're up early. Went to discover the way to the beach, did you?" he asked.

"Yes, and I wanted to see where they have started to put up the restrictions. It's right down by the social centre and appears to run north from there to the sea," he replied, looking confused.

"Yes, that's what we thought as well. There's nothing down there except a deserted beach," said Ralph.

"Good for landing illegal migrants," James replied.

"Shush, keep your voice down. If we want to find out more, we will have to work with my fishermen friends today to get a place on one of the boats tonight," Ralph replied.

"Yes, sure, can I just go back and eat some breakfast before?"

"Sure, eggs and baked beans, is it?" he said, looking at the bag. "When you're ready, walk over to the fishing boats by the big crane and I'll meet you there," he said as James nodded, got up, and left to walk home. As soon as he passed Wilma's house, she ran out to talk to him.

"Good morning, James! No, no, I cook for you," she insisted, taking his shopping bag and pulling him inside the house.

"James, you need a woman to take care of you on this island. I will cook your breakfast today and every day you are here," she demanded.

"Now, do you want a beer or some red wine?" she asked.

"Do you have any coffee?" James asked.

"Coffee, very expensive here, so it's a beer then," she said, as her husband hobbled out with his artificial leg, wheeling a bicycle. He smiled at James as he left. James ate his breakfast outside on the terrace, scrambled eggs on toast with baked beans, after which he was finally able to escape back to his apartment to shower and shave.

He changed back into his work clothes for his meeting with Ralph. Feeling more confident that his plane was safely hidden away, he left his apartment and walked towards where the fishing boats docked to unload their catch. It was still early in the morning when he saw Ralph engaged in a conversation.

He guessed the man was the skipper of the fishing boat that had just docked. James hung back as he looked closely at the boat in more detail. The name on the side was the *Carlos Orlando* with a traditional wood hull about 100 feet long, he guessed. The hull was painted white, with a blue deck and a central wheelhouse. What made the boat distinctive was a forward mast with ladders on each side going to the top, with a wire to the bows to hold it in place. Looking towards the stern of the boat were two traditional smaller posts to haul the catch and lift it onto the boat, he thought. James waited until he was invited to approach and Ralph spoke to him.

"Hi, James, we've reached a deal here. If we help unload his catch and prepare it for sale, he's agreed to take us out tonight on his boat. Is that okay?" he asked.

"Yes, sounds good. What do I have to do?"

"Come with me and I'll show you," he replied, and climbed down a ladder onto the deck of the fishing boat.

"Down here in the hold is last night's catch of fish: shellfish and clams all mixed up and contained in these plastic boxes. Come down here and have a look," Ralph asked, as James followed him down a ladder onto the boat, and Ralph jumped down into the hold.

"Look, I'll pass the boxes up to you on the deck, if you can put them up on the quay," he explained. After half an hour, there were over ten boxes on the quay and James was feeling the heat in the sun.

"Now we take one of the four-wheel carts to move them over to those huts in the shade," Ralph said, pointing to a row of flat carts left outside in the sun.

They both walked over to the huts as Ralph explained he would take care of the big fish, while James could sit in the shade to sort out the shellfish. His job was to bag them up for the fish market. With that, Ralph disappeared, with a trolley loaded up with the best of the catch, leaving James to work on his own. When Ralph returned, he helped James finish filling the sacks and, after locking up the shed, they both went for a beer in the local Janoca restaurant. Sitting together on the terrace outside it was quiet, while most of the local fishermen sat inside watching a football match on the TV. Ralph ordered two of the local Sagres beer, while James waited for him to explain the evening's event.

"It's best if you go home and take a shower to wash the smell of fish off your hands and body, James. Then take a nap in the afternoon, as we're going to be on the boat most of the night," he said.

"Okay, so what time do we leave?" James asked.

"Skipper asked us to be down at the boat just after sunset. Help him prepare the nets and bring back the boxes for the new catch."

"Okay, sounds good. What about the weather tonight?"

"Yes, he says there may be a bit of a storm later tonight, so we may get a bit wet. Don't worry about handling the nets. I'll help him with that. Better if you stay in the wheelhouse to keep the boat on a straight course. Do you think you can do that?" replied Ralph.

"Yes, of course. So, where's he going to fish tonight? In the channel over by the lighthouse or go out into the sea?" James asked.

"Depends on the weather. It can get quite rough outside. That's the Atlantic Ocean, but where some of the best fish are. If he sees a storm coming, he can always head back inside for shelter," Ralph replied as they finished their beers, got up to leave, and went outside.

"Remember, walk around the church. You don't want my mother to see you or you'll be stuck for another hour." Ralph laughed as James smiled and set off to walk in front of the church, back to his apartment. James took a shower, changed into shorts and a t-shirt, and went upstairs to his bedroom, where he closed the shutters and sat on his bed to think.

On the one hand, he was happy that the plane looked safe on the island, but on the other, he was concerned about what they might find out tonight. He took out his medallion and changed his emergency setting to his current position on the bed. Feeling more secure, he settled down to sleep on the double bed. When James woke, he threw open the shutters and walked out onto a roof terrace. He saw the sun was going down in the west and went to eat a snack before he left. Changing back into his work clothes, he left the house and walked back towards the restaurant, only to find Ralph coming out of his house.

"Well, that was good timing, James. What do you think we are going to see tonight?" he asked.

"Oh! Probably a lot of water and some fish," he replied, laughing as they walked down towards the port. On arrival, they found Captain Carlos already on his boat arranging the nets at the stern. He looked up and said something in Portuguese that Ralph translated for James.

"He's asking if we really want to go out tonight, because there's going to be a storm," Ralph asked James.

When he looked around, all the other fishing boats were still tied up with no one onboard. Then James thought of all the time they had spent working in the morning and the security on the island and replied, "Tell the captain he may get his biggest catch of all time tonight."

"Carlos thinks you're crazy, but we're going out tonight," Ralph replied, as they both climbed down onto the boat, already afloat with the rising tide. Ralph went forward to cast off while the skipper started the engine and went aft to let the ropes go. The boat went in reverse, turned, and headed out of the port.

Once outside, they turned west to head down the coast towards Farol at the end of the island. James stood on the deck and watched as first they sailed past the old base and then the bay that had been cordoned off. Both places looked deserted as Ralph joined him.

"So, James, looks like we're not going to see much action tonight," he said, as they both watched a red ball of sun setting over Faro. Once it was dusk, there were loads of lights on the shore. There were lights on other boats, lights from the channel marker buoys, and the high up ones on the lighthouse on Farol. It was then that James noticed a bright orange light coming in from the west. It just hung there. James thought it must be a light on a boat hidden in the darkness, but the light seemed to get bigger as James pointed it out to Ralph.

"Look! That light that just came out of the sunset," he said.

"James, that's just another EasyJet flight taking off from Faro," he replied, as the light got bigger and they both realised it was moving at some speed. As the light got closer, it became a bright orange ball, a ball of fire around another ball, as Ralph looked distraught.

"Christ, James, whatever is that thing?" he asked as the ball came over the boat and hovered there for a few seconds in an orange fiery glow with the air charged by static electricity. Then the engine of the boat stopped as Carlos finally came out of his wheelhouse to ask what happened.

"Tell him it was a plane taking off from the airport. Everything looks alright now; he can restart the engine," James said, asking Ralph to translate for him.

Then they watched as it shot off at great speed to the east and descended into the sea. But James knew exactly what he had seen. It was the same as when his plane re-enters space time. He knew some kind of alien craft must be back. Perhaps looking for his plane or, more likely, somewhere to land on the island again. *Standard operating procedure,* James thought to himself.

As soon as the engine of the boat restarted, they were underway again. James and Ralph sat on the foredeck watching as they passed the lights from the village of Farol and then the boat turned south out into the darkness of the Atlantic Ocean. At first James could see nothing except the regular flashes of the lighthouse behind him. Then, as his eyes became accustomed to the darkness, he could make out white surf breaking on the beach, until that also disappeared as they sailed further out to sea and Ralph came over to talk to him.

"Carlos wants you to take the helm while we prepare the nets for fishing. Come up to the wheelhouse and I'll show you what to do," he said. James followed Ralph inside the small cabin, where a dim light shone on the magnetic compass in front of the boat's steering wheel. As they entered on one side, Carlos left by the other door, as Ralph explained where to steer.

"Look, James, it's easy, as it's calm with a small swell. Here, take the wheel and keep the bow of the boat on the big E on the compass card. There's a southerly swell and some current pushing us towards the shore, so you need to keep correcting the course by turning the wheel to starboard. That's clockwise a few spokes on the wheel. If you overcorrect, turn the wheel the other way and let the boat come back to the East point on the compass card again," Ralph explained. After a few minutes watching, he left James to steer the boat on his own.

James found the steering easy to do and tried to visualise where this course would take them. If the beach on Culatra Island was roughly a straight line running from NE to SW, then an easterly course would take the boat further and further away from the shore. All went well, until he felt a huge drag on the boat and the wheel spun out of his hands.

What he didn't know was that the big fishing net had just been lowered into the water, causing a big drag on the course and speed of the boat. James fought to get the boat back on their course, when Carlos came back, smiling at him. He took control of the boat again and increased their speed to start fishing. When James came out of the wheelhouse, he couldn't see Ralph on the foredeck, until he looked up and saw his figure halfway up the ladder on the foremast.

"Ralph, whatever are you doing up there?" James shouted at him as he was almost at the top of the ladder.

"I'm up here to try to spot a shoal of fish. You can climb up on the other side and help if you like," he replied. James carefully watched and climbed halfway up to have a look. From here, he could see the island far away in the distance.

"Ralph, do you know where our position is from the island?"

"Roughly. We've just passed the Molhe Leste Club if you remember the beach over there," he replied.

"Of course, but there's a lot of coloured lights further down the beach. It's almost like an aurora of colours in the sky," James replied.

"There's an old military bunker down there. Must be some kids with fireworks," he replied. When James looked more closely, the colours were not fading but going higher up into the sky.

"James, I've just pointed out to Carlos there's a big shoal of fish on our right. You had better climb down as the boat will be turning shortly," he said, jumping down from his ladder, and James followed. The next moment, the boat increased speed and turned violently towards what Ralph had seen.

"You see, if we can trap the fish between us and the shore, we will make a huge catch. You will be a popular crew member with a bonus," Ralph said, smiling at him as the boat raced towards the fish and then slowed down again as the nets at the stern started to take the weight of a big catch.

"Now, James, you need to get out of the way as I need to help Carlos prepare the hold for the catch. We will use the winch aft to bring the fish onboard. It can be dangerous, so please go up to the wheelhouse and watch the operation from up there," he asked, as the boat came to a complete stop in the water and the winch started to haul the catch towards the stern of the boat.

When it was lifted out of the water, it was the biggest catch of fish James had ever seen. Most of the catch was dropped into the hold of the boat. Some fish were jumping around on the deck in complete madness. Most of them were thrown back into the hold. But James was also watching the sky in the west, where black clouds were racing towards them with flashes of lightning. When Carlos returned to the wheelhouse, he kissed James on his forehead at his success.

James pointed to the black sky coming towards them, but Carlos just nodded. He started the engine, turned the boat towards the flashing lighthouse of Farol, and increased the speed to full ahead, as Ralph joined them in the wheelhouse.

"James, you have brought good luck to us all today. You really should come out every day. That's the biggest catch I've ever seen."

But James was watching the storm coming towards them in fear.

The boat passed under the lighthouse at the end of the island and entered the channel with red and green marker buoys flashing in the darkness. There were fewer lights showing at the village of Farol as they passed the lights of the landing stage with a few boats moored close by the pier. No one was around as they made a final course correction back along the coast towards the port of Culatra. Finally, the strong wind from the northwest hit them as an electrical storm of lightning passing overhead.

"Going to be a strong one," Ralph exclaimed, closing the windward door of the wheelhouse while James watched the shore of the island from his side of the boat. As the boat passed a small bay, he saw the coloured lights again and walked out onto the foredeck to get a better view. Ralph followed him outside as James started to climb the ladder on the mast to see where the lights were leading.

"James, come down before you fall overboard," he shouted, but his words were lost in the wind. Suddenly, a bright beam of light shone down onto him and James was lifted into the air, only to disappear into the low clouds above them. When Ralph looked up, he saw a large cylindrical craft descending through the clouds to land on the island.

"Man Overboard," Ralph shouted at Carlos, pointing into the water where he had last seen James.

"Pare o motor. James caiu na água!" Ralph repeated in Portuguese and ran to the wheelhouse. Carlos stopped the engine and turned on a searchlight to scan the water where Ralph was pointing but could see no one in the water. It was at that point that sheets of rain hit the boat and visibility was reduced as the squall passed over the boat.

Carlos was now worried about his boat being stranded on the falling tide and, looking at Ralph, he started the engine again. Ralph breathed deeply and thought that maybe James had swum to the shore to check out the lights for himself. He didn't want to tell Carlos what else he had seen just before James disappeared. The boat finally passed the ferry terminal of Culatra and continued to safely enter the fishing port to tie up after a long night's fishing.

25 – ABDUCTION

When James awoke next, he sat facing Nathalie in an armchair.

As James looked around, he saw a control room with screens above a circular desk. There was a person watching a screen that he thought he had seen before. Above her were three rows of viewing ports and on one side he saw a sofa bed for sleeping.

"Hello, James, long time no see! Whatever were you doing on a fishing boat? Since when is that part of your agenda to save the planet?" Nathalie asked sarcastically.

"Wait, I recognise this craft. The last time I saw you was in 2031; same island, wasn't it? You were bringing back the team from the airbase with an alien, if I remember correctly," James replied.

"Yes, but we were forced to do that in order to let them return to the planet," Nathalie replied.

"So, where are we now?" James asked.

"You're right, we just landed on that island again. Look, James, I'm sorry about picking you up with our tractor beam, but we need to discuss more important matters," Nathalie replied, handing James a bottle of water. "There's a galactic war coming that you should be aware of."

"Yes, well there are about five wars on this planet since I've been back in 2024," James replied.

"No, James, I'm not just talking about the comet impact in 2030. Remember, the alien invasion occurred shortly after that."

"Yes, I remember it well, but are you sure that will happen? I thought you were on the side of the aliens, rather than trying to save humanity," replied James.

"No, we're not. Look, we realise your scientific community is stuck in the past. They still haven't found a way to produce free energy from the vacuum. Still launching rockets with a chemical engine and an obsession to visit another planet," she said.

"Correct! We have EVs. Electrical modes of transport from twenty years ago, to *err...* save the planet," he replied.

"It looks to us from the outside that you have a CULT of political people who can't move forward with the science. And all that despite providing you with an anti-gravity plane. You still do have it, don't you?" Nathalie asked.

"It's hidden somewhere here. Before that, it was on that Caribbean island under the control of the US Government. Been like that since I brought Susan and Bee back. I've been allowed to take it out for a spin, to let Janet attend an investors conference in London. After that, they want it returned to the island," James explained.

"Really, so you're all back on this island together."

"Yes. Susan has been working up at the observatory on the island where they've seen a number of strange events. There have been auroras and I've even seen Elizabeth up on the space station."

"You've seen her personally?"

"Only briefly. Sometimes, the station passes over that region about eighteen times a day, and yes, it was her. What is she doing up in space, Nathalie?"

"I have no idea. So, you think these aliens may be back on the island already?"

"Susan does. They recovered Kiya's body up on a hill. She was still recovering when I left, so we don't know all the details of what happened yet," James explained.

"Yes, I remember Kiya; an advanced humanoid hybrid. She looked like a young girl but was, in fact, around seventy Earth years old," Nathalie replied.

"She wasn't on your flight and now reappears on a Caribbean island in 2024. Were you involved with that?" James asked.

"No! Things sound much worse in 2024 than I thought. Look, as you may remember, this craft has a small transportation space, and we have brought back some scientists. We hope they can help speed up the transition to finding free energy. We have also returned with two people you will also remember," Nathalie explained.

"Let me guess, Ben and Michelle?"

"No, it's Anita and Claude."

"Sorry, but my craft can't carry that many people," said James.

"James, we only want you to take two people with you when you return to London. Maybe you can you persuade Janet to let them stay in her house, at least until they see what's happening in London," she asked.

"Alright, I'll try but can't promise anything."

"Good, then it's agreed. What time do you leave?"

"Wednesday next week are my orders. I can meet them outside where the plane is hidden, sometime after noon," he replied.

"Ah! Yes, the old, ruined base. We saw it as we came in to land. Most enterprising of you, James," Nathalie replied, reading his mind.

"Now, we can let you walk back to your house, or you teleport. If you do that, there may be some time dilation," she warned.

"That's okay, I set my medallion to my bed and don't want to waste any more time fishing," James replied.

"What exactly were you looking for on that boat, James?"

"Strange as it may seem, I was looking for you. Or any other aliens who were going to land on the island," he replied, smiling.

"Good luck, James," Nathalie said as he pressed the button on his medallion and was gone in a blue flash.

***

When James awoke next, he was back in his bed in the apartment feeling the worse for wear on his journey. He sat up in bed and reached for his travel bag on the floor. He took out two aspirins and swallowed them from the bottle of water, when he heard someone banging on the door downstairs. Slowly, James got to his feet and half staggered down the stairs, only to find Wilma at the door.

"James! James, you're back!" she exclaimed.

"Yes, what time is it? I must have overslept this morning."

"It's your last day here at this apartment. You need to pack and leave on the noon ferry back to the mainland," she replied.

"Leave today, okay, that's fine," he replied.

"Did you eat any breakfast?"

"No, I just woke up. Can you bring me something to eat?"

"James, I filled your fridge with fish, but when you didn't come back, I put it all in the freezer. Do you want me to take it and sell it to the Janoca restaurant?" she asked.

"Absolutely! Can you exchange it for sandwiches and a bottle of wine before I leave?" he asked. Wilma took the fish out of the freezer in a plastic bag and bolted out of the door while James went upstairs to pack. Before he changed, he needed to talk to Janet on the burner in his travel bag. He pressed call and waited.

"James, there you are. I was just going to call you. The conference is over. Are you ready to pick us up around midnight tonight?" Janet asked.

"Yes, of course, I'm packing up here now," he replied.

"Well, I hope the plane isn't damaged. What have you been doing for the last week?" she asked.

"Actually, I met Nathalie, who landed with her spacecraft."

"What! That horrible person who nearly got us all killed?"

"Janet, Nathalie is my daughter, if you remember?"

"Alright, what does she want this time?"

"She brought people back to our planet to try to solve some of our most pressing scientific problems," James replied.

"*Err…* and what else?"

"She wants me to bring Anita and Claude back with me to London, when I land tonight, alright?"

"What? And where are they going to stay in London exactly?"

"I've been asked if they could stay at your house in Windsor. At least until they get settled back in the UK."

"No, no, absolutely not. You think I'm running a bed and breakfast for all who turn up uninvited? That's a no, thank you," she said as the line went dead.

James raised his arms up into the air and threw the phone back into his travel bag. He stood up and went to get shaved and showered. Once changed into some more casual attire for a tourist, he took his things downstairs to wait for something to eat. He didn't have to wait long before Wilma returned to the door.

"James, I've brought you six cheese rolls and a bottle of wine, because you're rich," she exclaimed and continued.

"The bonus from the huge catch you made was a hundred euros and I've brought you the money here," she explained.

"Wilma, I can't take this money! Alright, I tell you what. You give me the euros and I'll exchange it for a hundred-dollar bill. Okay?"

"Well, I don't know, but Ralph always said you would come back. Look, he even left you a note," Wilma replied, passing over a piece of paper to James.

Hi, James, I know you are safe somewhere after what we saw on the boat. Obviously, I can't report this on my news channel so I'm leaving here tonight. Take care and it was great meeting you.

You will receive a bonus from my mum. Regards, Ralph.

"Wow, that's great. Thanks, Wilma. Do you want to join me with a glass of wine before I walk down to the ferry?" James asked, as Wilma smiled and James opened the bottle of white wine.

After James had eaten his cheese roll and finished a glass of wine, he put the remaining food and the bottle into his small case, closed it, and stood up to leave. Then he said to her, "Thanks, Wilma, for all your help and please give the dollar bill to Ralph. Hope to see you again." He followed this with a big hug and left her standing alone in the house. He walked down the path, pulling his suitcase behind him towards the jetty for the noon ferry. There was no one at the ferry shelter except a young woman sitting in a ticket kiosk.

"Leaving us already are you, Mr Pollack? It's a single then back to the mainland? That will be one euro twenty," she asked. James was surprised that she was speaking to him in English.

"Thank you. Yes, my visit here has been most interesting," he said, placing his small change on the counter.

"Well, you're a bit early for the ferry at twelve. Might be better if you sit in the shelter than stand out in the wind," she advised.

James took his ticket and sat in the shelter waiting for other passengers. Once a crowd of people had arrived, he quietly walked around to the far end of the shelter, carrying his case. Then he climbed down the bank onto the beach below and walked away. He needed to walk all the way back to the ruins where his plane was hidden. He hoped not to meet too many people on the beach. There was a westerly wind blowing as he watched a lunchtime passenger jet flying low over the channel to land at Faro Airport.

James passed the wooden boat up on the sand and continued until he guessed he would be in line with the ruins, and scurried up the bank, pleased to find the outer wall was but a few hundred yards inland across a landscape of sand gullies, tufts of grass, and spring flowers. Looking around he saw no one and pressed on to the ruined building. When he reached the far entrance, there were two people waiting for him both dressed in partial uniform. Anita was wearing her khaki army shirt and pants with commando boots. Claude had on a navy blue shirt, long trousers, and boots. They both smiled and waved as he approached.

"Well, James, this is much better than when we met on the island last time," Claude said shaking his hand, while Anita came and gave him a big hug.

"You know, I never really believed that you existed in the future, but where's the plane?" she asked.

"All in good time, guys, let's go inside and I'll explain," replied James, as he led them into the main building with its broken roof, a few old chairs, and lots of rubbish left over from teenage parties. James found a chair and sat down, as they both looked for something to sit on.

"Let's start at the beginning. Can you explain where you have been since I was lifted onto her craft to meet Nathalie again?"

"Look, James, she's okay now and really does want to help us. After we arrived, we were taken across the sand dunes to what looks like an old military bunker. Inside there's a portal to a more modern control centre where we spent some of the days in one of those sleep chambers. We both found the time travel more exhausting than before. After that, we were told of a change of plans, to come with you to London," Claude explained.

"Is there a problem, James?" Anita asked.

"No, not for me, but Janet is not happy for you to stay at her house," James replied.

"James, do you have a phone or something we can call her on?" Anita asked.

"Yes, I was given a burner, but was told its only good for one call," he replied, opening his case and passing the phone to Anita.

"Well, this looks good to me, let's give her a call," she said pressing the call button. Immediately, an answer machine came online telling them user was busy.

"So, James, this phone is good," she said as suddenly it rang again.

"James, I told you not to call me again," said Janet.

"No, it's me Anita. Lovely to hear your voice again after so many years..." Anita began and then got up and walked away. James and Claude were unable to hear the rest of the conversation, until Anita returned with a big smile on her face.

"Janet's agreed for us to stay at her house! Of course, just initially until we get settled again. Do you have any other problems to solve, James?" she replied tossing the phone back to him.

"Yes, in fact I do. Maybe you can help me finish this bottle of white wine and some rolls, if you're hungry," James replied, laughing.

"I knew it! I said he would come with some supplies, Claude. Yes, we're both starving," said Anita, smiling, as James passed around the bottle and gave the rolls to Anita. When they finished, James took out the burner phone again, placing it on a piece of wood, and hit it with the empty bottle several times, then threw the pieces into the trash.

"James, whatever are you doing?" Anita asked.

"You don't know. Everything is connected on this planet now. All mobile conversations are recorded. When we brought Susan back, they even had a satellite over the house to take all our photos."

"You mean everything we did at that base was recorded and filmed?" Anita said and gasped.

"Probably, but only watched by the security people to check you hadn't run off up the beach," James replied.

"So, that's why you destroyed the phone," said Claude.

"Yes, no one is coming on the plane until you explain what happened. Where did you go after leaving the RAF base? How did you get selected for this mission and what's its purpose in 2024?" he asked.

"Alright, James, calm down. Both Anita and I were assigned to the NATO headquarters near Brussels and after settling into different units, we applied for this mission to come back here to 2024. We were told its purpose was to help the planet in the event of a comet impact," Claude replied.

"Okay, so you had months of training for this, with how many candidates? Exactly where were you going after you landed?" he asked.

"Well, James, some changes were made, even before we left. Originally, there were four other couples. We were all assigned to a geographical region depending on our nationality. I was going back to the US and Claude back to NATO. That all changed when you arrived on the scene shortly after we landed," Anita explained.

"So, what happened after you landed? You must have been a group of eight and you all walked across the island?"

"No, we were taken by these security guards in an open golf buggy type vehicle, towards the lights," Claude explained.

"These coloured lights were like an aurora, because that's what worried me. We had a similar event on Janet's island that Susan couldn't explain," James replied. "When you arrived, were you given a medical or something?"

"Yes, I was checked by a nurse and the men by a doctor. Then we were given an injection and led away to one of those sleep chambers for a couple of days," Anita advised.

"And it was the same people you trained with, that were on Natalie's craft, like last time?" James asked.

"Yes, James, except when we were woken up, Claude and I were the only two left at this place with a couple of security guards. It was only when we went outside that we saw it was a disused military bunker."

"So, you were allowed out when exactly?"

"We went up some stairs for a swim just before sunrise. It was only later we guessed tourists were about a mile up the beach at a club."

"Really, and what did you wear? They provided swimsuits?"

"No. Claude and I just took bath towels with us, that's all. The guards never looked or bothered us at all. They were looking for beachcombers with binoculars," Claude said smiling.

"Great, so how did you know about the beach club?"

"Oh! They let us choose from a menu and brought us food from this club with a German-sounding name. We mostly ate junk food."

"Does the name 'Molhe Leste' ring a bell?" James asked.

"Yes, that was it, wasn't it, Claude? Have you been there?" Anita asked. Claude just nodded in agreement, getting frustrated.

"Look, James, what's this all about?" Claude asked.

"Alright, I'll explain. I asked the same question to Nathalie after you landed and she said: 'We have brought back some scientists, to help speed up the transition to finding free energy,' to quote her words," James replied and continued.

"Now I've heard your story and can believe it. But were there really four other scientific couples to help find free energy after you landed?" James asked, as there was silence from them both.

"Oh my God, James. You think we are an advance party to see if the planet will be ready for an alien invasion?" Anita asked.

"I don't know! But I don't think Nathalie has been honest about the purpose of your mission. Anyone recruited at NATO is military, not a scientist. So, are you ready to join Janet and me?" James asked.

"Yes, of course we are. We just thought 2024 would be better than what happened in the future," replied Anita.

"Thanks, James for the warning. But you look to be playing the part of a tourist here as well," replied Claude, pointing to his clothes.

"Yes, I've had to do that all my time here. I even bought a ticket on the ferry to the mainland this morning. I was staying at an Airbnb apartment that Jana had booked. You do remember her, don't you?"

"Yes, I remember. Bee worked with her on a tablet that showed her some past events with Nathalie," replied Anita.

"Exactly. Tell me, did your training include anything about climate change or Net Zero? Nathalie mentioned a CULT of political people who can't understand science to me," James asked.

"No, we only heard about this on the TV after we arrived back here… but yes, it does sound like a cult to us," Claude replied.

"Well, I'll be glad to get out of this place," James explained.

"Do you have any cash we might be able to use in London?"

"In fact, I do. I was given a hundred euros from my work fishing. That's how you work undercover. You need to think of a cover of how you returned from a holiday in Portugal," James said, taking a wad of notes he kept inside his passport, and handing them over to Claude.

"Thanks, James, but when I looked around in this building, we couldn't see your plane," said Claude.

"That's because it's not in this building. It's hidden in the walled courtyard outside. Now, I think we've finished. Let's go and have a look," James said, closing his case and standing up.

"Follow me, there's a door outside that I blocked up to keep the local kids out." James led them to a door in the wall. He pulled away the pole and asked Claude to remove the door.

"Oh, this is a job for the army," said Anita, who rushed forwards and pulled the door away. When they looked inside, both Claude and Anita looked on in astonishment.

"What the fuck is that thing?" Anita exclaimed.

"That's the hover plane to take us back to London," said James.

"We didn't see it on the island last time," said Anita.

"No, but we know it flies because they brought the children back to the airbase, remember," Claude replied, as he ran his hand against the smoothness of the fuselage.

"James, this is an alien design, isn't it," he asked.

"Yes, a much earlier model than the one you flew on with Nathalie. I don't think it was ever designed on this planet. It flies with anti-gravity and almost instant travel," James replied with confidence.

"Okay, so how do we get onboard," Claude asked, as James opened his medallion and activated the plane.

"Wow, this thing has come alive," exclaimed Anita, standing back, afraid of the power. James opened the passenger door at the rear and then his canopy for the pilot.

"We have one small problem with our timing. Janet wants to be picked up after midnight tonight and it's still only two in the afternoon. I don't want to arrive in London during daylight," James explained.

"So, when do you want us to leave?" Claude asked.

"We have to sit here for another ten hours?" said Anita.

"No, I have another idea," replied James, throwing his suitcase into the passenger compartment.

"Why don't we walk back to the military bunker, as I'm sure I can get inside with my medallion," he asked.

"I'm not sure I want to go back there. Anyway, not dressed in this uniform. That's all I have to wear," Anita replied.

"Alright, jump up into the back and change into my spare shorts and t-shirt in the pink case. After that, Claude can change into my old work shirt and trousers. Then you will both look like me. Almost as tourists," James suggested.

"Well, Claws, what do you think?" Anita asked.

"Yes, why not, better than sitting around here all afternoon," he replied, laughing. Anita pulled herself up into the compartment to change her clothes.

"James, everything's too big for me. Can't keep these shorts up. We need to find a belt," she shouted down.

"That's alright, come on down and we'll look for some rope or something for that," James replied as Claude helped her climb down.

"Now it's your turn, Claude. I'm afraid my clothes may still smell of fish, but should be a better fit," said James.

Claude pulled himself up into the plane, and as soon as he had changed, James closed the plane again. As he walked back inside, Anita was tearing strips of cotton from a broken chair and, tying them together, she made a colourful belt. Claude replaced the door and the three of them walked back to the entrance of the ruin and looked across the sand and grass to the old bunker.

Claude set off walking, with Anita behind and James at the rear. After ten minutes, they came to an area where the grass had been flattened by something heavy and the sand was all churned up.

"Look, we must have landed here as these are the tyre marks in the sand from the electric carts they used to take us to the bunker," he said, pointing to the tracks in the sand. James was beginning to believe their story.

"Hang on a minute, let's just sit and you tell me what happened when they let you go," James said, as they all stopped and looked at him. Anita looked around for a gully they could hide in.

"Come over here, James, you can get a better view from down here. You're right, I should have thought of that before. Anyone could see the three of us from half a mile away. Tell him, Claude, what happened earlier today," Anita asked.

"When we awoke, they brought us our uniform clothes. After we changed, they led us outside and told us to walk to that old ruin where we would be met. Then they threw us our boots, turned, and went back inside," said Claude.

"So, you see, James, at least two of those security guards must still be in there," Anita added.

"Okay, but with my medallion that shouldn't be a problem. For you two it might be better if you head straight for the beach from here. Crawl on your hands and knees through the sand from here, while I'll follow the tracks to the bunker," said James.

"What happens when we get on the beach?" Claude asked.

"Before you get down to the beach, wait until others are walking towards the beach club. Then go and talk to them; tell them you just arrived and behave like tourists," James said.

"Okay, but how do we meet up again?" Anita asked.

"Relax at the club until after sunset. I saw a wooden walkway across the sand back to the village. At the end, there's a modern-looking social centre and you walk west from there, over to the ruins. We'll all meet back there, got it?" said James.

"Yes, so basically, we move around in a circle. South down to the beach, walk east to the club, eat a snack, and relax. Then north on the walkway and finally west again to our RDV," Anita confirmed.

"Yes, and remember to hold hands all the time," James replied, laughing, as the two of them started to crawl off towards the beach.

James waited five minutes, until he could no longer see them. Then he stood up and followed the tracks towards the bunker. As he approached the concrete structure, the first thing he noticed was that the entrance was not facing the sea. The outside was covered in faded graffiti with rubbish scattered around outside, probably left by local kids. The tyre tracks had stopped some distance from the main building, as he looked around to see if there were other people around. He could see the way to the sea was around the back, so he went to check that out first. Here he saw many footprints in the sand and realised the bunker was partly hidden from the beach by a massive sand dune. Creeping back along the front wall, he reached the entrance and went inside. Here he found a small empty concrete room, and little else of interest.

It was at this point that he was beginning to doubt Claude and Anita's story as he pointed his medallion at the back wall to see if there was another chamber behind but found nothing. Feeling confused, he sat down on the sandy floor to think. Then he remembered Anita said they went upstairs to go for a swim. When, in fact, there were no concrete stairs here at all. He had seen Ralph's note about something so frightening he had left the island, but carts being driven across the dunes to bring people to this place was impossible. Unless the bunker and the beach had been moved to another dimension of time, he thought.

James got up to walk outside and, standing next to the entrance, he thought of his options. He remembered that after his meeting with Nathalie he had jumped back to the apartment, but only remembered waking up on his departure date. Someone had interfered with his timeline. He had lost four or more days of his time on the island, and he wanted to know where he had been.

The best solution was to reverse the time jump on his medallion when he was on the spaceship with Nathalie. Knowing this might be dangerous, he set his current position and time outside the bunker. Just in case he needed to return in an emergency. He then went back to find his last time jump, pressed reverse, and waited to see what would happen. At first, he saw nothing. It was dark and then lights appeared coming towards him across the sand. The next thing he heard was a group walking towards him, as James stood against the wall and watched.

The images he saw looked almost like ghosts. People with grey-coloured clothes being led by someone who could have been a guard. James counted them going inside and saw them descending a stairway. No one appeared to notice him standing at the side of the entrance. When he looked at the last person, he thought it was Claude. James jumped in front to stop him, but he just walked through his body. James followed him down the stairs as well, as he realised that no one could see or detect him in this dimension.

At the bottom was what looked like a control room of sorts with a semicircular desk facing the sea and a bank of four monitors on the wall. James watched as the group lined up, five men on one side and the women in another line, as each was scanned and as Claude had said, given an injection. He walked forwards through the men and watched as they were taken to a sleep pod and made to lie down inside.

James realised they must have been drugged as all appeared in a trance. Finding this to be most horrific, he moved back to the control room. He needed to find the year of this illusion, but all the papers on the desk were a blur to him. Then he remembered the wheel on his arm that he had used to access the fifth dimension in the past and thought this might enable him to see more clearly. When he activated this wheel, everything in this dimension became clear and he read on the desk the name "Manual to Enforce Agenda 2030," before a high-pitched alarm sounded. He picked it up and pushed it down the back of his shorts as he could hear a guard running to locate the breach of security.

James pressed on the wheel again and he was back in his world of ghosts. He could make out that the security monitors had lit up, but the guard had run upstairs. *Interesting*, thought James, *this is going to be fun*, and he moved to check out another corridor to his right. He found a number of small rooms with table and chairs, and right at the end was a door that looked more solid. When he walked inside, he found it was furnished with a desk, television, and a large double bed.

This could have been where Anita and Claude were held, so he pressed the wheel again to see if he could find any traces of them. Alarms sounded again that James ignored, as he stripped the bed and then went to look in the en-suite shower. High up behind the curtain he found someone had scratched the initials A*C in the wall. That suggested they had stayed in this room. Not wanting to encounter any of the guards, he pressed the wheel again, and then the button on his medallion to take him back outside the bunker in 2024.

Outside it was all quiet, a starlit night, with the litter blowing around in a gentle breeze. Then he noticed a tall dark shape standing on the edge of the dune looking out to the sea.

"Hello, James, I see you've taken an interest in the fifth dimension again," he asked, turning around.

"Good evening, Deepak, what brings you here tonight?" James asked, knowing that his guardian would not be pleased to see him.

"James, I didn't give you access to the fifth dimension to look around bed chambers. Now you have alerted Nathalie to your action here, and she will change her plans again," Deepak complained.

"I just wanted to be sure of their story…" he replied.

"Really? By wasting your time here, you are going to miss your next flight, and that's a lot more important," he advised. James looked and his medallion showed it was already past midnight.

"Good night, James, and be more careful," Deepak replied and left him standing alone above the beach.

26 – SPACEX

James quickly set the medallion to his first visit to the ruined house and hoped he would find the other two still waiting for him there. He jumped back to outside the outer wall of the ruin. He looked around only to see the manual lying on the ground, and, picking it up, he briskly walked around to the entrance where he found the others most upset.

"James, where the hell have you been?" Anita asked while Claude stated the obvious problem.

"Well, we've missed your midnight deadline so are we still going to leave for London now?" he asked.

"Yes, it's past midnight in Portugal, but London is one hour behind. Time here is CET while UK is on BST," he said.

"We can still make midnight in London if we leave in the next ten minutes," James replied, walking into the building as the two others followed him.

"Yes, I remember that's correct. But did you find out anything new?" Claude asked.

"Yes, Claude, I've brought back the Manual for Agenda 2030. Now can you please remove the door again," James asked him.

"Thanks, now let's all get on board again," James said, activating the plane and opening the rear access door.

"Anita first, if you can help her, Claude," asked James.

"Right, now come and give me a leg up to the cockpit, and we can get on our way," he said.

"Sure thing. Are you sure you can manoeuvrer the craft out of this courtyard in the dark?" he asked James.

"Don't worry, should be easy. Listen, there's a headset in the back so you can talk to me when we arrive. Janet's house is close to the river, so I'll take the plane down and wash it in the water before we land. That's normal operating procedure for every flight," James said.

"Confirm on the intercom when you're onboard and I'll start the engine," he explained. James waited until he saw the all clear, started the anti-gravity lift, and the plane rose 300 feet above the island. Then he selected the coordinates for Janet's house in Old Windsor and, pressing the activate button, the plane disappeared in an instant.

The next thing everyone saw on the plane was darkness outside as James looked for the lights to the river. Then he heard Claude's voice in his ear.

"James, is that it? Have we arrived already?" Claude asked.

"Yes, can you see any lights below us?" James replied.

"There were lights behind us before," he replied.

"Turning now. Yes, I see them going down to the river now…" James let the plane down into the water to remove all the dust and static electricity and then he reset the destination to Janet's house again. A few minutes later, the plane landed safely on Janet's driveway, and he saw people coming forward with a ladder for the people at the back. James waited patiently in the cockpit until he heard a voice in his ear he recognised.

"Welcome back, my love. I've really missed you," he heard Jana say on the intercom.

"Same here and what about our big boy? How was the conference; anything new?" James asked.

"He's fine, and the conference is all sorted. NASA paid up and want to involve SpaceX in the project. You won't believe it but they're going to be meeting us when we land in Montserrat," she explained.

"You don't mean Elon, do you?"

"No, not personally, just his rocket engineers."

"Jana, do you know what I'm wearing?"

"Shorts and a flowery tee!"

"Look, I must change. Is your pink case in the compartment? Claude's navy kit should be in there," James asked.

"Yes, it's here," she confirmed.

"Okay, can you move the ladder to get me out of here? I need to come and change," she heard. Jana moved the ladder to the front of the plane and helped James down onto the ground, where they hugged each other. When they kissed, Jana's eyes lit up with surprise.

"You went fishing!" she exclaimed.

"Yes, and I met Nathalie, remember from our past, her future!"

"Hurry, James. Janet's only gone to show Anita and Claude the house. You need to get changed quickly," she said as they both climbed back up to the rear compartment, when they heard a voice from below.

"Everything all right, Mrs Jana?" asked Janet's housekeeper.

"Yes, just having some private time with my husband. Please can you bring my baby, with our luggage, when Janet's ready to leave," she asked, to get rid of her.

They both giggled as Jana pulled the shirt off James and when they finished, James was dressed in a navy shirt and pants.

"Look, I have to tell you about this document. It's called *Manual for Agenda 2030*. I stole it from Nathalie's base on the island. Don't tell Janet until we have reviewed it," James asked.

"You went into the fifth dimension to get this?"

"Yes, and I got a reprimand from Deepak as well. It's a complicated story but I needed to find out what's being planned for this planet in 2024," James said.

"So, you didn't see her cylinder ship land then?"

"No, they picked me up with a tractor beam from above. They must have been coming in to land. The next I remember was sitting talking to Nathalie in the control room of her ship," he said.

"It's alright, James, I can read the rest of this from your mind. Leave the manual with me. I'll put it in the pink case and we can discuss it when we get back home," said Jana, when the housekeeper returned to shout up to them again.

"Mrs Romford is asking if you will come and take your baby."

"Alright, I'll be right down," she replied, then seeing a red passport on the floor she gave him more advice.

"James, you will need your passport when you arrive back on the island. Also, don't forget to delete all the coordinates on the plane, except this one here and Osborne Airport, to hide where you've been," she told him. Then she climbed down the ladder from the compartment, followed by James. Outside in the cool London air, they found Janet talking to Anita and Claude next to the plane.

"Ah! Well done, James. I've been hearing about how you have been looking after my plane, or rather hiding it. I thought you might want to say goodbye after your adventures together," Janet said, smiling at him.

Anita stepped forward, still dressed in oversized shorts and a tee, with only the lights on the drive shining on the plane in the darkness. She gave James a big hug, while Claude shook his hand. They both wished them a safe journey home. Jana reappeared holding her baby and James gave his son a kiss before they both climbed back onboard. Then Claude moved the ladder and helped James up into the cockpit again. Finally, several more cases were loaded onboard, and they were ready to depart. James was ready to start the engine when Janet came on his intercom.

"James, we need to delay our departure. Jana told you that there will be SpaceX engineers waiting at Osborne Airport when we land. So there will be no dip in the sea. We land at the airport, where Sam has prepared fire trucks to spray the plane," said Janet.

"Okay, normal operating procedure, isn't it," he replied.

"James, this is the first test flight of a plane to be further developed by SpaceX. Don't mention any alien design at your post flight briefing," Janet demanded.

"Really, so you want this to look like a flight of a really fast plane, nothing more?" he replied.

"Yes, is there any way you can reduce the speed of the plane?"

"Not, unless we stop off in the ocean somewhere. But once we go down, they can't track us anymore."

"Really, so that's the answer?"

"Not really, I have thirty minutes of oxygen in the cockpit, but you would all be dead," he replied.

"Think, James, how can we make the flight duration with a speed of say Mach40, so it's not alien?" Janet asked.

"Alright, ask Jana to explain the fifth dimension," he said, as the line went dead for a few minutes, and James shut the engine down again.

"Hello, Houston, we have a problem," James said when Jana finally came back on the intercom again.

"James, the only solution is for you to press the access to the fifth dimension and then input the coordinates to Montserrat as normal. Every time you have been in the fifth, time has slowed down in that dimension," Jana suggested.

"Okay, pass me back to Janet," James asked.

"James, I'm sorry. Unless we deliver this plane undamaged to the airport on Montserrat, NASA will not release the final 50 percent to my investors. What are the risks to you and your son?" Janet asked.

"Understood! If I limit the time in the fifth to a few minutes, the flight may take less than a few hours."

"No, that's too long. We need it to be less than an hour."

"Alright, I can try less, but, Janet, nothing is certain in the fifth," replied James, as he restarted the engine and pressed the wheel on his arm and waited. Then, before he let the plane climb in the dark to hover above the house, James input the coordinates for Osborne Airport on Monserrat. Looking at the wheel on his arm, he wondered if this was really such a good solution. He waited a few seconds and deactivated it again, but nothing happened. He realised he would have to press two together and when he did, time paused until he hit the wheel again.

The next moment, he found the plane was hovering some 300 feet above Osborne Airport on the island of Montserrat in late afternoon sunshine. Below he could see fire trucks waiting for him to land and started to descend. Only then he saw men in white suits waving the plane down onto his usual landing pad, until he touched down.

Once landed, the plane was sprayed with water as steam rose into the tropical air. A stage was brought to his cockpit and the men in suits helped him leave as if he was an astronaut. James realised this was a show for the media as if he had re-entered from space. Then he wondered what had happened to the passengers in the back.

Finally, he was taken in a wheelchair towards the hangar and given a bottle of water to drink, as doctors rushed up to check how he was still alive. James was not amused until he saw Sam and beckoned to him to come and help.

"Sam, please can you explain what's happening here, and where are all the passengers from the plane?" James asked.

"James, this was a test flight for SpaceX. No passengers would be allowed. I expect Janet, and the rest of your family will arrive on British Airways in the next few days," he replied, smiling.

"No wait, something went horribly wrong. Can you give me your phone, I need to call Jana in the UK. I need to speak to her urgently," James asked.

"No, James, I can't do that with all these people watching you. What do you want me to say," he asked.

"Call her and tell her that I arrived safely and ask if she has started packing," he replied.

"Okay, I can do that. Look, remember Justin? He's our new Superintendent of Police and he's coming your way now," Sam replied, who faded away to make the call.

"Hello, Mr Pollack. I need to do an identity check, if you have your passport," he asked.

"Justin! What a pleasant surprise, all of us together again? Passport, yes, I think I can help you with that. I'm a British citizen and now resident on the island here," James replied, handing over his UK passport to him.

"Very good, I need to check with immigration if they can confirm that and will return your ID," he replied, as Sam came back with a reply.

"Jana was relieved you arrived safely and sends her love. They haven't started packing yet, as Janet now wants to stay at her house until after the election in July," Sam replied.

"Thanks. Justin wasn't very friendly; can you tell me what I've done wrong, Sam?" James asked, getting more concerned.

"It's the plane, James. You were being monitored by NASA and SpaceX and you flew from London to Monserrat a distance of about 4,000 miles in six minutes," he replied.

"Well, yes. Janet asked me to slow it down a bit, and they're worried about the speed?" James laughed.

"Think, James? The space shuttle was travelling at Mach25 when it broke up. That's over 18,000 mph and you were travelling at twice that, around 40,000 mph to arrive here in six minutes."

"Sam, we both know the reason for that, don't we."

"Yes, but you can't say anything like that at the briefing. The question they can't understand is how you're still alive."

"Got it!" James replied.

"They're going to want a lot of answers at the flight debrief, and that's going to start in a few minutes," Sam explained, as Justin came back with his passport.

"Thank you, Mr Pollack. Can you follow me now," he asked, nodding at James. Sam pushed James in his wheelchair and followed Justin into a private space at the back of the hangar that must had been constructed for the debrief. Sam left James in front of the panel of five experts, while Justin made the introductions.

"Gentlemen, the pilot of the plane is here and ready to answer your questions," Justin said in his Montserrat Police uniform. Then he turned and wheeled across a bedside table with a bottle of water, that he placed in front of James, still sitting in the wheelchair.

James nodded, took a drink from the bottle and, placing his arms on the table, looked at the woman sitting at the centre of the panel.

"Thank you, Superintendent, you can leave us now," said the woman who appeared to be the chair of the panel.

"Welcome, Mr Pollack. My name is Dr Stacy, the deputy director of National Intelligence and probably like you, I feel a bit jet lagged after my flight down to this island," she said introducing herself.

"Please understand, this is not an interrogation. I'm here on this panel with engineers, two from NASA and two from SpaceX. I'm going to start the discussion and then let my colleagues ask questions. If you don't want to reply to them, just answer 'no comment'. Will that format work for you?" she asked, and James just nodded.

"So, let's get started. We understand that you are the test pilot for Clear Water Investments. A UK company owned by Janet Romford. Is that correct?" she asked to which James just nodded.

"Please, Mr Pollack you must answer yes or no," she asked.

"Yes," replied James.

"And the test base for this plane has been at Mrs Romford's house in Windsor near London, is that correct, Mr Pollack?"

"If you say so. If you look on Google Maps, it's just a country house, with a garden running down to the River Thames," he replied.

"So, it's not a test base at all?"

"No," James replied.

"So why were you at this location then?"

"I can only assume that was agreed with the representatives present here today," James stated. The chairwoman looked at the men on each side of her and they nodded.

"Very well. Now your flight was scheduled to leave at 18.00 hrs BST, but it was delayed. Were there any mechanical difficulties with the plane?" she asked.

"No, none whatsoever."

"Did Mrs Romford explain this was a test flight to return the plane to NASA here at the airport?"

"Yes, she did. She said that was agreed at a conference with the two parties sitting here today."

"And did you go to this conference in London?"

"No, I did not."

"So where were you when you got these orders to return to London?"

"I was on holiday. I went on a fishing trip to Portugal."

"Really? And from the satellite images when the plane arrived at just after midnight, you brought two persons back into the UK with you. Is that correct?" she asked.

"Yes, they were my fishing friends I knew from the past. Both were invited to stay at her house in England."

"Finally, Mr Pollack, about the flight. We tracked you from London back to the airport here. Is there anything you want to explain?"

"Not really, what's your problem?"

"The plane flew 4,000 miles in six minutes. Do you have oxygen on the plane for the pilot?"

"Yes, of course, but I rarely use it. You will find this plane is like the reusable X-37B. It's about the same size as that from the outside.

When that lands back on Earth, I'm sure it exceeds the Mach40 speed you're referring to."

"Yes, Mr Pollack, we know all about the capabilities of the X-37B, thank you. So how are you alive today?"

"Well, this plane has several distinct features. It must generate its own local gravity, or the pilot would not survive."

"Really, can you explain more?"

"I'm not sure I need to, after the AA Weapons system project was restarted last year. You will have all the operational characteristics of these UAP craft in your files. Wasn't that study done by your Secretary of Defence?"

"Yes, it was, I just wanted your opinion of how it flies?"

"Look, I'm just the pilot. I have no idea how it's been engineered. You need to ask the NASA representatives how that works."

"All right let's ask them for answers then," she said, turning to the two men on her left.

"We have no questions for the pilot, thank you," the first man replied and the second confirmed the same 'no questions'. Then the chairwoman looked at the two SpaceX representatives and asked, "Well, do you have any questions?"

"No, not until we examine the craft, we have no questions for the pilot either," they both confirmed.

"Very well then, let's all go and look at the plane outside before it gets dark," the chairwoman said standing up as the meeting ended. When the doors opened, Sam returned to take James in his wheelchair towards his car parked not far from the hangar. When James stood up, he saw a crowd around the plane and got into the car.

"So, James, how was the debriefing?" Sam asked.

"Not so bad after all. They wanted to know all the technical details, so I referred them to their weapons system inquiry they ran in 2023. It's obvious they have all the data but no idea about the specifics. Just hope this won't be filed as 'unconfirmed,'" replied James.

When they reached the security gate into the terminal, there was a Montserrat Police sergeant waiting to check them out.

"Lot of security here at the airport, Sam?"

"Yes, I was told to close the airport at 5 p.m. Justin, our new 'Sub Ops', was ordered to deploy his force here to keep out the public."

"What about the Chief of Police here as well."

"Most likely up in the control tower, so I'm not really needed."

"Well, we both know why this plane is being kept here on this island. You know they sent a Deputy of NID down here to question me," replied James.

"Yes, I know. I was here when her helicopter touched down with her team who came in from Antigua. She's a bright engineer by training, James, and you have just exposed a huge black operation at NASA. Did they have any questions for you?" asked Sam.

"No, none, nor the SpaceX guys. It's about time this technology was exposed to the public, or at least the governor."

"They can't, James. The governor was never invited," Sam replied, as he restarted the engine and drove out of the terminal.

"Don't you worry about the governor, James. I'll take you home, as you need to sleep for a couple of days after that flight," Sam said, as he drove down towards Salem, to take him back to the house on the Old Bluff, as James fell fast asleep. Then Sam stopped the car and carefully lifted the medallion over James's head and put it in his pocket.

On reaching the top of the Bluff, he saw there was a military helicopter parked outside the house. That had been ordered to take

James to a French island, where he could do no more damage to the American power in the region. This was not something that he wanted to do as two armed commandos and a woman approached the car, who he recognised as Elizabeth.

"So, Elizabeth, you finally got your man," Sam announced.

"Yes, it's taken four years, and my government doesn't want him around on this island anymore," she replied.

"Very well, take the man. He's been sedated, as I'm not sure he would survive another flight tonight," Sam replied.

"Good, then we'll take him now and his medallion," she asked.

"Didn't have it on him when he landed," he replied.

"You're lying," Elizabeth replied.

"Take your target and leave," Sam insisted.

"What if I don't agree," she replied.

"Well, I happen to have a rocket launcher in the car, and I'll blow your chopper up before any of you can leave," Sam replied, getting out of the car and pointing the bazooka at the helicopter.

"Look it's a twenty-yard hit to the target. I'll wait till you all get on board and then fire, and there won't be any survivors, Elizabeth."

"You wouldn't dare," she replied.

"Oh, yes, I would. You want to call my bluff?" Sam replied.

Then she told the two soldiers to take the man out of the car and carry him to the helicopter.

"Always nice doing business with you, Elizabeth," Sam shouted as the rotors started and as soon all the persons were onboard, the helicopter lifted off and disappeared into the night.

PART SIX
THE TRUTH IS OUT –
July 2024

27 – MUSEUM

When Janet woke up, she saw it was the morning of 19th June, and she was at her house in England. Opening the curtains of her bedroom, she saw it was going to be a fine summer day and, humming to herself, she went downstairs to make a nice cup of her favourite tea. Entering the kitchen, she found Jana with a cup of coffee already.

"Good morning, Jana. Everything alright after we missed the flight last night?" she asked.

"Just great thank you. Oh! Sam called last night to say that James had arrived safely, and asked if we had started packing?"

"Good, so what did you say?"

"That we're staying here until the election on the 4th of July. That's right, isn't it?"

"Yes, my dear. Now tell me what you think happened to us on the plane last night. I'm a bit confused."

"You remember James tried to slow down his flight by engaging his fifth dimension for a few minutes. When he reversed that, it left us sitting on the drive with all our luggage and the plane flew away," she explained.

"I see. Most dangerous if you ask me! Do you have all your luggage?"

"Yes, everything except the pink travel bag I gave him. You know… the one with the document he found?" Jana asked.

"Oh! That bag. I will call Sam later and ask him to get it back from that technician at the airport. I need to call Sam anyway to hear if the plane's arrival was the success we had planned."

"Thanks, so what do we do with the other two sleeping upstairs?" Jana asked.

"I'm still suspicious why Nathalie wants them to come to London and stay at the house in Windsor. Perhaps you can find out more with your tablet? See if they were given any instructions of what they were to do in London," Janet asked.

Before she could answer, the intercom rang for a delivery at the house. Janet went to look on the screen and, seeing it was someone from the military on a small motorbike, she opened the gates and waited at the front door.

"Mrs Romford. *Err*… Mrs Janet Romford, we have an express delivery for you. If you can show me your ID and sign for it," he asked.

"Yes, of course. I only returned last night, and my passport is on the hall table. Here you are, where do I sign?" she asked.

"Thank you. Sign here, and have a nice day," he replied, handing over a large envelope and then left, riding his bike down the drive.

"'Curious and curiouser,' said Alice. Now I wonder what this is all about?" she said returning to the kitchen.

"I watched him from the window. You know, I think that was a NATO uniform he was wearing," Jana said. Janet opened the envelope and out fell two NATO ID cards onto the table.

"Well I never!" exclaimed Janet, as they looked at the cards, only to find the names of Claude and Anita, the new arrivals upstairs.

"Captain Claude Duquette (Fr) and Anita N. Seal (US)," Janet read on the ID cards. "But where did they get the photos?" she asked.

"Not bad for a military satellite. It's a nighttime shot turned into daylight, with good photoshop," Jana replied, sounding bored.

"You mean, last night, when they landed with James?"

"Yes, and you know what that means, don't you?"

"Police. And coming here next," replied Janet.

"We need to get those two love birds out of bed and into some proper clothes. They looked like beach bums last night," Jana replied.

"Okay, let's not panic. I'll go and give them the good news, as I need to get dressed first," Janet replied walking towards the stairs.

"I'll go and find some of James's old clothes. They might fit Claude," Jana replied, following her upstairs. Once she had found the clothes, Jana waited outside the bedroom door for Janet to arrive.

"Right, I'll knock first then we enter the room," said Janet, but they found the two fully clothed and still asleep as if in some kind of an unconscious trance. Janet tried shaking Anita's body, but nothing happened.

"Wait, let me try and see if I can connect to Claude's dreams with the tablet first," insisted Jana. She sat down on the bed next to Claude and, touching his head, turned on the tablet to find an image. After a few minutes, a grainy picture appeared of a large building that she thought must be in London.

"I know that place!" exclaimed Janet.

"That's the Natural History Museum in Kensington! Can you try with Anita and see if she sees the same image?" Janet asked, but this time Jana found nothing, and Janet gave up waking them.

"Let me get a jug of water and pour it over their clothes. That will wake them up. Then they will have to change into proper clothes," Janet said. They watched until Claude and Anita started to stir and then left the room, leaving them to get dressed.

By ten o' clock, the pair were downstairs, properly dressed and drinking coffee when the intercom rang again, and Janet saw it was the local police at the gate. Janet waited at the door as a police inspector came inside with two assistants.

"Hello, Inspector, it's been a long time since you last came here," Janet said.

"We've had reports that two persons arrived last night through irregular channels. Are they still with you at the house?" he asked.

"Why yes, they are in the kitchen drinking coffee if you want to meet them. Come this way," Janet said and introduced them to him.

"May I see your passports or ID please," he asked.

"Yes, of course, we're both on leave now, but serving officers with NATO," Claude replied, handing over two ID cards.

"Very well. What about the luggage I saw in the hallway?" he asked looking at them both.

"Oh! That's my luggage and the suitcase of my assistant. We missed our flight last night and have delayed our departure. Of course, you can look inside if you really need to," Janet replied.

"Yes, open the cases now," he replied, waving at the assistants to check inside. After five minutes of searching, they had only found clothes, boxes of baby foods, and some women's magazines.

"Will there be anything else, Inspector?" Janet asked.

"No, that will be all. Just make sure your guests don't overstay their visit to the UK," he replied, walked to the door, and left.

"Listen up, everyone. I have a business lunch in the city. I've decided to close my office here with this new government coming to power. Think it may be better to move everything offshore. Jana is going to take you two on a cultural tour of one of the oldest museums in London, if you can explain, Jana," Janet said and left wishing everyone a good day.

"We're going to take the train into London to visit the Natural History Museum, in Kensington, West London. Do you have any money or a bag to carry your things in?" Jana asked, as they both shook their heads in surprise.

"What's so special about this museum? Why do we need to go there?" Anita asked.

"Good question. This museum is the most popular venue for people wanting to learn about climate change and the Green agenda. It even has a garden devoted to dinosaurs outside the museum," said Jana.

"I think I've seen that in my dreams," said Claude.

"They are excavating the grounds of a five-acre site and Janet wants to know what you can find. I'll see if I can find you a couple of backpacks for your work," Jana explained. When she returned with the bags, Anita looked inside with surprise.

"Torches, hammers, wire cutters! What are we really doing?"

"Let's say it's a bit of an archaeological dig, and should be fun," Jana replied, as they all left the house to take the fast train to London. After arriving at Waterloo Station, they took a taxi to Cromwell Road and stepped out in front of the museum.

"Wow, this place looks most impressive, but there's a big queue to get in. Did you book us any tickets?" asked Claude.

"Don't worry about that. I called before and we're expected in the grounds. Come on, follow me to the gardens that are still being transformed. That's where we are needed," Jana said.

"Hang on, so we're not going inside?" asked Claude.

"No, we walk west to the museum's Darwin Centre to find the Jurassic Garden where we will meet the foreman who I spoke to this morning," explained Jana.

"So, we're on some kind of an exploration dig with the tools you gave us?" Anita questioned.

"Yes, you could put it like that," replied Jana as they arrived at an area still being excavated with a small Portakabin and a large man standing outside.

"Well, I never believed you would come. These are your two experts to solve our excavation problem?" he asked.

"Yes, they arrived in the UK last night from NATO and think they can solve the problem," Jana replied as they all shook hands and introduced themselves, showing their ID cards, as the man began his explanation.

"We were digging out the supports for this big Diplodocus dinosaur that needs to sit at the centre of the garden. Then we came across an old entrance to some old ruins, and none of my men would go near it," he explained.

"Does that happen often here in London?" Anita asked.

"Yes, quite a lot. I called in the bomb squad yesterday who came and said there wasn't a bomb. But none of my men will work to open this mound. You can see it over there," he said, pointing to across the site.

"Right, so there's a metal door that needs to be removed from the mound in order for you to flatten the site?" Jana asked.

"Yes, but don't tell any of those archaeological types or the site will be closed for months. These gardens must be ready to open to the public in the middle of July, and I can't afford any more delays," he explained.

"But what are the workers afraid of? Don't you have the plans for this site from the past?" Claude asked.

"We have plenty of plans of the museum from over a hundred years ago, but nothing special is marked on the grounds," he replied.

"Alright, what work do you need us to do?" asked Claude.

"You see that JCB over there? Do you know how to drive it?"

"Sure, if you show me how to start it," replied Anita, as the foreman smiled and led them out into the grounds to the machine. Anita climbed up into the driver's seat, while the foreman stood outside on the platform to instruct her.

"Okay, turn on the ignition and let's see what you can do."

"Yeah, looks easy to me," she replied, with her American accent.

"I have attached a wire to the door that runs back to the JCB. When you're ready, engage reverse and take up the slack in the wire," he explained. Anita could see Claude was standing too close to the wire, when Jana ran out and pulled him back beside the JCB.

"Ready, everyone? Going for a big burst of power now," shouted Anita, as the machine jumped backwards and the door flew through the air, landing in front of them. Everyone watched as a cloud of bats rose up into the sky from the open entrance.

"Bats! Not much more down there then," Claude shouted.

"No, Claude, we need to go and see what else is down there," Jana replied, pointing to an open hole in the mound. Anita jumped down from the machine as they all ran to see what had been exposed.

"Looks like a damaged stone staircase. Do we have to go down there to check it out?" Claude asked.

"Definitely, Claude, that's why you've got lights for your head and torches in the backpacks," replied Jana, and led them back to the Portakabin to speak to the foreman.

"We're going down inside to check out what's below, if you can give us another half on hour," Jana asked.

"Okay, but it will only lead to the underground sewers that run down to the Thames. Do you really want to do that?" he advised.

"Yes, we've come this far and want to be sure."

"I can give you until 2 p.m. when the men come back from lunch. After that we're going to demolish the entrance and flatten the ground. But it's up to you," he replied.

"Okay, guys, get your backpacks on and follow me. We're going down to check this out. Any questions?" Jana ordered.

The three of them walked over to the exposed entrance with Jana leading the way. Claude pushed some small rocks out of the way to make the access wider as Anita squeezed down into the stone staircase and disappeared underground. Claude followed, passing his backpack down first and Jana followed them down. When they reached the bottom of the staircase, everyone stopped to put the small lights on their heads and took the handheld torches out of the backpacks. After that, Anita led the way down a passageway that was going south and deeper underground, when they heard a strange noise.

"Stop, everyone. Do you hear a rumbling sound? Let me look at my underground map," she said, as everyone turned and looked at her.

"Yes, we must be somewhere above the South Kensington tube line. If we keep walking south, we should reach Old Church Street shortly in Chelsea," said Jana.

"What do you expect to find there, Jana?" Claude asked.

"Well, we're on our way to the river, so we're on the right track," Jana replied, and told them to keep going. The passageway started to drop down much deeper and then they heard rushing water as they shone their torches and saw a fast-flowing sewer ahead.

"There's no way I'm going in that," shouted Anita, as they all came and looked at a larger tunnel full of water.

"Sorry, Jana, it looks like we've reached a dead end," said Anita, but Claude was looking at the wall that he thought was a new brick construction and hit it with his hammer.

"Wait, look at this; it's been constructed recently. Help me break through this wall as I think there may be another way out," he said, sounding more positive.

Jana and Anita helped and they soon broke their way through to another space. Once the hole was large enough, Anita crawled through followed by the other two, and they shone their lights on a strange scene. When Claude climbed into the chamber, he exclaimed out loud, "What in God's name is this place with all these sleep pods?"

"Exactly. I knew there was something down here, but didn't know how to find it. Well done, Claude," remarked Jana.

"Look, Claude, these are the same pods we saw on that island with James. So why are there hundreds of sleep chambers stored underground in London?" Anita asked.

"I think we have found something that most Western governments want to hide from their people," Jana replied.

"Alright, can we open one to see who or what's inside," Claude asked, as they all looked in horror at him.

"Well, I'm not sure that's a good idea, but let's unplug this one first and see what happens," Jana agreed, as Claude hit the electrical connection with his hammer and they waited.

"See… nothing! Let's open the lid and see who's inside," he said, levering the lid off and they all peered inside to see the face of a large grey-haired man.

"Alright, I'm going to look in this chamber here," said Anita, who prised off the lid and found the same man inside.

"I think these men are all clones," said Jana, as she opened a chamber in the third row and found the same-looking person.

"All right, Jana, you had better explain what's going on here as there are hundreds of these chambers. This looks like a full alien invasion to us both, doesn't it, Anita?" Claude asked.

"Well, I don't know everything. We've had problems on Janet's island and Susan thinks the aliens are back there. But this is completely mind-blowing. I think we should destroy the lot before we leave," explained Jana.

"Alright, and how do we do that?" Anita asked.

"Well, there are three rows of these chambers and three of us. We each walk down one row and destroy the electrical connections to each chamber," Jana said hopefully.

"Good, I like hitting things with my hammer," replied Claude.

"Yes, that's the best we can do today. Let's get started, as it's going to take us some time to do this properly," Anita agreed.

"Right, but don't rush; make sure each chamber is fully disconnected as well," Jana replied. The three of them worked for over an hour and on reaching the far end of the cavern, they looked to find a way out to the surface again.

"Jana, do you have any idea where we are now on this Old Church Street you mentioned?" Claude asked.

"Yes, if we can find the stairs, we should come out inside Chelsea Old Church. It's on the map as an ancient Anglican church visited by Henry VIII and Elizabeth I. If that's correct, then this is the ancient crypt of the church," replied Jana.

"But that would mean the church is involved in this as well?"

"Some in the church actually want to see the country overthrown by invaders; that's the reality in 2024," Jana added.

"Well, there's a solid wooden door over there that must lead somewhere. Perhaps up to the church," Claude announced to everyone. Anita took one look and inserted a screwdriver in the keyhole to lift the latch on the other side and the door opened.

"Thanks, Anita. You go first and don't forget to say a prayer in the church," said Claude.

"Oh! I think we're way past saying any prayers in this country after what I've seen today," Anita replied, as she climbed the stairs, followed by the others. There was no one inside the church, and Jana guided them outside, to make their way out along Cheyne Walk to Albert Bridge. She hoped there might be a pleasure boat to take them back up the river to Windsor.

"Come on, you lot, we need to walk through the Albert gardens to find the pier, and a ferryboat," Jana said as they all broke into a run at the sight of the river until they reached the pier.

28 – THE FLOOD

"Well, it said in the guide to walk down to Cadogan Pier where we can board a pleasure craft to take us down the river to the Tower of London," Jana read.

"No, Jana, we want to go up the river, not down. So where are all the boats?" Claude asked and sat down in disappointment.

"Something will turn up soon," Jana replied, when she saw a fast speedboat approaching them. They all stood up and waved as the boat slowed down to talk to them.

"You want a lift? We're going up as far as Richmond," they shouted.

"Yes, please! We can pay you for the fuel," Anita shouted back.

"Nah, no problem. Climb down and come aboard," he replied, and they all climbed down a ladder onto the boat. Once onboard, the boat sped away past Battersea, under Putney Bridge, and on westward towards Richmond.

"What were you three doing hanging out on that pier? The pleasure boats never stop there now," the helmsman asked.

"We're tourists and went to visit the Nat History Museum this morning. Then we walked down to the river," Anita replied.

"Really, because there was a big electrical storm over West London this afternoon. If you look back, you can still see the thunder and lightning over Kensington," he replied, pointing it out to them.

"Yeah, when I saw that on my phone, we decided to go back home. It's been on the news; there were massive floods on the roads," said his friend. Claude and Anita looked at each other, alarmed, and Jana signalled them to say no more.

"You were lucky to have missed that. In fact, I only picked you up after seeing you running through the gardens. I thought you might have been people from the floods. Strange that happened isn't it," he commented. Half an hour later, the boat arrived at a landing stage near Richmond Bridge and they got ready to leave.

"Thanks for the ride. Can I give you some euros seeing as we much appreciated you stopped for us?" Claude offered.

"No, keep the cash for your holiday," he replied and waved them goodbye. Anita helped Jana onto the jetty and Claude followed as they walked towards the Richmond station.

"Do you think we caused that storm, Jana?" Claude asked.

"Looks quite likely, and if we were trapped in that tunnel, we probably would have drowned and be dead by now," she replied.

"From now on, we have to be much more careful and not go back to London until all this has died down," replied Anita.

"Don't worry, we'll take the first train to Windsor Riverside, and I need to report this to Janet and James," Jana said as they walked to the station in Richmond. They boarded a train, then took a taxi at the station back to Janet's house, and arrived at around 6 p.m. Jana went straight to find Janet to tell her the news.

"We found a huge crypt under the Old Church in Chelsea with three rows of those sleep pods, so we destroyed the lot," Jana reported.

"Calm down, Jana. You said there were three rows of these sleep pods piled three high? That would make a total of nine hundred clones, or hybrids. Frankly, I find all this hard to believe," Janet said.

"Then there were floods in Kensington and we barely escaped with our lives," Jana continued.

"Yes, I heard about that. A local thunderstorm. Fortunately, I also missed that as well. All right, tell the others we meet in the dining room at seven, as I want to hear their story as well," she insisted.

Janet arrived five minutes early and found them already there, with Anita in tears, Claude drinking a glass of whisky, and Jana looking worried.

"I saw him on the television tonight. It was the same person we found in those pods under the church," Anita blurted out.

"Excuse me, can someone tell me what's going on?" Janet asked.

"We were watching the evening news when we got back about two people who drowned in the flood and a lot more taken to hospital. When we looked online, we saw a short clip of questions in the House of Commons. I didn't know the UK had an Indian PM, but the leader of the opposition was the same man we all saw in three of the pods," Claude explained, taking a swig from his glass of scotch.

"I see. I think, Jana, you had better explain this story from the beginning," Janet asked.

"Alright, so after we saw the History Museum on the viewer tablet, I checked online to see the latest news. It was mostly about a bronze cast of the museum's dinosaur going to be installed in the Jurassic Garden. Then there was a note at the end to say a bomb disposal unit had been at the site. So, I called the museum and asked to speak to the works manager. I told him I had a solution and was put through to the garden foreman, who agreed to meet us. But we needed to arrive at the site before midday," Jana explained.

"And when you met, Claude and Anita showed him their NATO ID and you got to work by exposing the entrance to a tunnel."

"Yes, more or less. We walked underground to the end of the tunnel where we found a sewer outlet that, even then, was flooding with water into the Thames," Jana explained.

"So, really, you had no idea where you were then?"

"I had a map and knew we were going south. The tunnel was going downhill all the time, so I knew that it would come out roughly somewhere in the Thames River," Jana said.

"Interesting. I looked on Google Maps and you must have walked about a mile underground. But how did you find the Old Church in Chelsea?" replied Janet.

"Oh! You'd better ask Claude about that," said Jana.

"When we reached the dead end at the sewer, I noticed there was a new wall of brickwork. We broke through that with our hammers and found this cavern full of plastic pods – you know those plastic sleep chambers – hundreds of them," he said.

"Alright and how high was this hole you made above the level of the water in the sewer," Janet asked.

"Not more than a foot or so. We knocked the bottom of the wall down first and the rest fell apart. Why's that important?" he asked.

"Because I think I know what happened after you left the church in Chelsea. You're sure it was the old church?" she questioned.

"Yes, Janet, we're sure," replied Jana.

"Do any of you remember how many steps there were from the bottom to where you came out in the church? Claude, Anita, can you take a rough guess," Janet asked.

"I would say it was about twenty steps. Janet, where are you going with this," Claude replied, sounding tired of the questions.

"It's important, Claude, because water on this planet only flows downhill. When the storm broke over Kensington, that sewer would have been unable to take all the rainwater. The water would have backed up to fill the tunnel and then overflowed into this chamber."

"You mean the crypt under the church?" Claude asked.

"Yes, this floodwater would most likely have broken up all the neat rows of sleep pods and none of you were responsible for their destruction," Janet explained smiling, as everyone looked a bit happier.

"If you'll excuse me a moment, I'm going to call a private investigator to go down to the church to talk to the locals to see if he can find any damage. Jana, can you pour everyone a glass of wine while I'm gone," she said, and then poked her head around the door again.

"Can someone tell me where the door inside the church is located?" Janet asked.

"Yes, it's a very small door under the pulpit. The door was locked so I broke it open with my army boot, and then we all crawled out," Anita answered.

"Thank you. I'll get the kitchen women to bring you some nibbles, as we're not having dinner before eight," replied Janet, who then disappeared.

"Well, Claude what do you think of this latest development. Is the man on the TV tonight a real human or an alien?" Anita asked, as the housekeeper arrived with a bowl of crisps and one of nuts.

"You'll be eating dinner in the conservatory tonight at 8 p.m. so please don't be late," she asked. Claude waited until she left the room before he answered.

"Really, I don't know. We worked with those hybrids on the ship for months and they always helped us. But there were other aliens who they were terrified of. Frankly, I have no idea what we are dealing with here," he replied.

"Claude, you've had a few glasses tonight already. Would you be willing to help me understand by doing a session on my mind tablet? Remember I did it that time in Janet's house up at the airbase and it might help us understand what Nathalie really wants you to do here in 2024," Jana asked.

"Alright, but not now. I don't want any more shocks today," he answered, when Janet returned to the room looking happy.

"I spoke to my private investigator. He's free to look at the church this evening and will send me his first report later tonight," she said, smiling.

"Now, dinner will be served in ten minutes, so if any of you want to freshen up or get changed, let's meet again in the conservatory next door," Janet announced.

Claude and Anita stood up and left to go up to their room, while Janet took the bottle of wine, poured herself a big glass, and looked at Jana to tell her the latest news.

"My man was able to tell me that the museum's Darwin Garden was supported by the Cadogan Charity, a part of the Cadogan Estate."

"Yes, I looked that up in my research and found they own all the property in Kensington and Chelsea, making it one of the richest estates in the country," replied Jana.

"Right, but what I didn't know was that ferry pier you were on is also called the Cadogan Pier. Their property goes right down to the Thames. Are you thinking what I'm thinking," asked Janet.

"OMG! That's not possible, for such rich people?"

"No, but the church cannot be independent in all this, can it? The only way to move that number of pods would be on the river."

"Then they will have to take the bodies away in the same way," she replied.

"Yes, that's what I've told my man to photo for me. You know, Jana, when I was a young girl at school here in England, I asked my father why we had to move to South Africa," Janet said.

"Really, what did he tell you?"

"You don't want to know. There were private parties in London at that time for the aristocracy. Sex parties, where young girls only wore masonic aprons," Janet replied.

"Really, but not in Chelsea? Still, I suppose the Cadogan's family must have known about that," Jana replied.

"Probably. Now we will reap the political storm that's coming. I've given up the lease on the premises in London today, and all the office equipment will be sent down here on Monday," Janet explained, as the housekeeper entered to say that dinner was served and they got up to join the others.

The conservatory was an addition on the side of the house with a view of the garden running down to the river. The room had a large dining table for eight persons and was still light in late June, before the summer solstice. They ate a light dinner of cold gazpacho soup, followed by cold salmon and a salad, while Janet explained the entertainment for the evening.

"My staff tell me there are rumours in the village about lights at the house last night, so we've prepared a small firework display tonight. We can start as soon as it gets dark outside," Janet announced.

"Any news about that church in Chelsea?" Claude asked.

"No, not yet, I'll let you know as soon as I have anything," replied Janet, helping herself to a glass of wine.

"Come on, Claude, can I offer you a glass? We all need to try to relax tonight, after a most stressful day today," asked Janet.

"Yes, I think I need a glass or two after today," replied Anita, who accepted a glass and continued.

"So why were there three clones of this politician we saw on the news tonight?" Anita asked.

"Well, that's the deep agenda's backup if those humans don't do what this cult wants," Janet replied.

"Okay, but what about the people in the other pods we saw?"

"Well, they are expected to win the election with a huge majority. Perhaps as many as four hundred, so they need backups for all of them as well," replied Janet.

"I think this is all madness, what do you say, Claude?"

"It sounds like a very dangerous scenario. If these pods were all intended for political purposes, I hope they have all been destroyed. Then real humans will have to fight to maintain control," he replied.

"Yes, but who is this CULT directing all this?" asked Anita.

"Oh! That's easy to explain. It could be something like the World Economic Forum? That's a fanatical political organisation, who used the COVID hysteria to make people think that they're the saviours, when it's a global public-private fascist movement, supported by the EU," Janet replied.

"Yes, this all goes back to the communists who helped form the European Union after the last war. I remember the history in the past in Chechnya and it didn't end well," replied Jana.

"You think the next government here will be a Marxist cult?" Claude asked.

"Probably. That's one of the worst political ideologies in history. It's always run by a small group of 'elites,' who consolidate total control over the countries' resources and people. Then they erode democracy and stop all freedoms to enable them to take over the assets of the state," Janet said.

"But then don't they go bankrupt?" Anita asked.

"Yes, of course. Communist governments always eventually collapse, but not until they have done a lot of damage," said Jana.

"And the global elite paid themselves billions after the COVID pandemic, taking it all from ordinary people like us," said Janet.

"Yes, I can't believe that two of us were in the room back in 2020, before the pandemic started," replied Jana.

"Look, I'm sorry but we can't solve this tonight. Let's finish the meal and go and watch the fireworks outside," Janet asked, as the housekeeper came to take away the plates.

"Would you mind if I go upstairs to bed? I think I may have to lie down for a bit," asked Anita.

"Of course, we understand it's been a long day for the both of you," Janet replied.

"Think I'll go upstairs as well," said Claude and the two of them got up to leave the room.

"Well, that's no surprise, Jana. Shall we take our coffee in the lounge?" Janet asked and got up to leave as well. They both watched as

Anita and Claude went upstairs and then retired to more comfortable chairs in the lounge.

"I still don't know about those two. I need to get Claude to tell us what they were programmed to do before we can trust them," said Jana.

"Don't rush him. He will tell us what we need to know when he's ready," replied Janet, as their coffee arrived.

"So what's all this about a firework display tonight?" Jana asked.

"Well, you may not have noticed, but that hover plane left four big holes in the driveway last night," explained Janet.

"You mean the craft must weigh more than a ton."

"Exactly, and possible radioactivity in the ground, as well."

"So, this is a cover-up operation," Jana asked.

"Yes, I instructed the gardener to dig another two holes in order to launch the rockets tonight. So instead of four, we now have six holes in the driveway. Those holes will all be contaminated with potassium nitrate, carbon, and sulphur, to lift the rockets in the sky," Janet explained smiling.

"So, you hope this will cover up most of the traces of the plane last night?" Jana asked.

"Hopefully, yes! It's not just rockets, but more fireworks and even a bonfire over a small area. Catherine wheels, shooting stars, the whole lot. That should make any forensic investigation more difficult," Janet explained.

"You really think they will come and check that?"

"Probably next week. Come on, let's go and look at the fireworks," Janet replied, and they got up to see the show outside.

29 – CONFESSION

The next morning when Jana got up to feed her baby, she could hear a mower cutting the grass outside. Looking out of her bedroom window, a gardener was busy on a seated tractor and Janet's housekeeper was filling the two holes on the drive. There was a big brown patch on the grass where the bonfire had burnt. Finally, as the baby fell asleep, Jana put him down in his crib and, taking a dressing gown, went downstairs to find Janet.

"Ah, there you are. Everything all right with the little one?" Janet asked.

"Yes, thanks, he's much better in this cool climate. Any news from the church?" she asked, helping herself to a coffee.

"Yes, I've got a few photos to send you, if you open your phone," Janet replied and sent the images with airdrop.

"OMG, the doors of the church were open, with a fire truck in the road outside!"

"Yes, and the next shows water being pumped out and into a drain in the road, so now I really can believe your escapades yesterday. But it gets more interesting as he took photos of a list of names he found in the vestry of the church. I'll send them to you now," said Janet.

"What! This list includes the names of leading politicians, some of whom are now dead. Look there's even the name of Gorbachev, and Vaclav Hayek, the first president of the Czech Republic. I'll need to check out the rest of the others," replied Jana.

"Well, it's most certainly not a list of the parishioners at this church. Looks more like a list of the Club of Rome to me? Although I thought that had been debunked years ago," asked Janet.

"No, it's still active from what I read online and has over a hundred active members, including support from the EU of course. In fact, they held a workshop in Prague last year with an Israeli delegation that surprised me," she replied.

"And its aim is still sustainable development with a limit on population growth in Europe that's been blown apart with this record migration from outside, hasn't it?"

"That's now the Open Borders policy of the EU."

"Alright, so what's this list doing in this church? Making clones of dead politicians from the past?" asked Janet.

"Really, I don't know. I need to have a session with Claude on the mind tablet. That may solve the question of why they were sent to London, and what was in the document that James found in Portugal."

"Ah yes. 'Implementing Agenda 2030' or something, wasn't it? That sounds more like reducing the population and splitting our species to have a scientific dictatorship to control the planet," said Janet.

"Oh! God no, I hope not. That document should be with James at our Caribbean house. Can I call Bee on your phone to check?" asked Jana.

"Well, not now, it's still nighttime over there. So, if she has your phone, where did you find that one?"

"I found it in my room. It's a model I've never seen before, so maybe only works on the UK network here," she replied.

"Let me see that right now, Jana," Janet asked placing a finger to her lips.

"*Hmm*. Yes, it's a government-issue phone dating back to before the pandemic."

"You mean it may have belonged to Elizabeth K?"

"Don't know. I've turned it off but even now they can listen to what we are saying. You do realise that, don't you? And it has all the photos sent from the church!"

"That's bad, very bad. Maybe it was a plant in my room to listen to our conversations. Except I don't talk in that room with the baby, so what can we do?"

"I know someone in the village who's a good tech geek. I'll ask him to come and check it out first. We need to find a list of the contacts and messages on the phone," Janet replied.

"I'm sorry, I should have thought before charging it up."

"No, maybe this is the breakthrough we've been waiting for. Still, I think it might be best if we both leave before the election next month," she replied.

"You mean before the fourth of July?"

"Yes. Can you book a ticket to Antigua for you and your baby boy? I don't want you involved in any police business."

"Really, you think it will come to that? What about a ticket for you," Jana asked.

"I've been thinking of going back through New York. I may need to look up this person if we can find out where she's located from the phone," Janet explained.

"Very well, I'll have to do it on my laptop. I'll let you know what the flight options are," Jana replied and watched as Janet placed the phone in an empty kitchen jar and on closing the lid, she started to call her tech guy in the village. Meanwhile, Jana went back upstairs to get dressed.

An hour later, Claude and Anita emerged from upstairs and found Janet in the kitchen with the man from the village looking at the phone sitting in the glass jar with an airtight lid. On entering the kitchen, she put her finger to her lips to tell them not to speak. Anita bent down, took one look at the phone, and asked for some paper to write on. Janet was horrified when she read what was written.

'*Old US military communication device. Destroy it now,*' to which she replied.

'*NO. It's important to find contacts in the US before that.*'

'*This guy can try, but probably encrypted. Please take it out of this room, we're hungry.*' Anita wrote, and on showing it to Janet, she showed the man out with the jar and they both left for the basement.

When Janet returned to the kitchen, she found Claude and Anita had eaten and were drinking coffee.

"Made any progress with that military phone?" Anita asked.

"Some, he was able to find a couple of locations in the States, where the user was based. Does JPL in Pasadena mean anything to you guys," Janet asked.

"Oh yes, Pasadena's just north of LA. That's where they built the Cold Atom lab that's been installed on the ISS," Anita replied.

"You want to meet someone there?" asked Claude.

"I'm not sure, but we have bigger problems here. Come and look at these photos that were sent to me at the church," Janet replied.

"Yep, that pretty much confirms that the basement got flooded, doesn't it. So, what's the problem," asked Anita.

"I sent them to Jana when she was using that military phone. I'm sorry but she gave her phone to Bee and said she found the device in her bedroom," Janet replied.

"OMG! So in a day or so they will come to arrest us all. Do you have any firearms in the house? Can we buy some guns at a store," Anita asked, getting more concerned.

"No, that's not possible in the UK. Only the police can carry firearms if they think they may be threatened," Janet explained.

"Look, lady, we're serving NATO officers who became involved in a covert operation yesterday. I think we destroyed hundreds of dead clones, so shooting a few more should not be a problem," she said.

"You mean shoot police officers here!" Janet said, as Jana appeared at the door, having overheard the conversation.

"I'm sorry, this is all my fault. Claude, you need to come with me now. We urgently need to discover exactly why you were sent to London," Jana said holding up the black mind tablet, as everyone turned to look at Claude.

"Alright, I'll come. Where do you want to do this?" he asked.

"We can go to the dining room where it's quiet. Leave Anita and Janet to continue her search," said Jana, and they both left the room.

"Well, do you have anything at all?" asked Anita.

"*Err*, yes maybe. There are some old relics from my husband in another building, if you care to come and look," replied Janet, and led her out of the house to an extension next to the garages.

"This was my husband's shooting lodge. He even brought some of it back from South Africa," Janet explained, unlocking two padlocks. When the door opened, Anita saw it was like a replica from the Boer War.

There was a large oak table in the centre of the room covered with a canvas sheet. There were six chairs and leather armchairs in the corners. On the walls were the trophy heads of wild animals from the Veldt and above an ornate fireplace was a massive hunting rifle.

"Now that's more like it! An elephant gun; never seen one before, can't wait to fire it," exclaimed Anita.

"Yes, we probably shouldn't leave it in here," said Janet.

"Any more firearms in this place?" Anita asked.

"Oh yes! There are more guns in the sideboard over there," Janet replied as Anita pulled open a drawer to find an ageing 303 rifle, and two handguns.

"You know if there's any ammo?" asked Anita.

"Yes, in the next drawer down," she replied.

"Wow, this is quite an arsenal, but we can't leave any of this in this place," Anita said, as she removed the canvas cover and started to place all the guns and ammo on the table covered with the canvas. Lastly, she placed the elephant gun on the top and folded the canvas into a bundle.

"Now we need to get this lot hidden somewhere safe. Something moveable like a car."

"Right, it's not too big, so it should fit in the boot of the Bentley. Wait and let me open the garage," replied Janet. Two minutes later, she returned and helped Anita carry the bundle to the boot of the car next door. When they closed the garage door, Janet stood and, looking worried, turned to Anita to ask what next.

"What are we going to do if the police arrive," she asked.

"I think you and Jana should book an airline ticket and get back to that Caribbean island by Monday, at the latest," she replied.

"Yes, we've already been planning to leave next week. And the hunting lodge? What should we do with that?"

"Don't keep it locked up anymore. We might all have a farewell party in there tonight. Cover up the traces from the past," Anita said in her American drawl.

"Good idea. I'll tell the housekeeper to prepare dinner there. But what are you and Claude going to do after we leave?" Janet asked.

"That all depends on what Jana can find out from our past. What were we really meant to do in London?" Anita replied.

30 – PARTY TIME

That Saturday evening, they all gathered in the hunting lodge for a final dinner together. Janet found Anita a summer dress to wear that pleased Claude, who wore jeans and a summer jacket that had belonged to James. The evening was warm for the last days of June and humid over the west of London. Janet was her usual buoyant self, while Jana was tired with the thought of her flight back home to the Caribbean the next day.

"Here we are, my darlings, the charcoal barbecue has been lit outside and a case of my best Bordeaux wine is on the table for Claude to open," Janet announced, as Jana arrived at the party.

"We're not going to drink a whole case of wine are we?" exclaimed Jana.

"No, my dear, let Anita explain," replied Janet.

"Earlier today, Janet and I found some old firearms in that sideboard over there, so we're going to splash a bit of wine around to liberate the drawers," explained Anita, and, taking an open bottle from Claude, she walked across the room spilling the wine on the floor.

"OMG, I'm spilling the wine." She laughed, as everyone else started clapping at her frivolity until she reached the sideboard. Then she poured the rest of the bottle into the drawers. In a final act of madness, she threw the empty bottle into an open drawer, turned, and bowed at her audience.

"Thank you, Anita, for your performance tonight. That should confuse any forensics who come to check this room," said Janet, while Anita made a curtsy in her summer dress and everyone laughed too.

"Now, I have an announcement to make to you all tonight. As some of you know, I came back to London to ensure that the second and final payment on the hover plane was returned to my investors. Last night, I received confirmation that it was deposited in my account, so I went out shopping," said Janet, as everyone looked puzzled.

"She's bought herself a real private jet!" Jana announced.

"Yes, thanks to Jana here, the company has purchased a Gulfstream 450 with a range to fly from the UK to the island without refuelling," Janet announced to applause from everyone.

"Right then, that calls for champagne," shouted Claude as the chef walked forwards with an open bottle, followed by the housekeeper and a tray of champagne glasses.

"Let's toast to our success in the future and hope that we never lose touch with each other," Janet toasted to all the party. Once that was over, everyone moved to the more comfortable chairs and sat down around the table. While Janet told the chef to start cooking on the barbecue, she returned to listen to the conversation.

"So, Jana, was Claude able to find anything on your magic tablet? Like, where you're going next, because he refuses to tell me anything," asked Anita.

"Well, that's been difficult. All I can find is that stupid museum in London, but something is blocking me from going inside," she replied.

"You mean you will have to go back in there," Anita asked.

"Yes, and we don't have much time left do we?" replied Jana, as Janet realised she needed to change the subject.

"Tonight, our chef is going to cook us all American dishes. So we're going to start with a Cobb salad, for those on a diet. Then barbecue T-bone steaks and Tater tots. If you can explain, Anita," Janet asked.

"Yeah, there're crunchy fried potatoes, but very good," Anita replied, smiling, and poured herself a glass of red wine. Jana thought this was all madness and got up to excuse herself.

"I'm sorry, but I have to go and check on the little one," she announced and left the party.

In fact, there was something she wanted to check out on the tablet again, as she ran back into the house and upstairs to her bedroom. She needed to call James for his advice, but not having a phone any more, thought she would try to connect on her tablet. After a few minutes of thinking about her man, grainy pictures somewhere on the island started to appear on the screen.

My God, why didn't I think of this before, she thought, and sat back in disbelief. There was nothing she could say tonight to spoil the party, but she would need to talk to Janet later. Closing the tablet, she checked her baby was still asleep and went back downstairs to rejoin the dinner. When she returned, a full party was in progress, with people eating the food with gusto.

"You know, Claws, you never told me why you wanted to destroy all those chambers in the cavern," Anita asked, sitting across the table from her.

"I mean, they were obviously not human, but why so determined," Anita continued, as Jana realised this was going to be another problem.

"Don't you remember from our future in 2030? These aliens – you know, what they call migrants now – wanted to take over our planet, and they succeeded," he replied, cutting a piece of meat from his steak.

"Stop it, you two. We are here tonight to enjoy, not to discuss your past events. I'll ask if we can get some music in here. Would some country and western be okay for you, Anita?" Janet asked.

"Yes, that would be great, if everyone agrees," Anita replied. Jana moved to a chair next to Janet and helped herself to some salad.

"Everything alright?" Janet asked, looking at Jana.

"Yes, yes. No, I mean we have to talk after. I found out what happened to James on the island and it was not good," she replied.

"Alright, but you can still go to the airport to finalise the purchase tomorrow? I'm thinking that it's better if we all leave this place before the country descends into chaos after the election," she said.

"Yes, of course. So, you now want to fly direct to the island and take the other two with us?" Jana asked.

"Well, after that outburst tonight, I don't think we have much choice, do we?" she replied.

"No, but there's something we need to discuss before we leave," Jana asked, as an old-fashioned gramophone was brought into the room and a collection of vinyl records handed to Anita.

"Later, Jana. Let's just enjoy the music," Janet replied.

Anita chose the best country music from 2015 that she remembered before they all left that year. The gramophone started to play songs like 'I See You', 'Lonely Tonight', and 'Take Your Time', and she got up to dance, waving at Claude.

"Come on, Claude, you have to come and dance!" she shouted at him and finally he got up to dance with her.

"Janet, do you remember how you found this music? It's so emotional and soul-searching, if you know what I mean," Jana remarked.

"Oh yes, this music belonged to Ben. As you know, he's still trapped six years in the future. It makes me want to cry just thinking about him," Janet replied, squeezing Jana's hand.

"Listen, we need to talk about changing the registration for the new plane. When you go up tomorrow to City Airport, start doing the paperwork so we can leave on Monday," Janet asked.

"Of course, but I can't say I've ever done that before. Isn't that something your lawyers usually do," Jana replied.

"Yes, all the legal transfers have been done. I really want someone to check that the registration is changed on the tail. You know it's a paint job to show it's registered in Montserrat. We also have the flight crew arriving on Monday morning at 8 a.m. I need someone to meet them and go over the details of their duties," Janet explained.

"I see, so I need to sleep onboard an empty plane, with my son. Is that going to be alright with the airport," Jana asked.

"Probably not, but that's the only way this is going to work for an early departure next week," she replied.

"Alright then, think I need to go and get packing again."

"Yes, and take plenty of baby food. Don't worry, I'll get the chauffeur to drive you up to the airport and answer any security questions. I've briefed him already on what we need to do," replied Janet.

"In that case, please excuse me and say goodnight to the others for me," said Jana, who got up and left the party. She even forgot to mention what she had found out about James. Now she planned to surprise them all on the plane before they left. Janet got up to dance with Claude and started whispering in his ear.

"I need you to go back to the Old Church in Chelsea to finish the job. You can leave with the removal men when they bring the office equipment early on Monday morning," she explained.

"You mean, we didn't…" he exclaimed.

"No, not according to my man who's been watching the church. The crypt was pumped dry of water, but he's seen none of the empty plastic chambers come out," Janet replied, as Claude raised her arm and twirled her around to the music.

"And after that?" he asked.

"When that's done, the delivery van will stop to load up the Gateway Food for our flight. I'm sure you can get onboard the plane without being spotted," she replied.

"Alright, sounds risky to me, but I'm sure Anita will make sure the target is destroyed this time," Claude replied.

"Well, you can't stay here as I'll be closing the house down as soon as we all leave for the Caribbean. The only other option would be to return to NATO in Brussels. Talk to Anita tonight and let me know what you decide tomorrow," she said, releasing his arm and giving him a kiss on the cheek, she turned and looked at him again,

"I hope you will come and join us on the island. We really need a small team of professionals to help us survive what's coming next," she said, and, turning around, she walked back to the table. Then she waved at the others still dancing, got up, and left to return to sleep at the house. Better to go to bed early and sleep.

***

Later, at six in the morning, she was woken by her mobile phone ringing. When she looked at the caller, it was Sam on the Caribbean island.

"Everything alright, Sam?" she asked, knowing there must be a problem.

"No! I'm afraid James has been taken by that Elizabeth woman, here on the island," he explained.

"What? And where is James now?"

"Last seen on a French military helicopter, flying south towards Guadeloupe," he replied.

"Really, so the Americans must have put pressure on the French to make such a covert operation. Where did this happen?" asked Janet.

"On the Old Bluff, right outside your house. I was bringing James back from the airport, and they were waiting for us. She and a couple of fully armed French commandos. I'm sorry but there was nothing I could do except take his medallion before he was bundled onto the chopper," he explained.

"Well, at least that's something. Listen, I'm planning to return on Monday, on a private jet I've purchased here in London. We might need to stop over in Guadeloupe to refuel," she replied.

"Understood. In the meantime, I'll report James as having been kidnapped and keep you informed," Sam replied, and closed the line.

This news really changed everything, she thought. Now she would need Claude and Anita's help. Taking her dressing gown, she went downstairs to make coffee and wait for Jana to arrive to tell her the news. As the coffee percolated in the kitchen, Janet could hear Jana carrying her travel bag down the stairs and then came to give her a big hug.

"I'm really not happy about going to the airport on my own," Jana said with tears in her eyes.

"Don't worry, you're not. I've had a call from Sam to say that James was kidnapped outside my house. It appears Elizabeth was involved with a French military helicopter," she replied.

"I knew it! When I looked on the tablet last night, I saw that he was no longer at the house on the island. Do you know where he was taken?" she asked.

"Sam said the chopper flew south. The most likely would be Guadeloupe, as that's the closest French island," Janet replied, as her phone rang, and she waited to answer it.

"It's someone calling from Europe, should I answer it?" she said and then she pressed accept.

"Hello, is that Mrs Janet Rumford?" the voice asked.

"Yes, indeed it is. Who's calling me," asked Janet, placing the phone on the speaker.

"I'm calling to warn you that you must leave the house by 8 a.m. this morning, or face possible arrest," the voice advised.

"Right, I understand. I was planning to leave anyway, so we can leave in an hour as you suggested," she replied.

"Good, and are two of our officers still with you at the house? We need them to finish their work in London with our removal men who will arrive after you leave," he asked, as Janet realised she was talking to someone from the military of NATO.

"Yes, they are still here and with us now," she continued as Claude and Anita appeared in the doorway, listening to the conversation.

"The two men who will arrive are the backup for this operation. Once the truck is unloaded, they should proceed with our men and destroy whatever remains of the target. Do they agree to finish the mission?" he asked. Janet looked at Claude and Anita who both nodded in agreement.

"Yes, that's an affirmative," Janet replied and with that, the line was cut dead while Janet looked at two in the doorway.

"Help yourselves to coffee. I have to alert the chauffeur to leave before 8 a.m. and start closing down the house," Janet said, pushing her way past them in a hurry, while Jana smiled and poured them coffee.

"Thanks, guys, for your support. I'll go and find a large canvas bag for the firearms and add your beach clothes to wear in the tropics. Come and join me outside by the garages when you're ready," Jana said, smiling, and left as well.

"You know, Anita, it sounds like we're invited to a beach holiday in the Caribbean," said Claude.

"Yes, but that's after we've eliminated the aliens; although I can't wait to try out the elephant gun. Come on, let's drink up and go and see what Jana's found," Anita replied.

At a quarter to eight, they were both standing next to the Bentley, waiting for the others to arrive. Janet came first with her housekeeper pulling a suitcase behind her. She was followed by Jana holding her baby and the cook with her suitcase, as everyone looked at Janet.

"I'm sorry that we've had to leave early and thank you, everyone, for all your help. It was a most enjoyable stay at the house. I really don't know when I shall be able to return," Janet said to her staff and, shaking each of them by the hand, she got into the car. Claude looked at Anita and rolled his eyes, as Jana rushed up to say goodbye.

"You two are going to join us at City Airport after we leave, aren't you?" she asked.

"Yes, of course we are. Where else would we go?" Anita replied, giving her a big hug and after a kiss on the cheek for Claude, she got into the car. The sound of a twelve-litre engine started as the car slowly moved down the drive and they waved as the gates opened and the housekeeper came to speak to them.

"You had better wait in the hall to open the gates for the removal men. I don't have time for that as we're busy closing up the house," was all she said as she walked away.

"Well, I think we know where we stand in this place," said Claude, smiling.

"Come on, Claude, bring the canvas bag. I want to see what clothes Jana has given us for our holiday," Anita replied, laughing.

"Yes, and I think we have time for some breakfast, at last," he replied, and taking her hand, they walked back to the main entrance of the house.

31 – OLD CHURCH

Early on Monday morning, the first of July, the removal men arrived at the house to deliver the last of Janet's office furniture.

Claude opened the gates while Anita went to talk to the men about the operation they were planning that morning. Janet's chauffeur arrived to tell the men where to unload the van. It was in an outbuilding, close to the garages. Claude arrived with the canvas bag of their clothes that were placed in the empty van. Then he went to recover the weapons hidden in one of the cars. They both thanked the staff for their help and said their final goodbyes, at leaving the house.

When they returned, they confirmed they were no ordinary delivery men. "We're your NATO support team for the operation today," he said as they both pulled out their NATO passes to show them.

"Now we need you to confirm where the target is in West London," he asked.

"Yes, that's easy to find, it's the Old Church on Cheney Walk in Chelsea," Anita replied.

"Very good, that's what we have marked on the plan. You do realise this will be dangerous and you may not come out alive, don't you," he said.

"Yes, but that was what we were sent to do," Anita replied.

"We've been dealing with these things since the first one was destroyed in the Arctic, so we know what the risks are. First you must wear the hazmat suits we have in the van and earphones to block out any signals that may be sent to confuse you. You can take the best of the firearms you have available, but you must let one of us come to set the final charges, understood?" he advised. Claude nodded his agreement while Anita wanted to know more.

"You've been doing this all across Europe, have you?"

"Yes, although here in the UK, this is only the third case. In some countries it's been a full-time job. Now, if you've got no more questions, let's get you in the van and get moving," he said.

Claude and Anita climbed into the back of the white van and found the protective suits. They pulled them on, on top of their work clothes, by sitting in the two chairs behind the front seats. Then helped each other fasten the suits right up to the neck, laughing.

"I'm not sure how we're going to get down the stairs at the church," remarked Anita as the men closed the rear doors and returned to the cab.

"If you're ready, I'll turn the van and we can leave," advised the driver. He drove up to the house gates that opened automatically and followed the road to the M4 into London. When the traffic became congested, they crossed the river after Putney and approached the site from the south bank. Crossing the Battersea Bridge, the van drew up outside the church in Chelsea.

"We've arrived at the target that looks quiet, with just two police officers outside. Now we'll change into our military uniforms and go tell them what's happening," the leader announced, climbing into the back of the van and taking off their overalls. Then opening the doors, they took out a few traffic cones and began to fence off the pavement in front of the church as the police officers came down to see what was happening.

"We've been sent here by the Government Agency Serco to check out the crypt of the church," he said pointing to the sign on the side of the van.

"Well, we didn't get any notice of that," replied the police officer.

"Perhaps you can stand down here during the process to control any crowd or press that arrive," he asked.

"Very well, how long will this take?" he asked.

"Shouldn't be more than half an hour, but there may be some toxic gas inside," he said pointing to a gas mask around his neck.

"We have our two specialists in hazmat suits to carry out the work," he replied, smiling, and walked back towards the van. Then, on opening the rear doors, he spoke to the two inside.

"Right, you two. Helmets on and bring your firearms in the bag we provided," he ordered. Anita jumped down from the van and, taking the bag, walked up to the church, followed by Claude. When they reached the door it was locked, so opening the bag, she found a small battering ram that quickly forced the door open.

"Was that meant to happen?" she asked. As she turned around, the support team were right behind them, and they entered the church. Anita walked straight to the pulpit and pulled the small door open.

"From here on we can't wear these helmets, there's not enough room in the staircase," she said.

The man replied, "Okay, but wear the headlights and take a torch each."

"Thanks. Oh great! I'm taking this double-barrelled elephant gun; what do you need, Claude?" she asked.

"I'll take the automatic machine gun, if we have the ammo," he replied. After they put on the headlights and loaded both firearms, they were ready to descend and got some more advice.

"Be careful with your shot. These things are known to have a force field that will return your fire," he advised.

"Right, ready, Claude, let's get back down there," Anita said, and started to climb backwards down the staircase first. When they reached the door at the bottom, Anita checked and found it was not locked.

"Claude, let me open the door a crack and shine your torch inside," she asked, opening the door.

"There's nothing but a huge pile of the sleep pods, nothing else," Claude said.

"No, that's not possible? There must be something more inside? Let me fire both barrels and see what happens," she replied, inserting two cartridges into the shotgun.

"Alright, but we keep the door closed as soon as you fire, remember what we were told before," he warned.

"Good point! So I'll only open the door enough for the barrel of the gun and we both crouch down as soon as I fire. Now I can't see anything, though," replied Anita.

"Oh! For God's sake, Anita, just fire, it's a shotgun!" shouted Claude. His last words were lost by a huge explosion and then the sound of the returning shot impacting the heavy wooden door.

"Wow! Whatever it is, that's most intelligent! You're not you hurt are you, Claude?" exclaimed Anita.

"No, not hurt, just deaf, despite the ear protection," he said, crouching on the step above her in the semi-dark.

"Right so, this thing must have a lot of power to return fire like that. If we can find the power source, we may be able to disarm it," Anita asked.

"What exactly are we looking for?" he asked.

"Well, look around you, Claude. See if there are any cables going into the cavern," Anita asked, when the leader of their backup came down to see if they were still alive.

"You guys alright down here?" he asked.

"Yes, fine. We need to find out where it's getting its energy from before we can disable it. Do you have any ideas?" Anita asked.

"We've seen this before. We think they were taking energy from the ground underneath them," he replied.

"And what's under the church here?" she asked Claude.

"Nothing I'm aware of. Let's cause a diversion all around the around the target and see what happens," he replied. Opening the door again, he took out two stun grenades and threw them down the chamber. When they exploded, there was no reaction, no shots, nothing.

"Look, I think it's safe to walk inside. If so, we can carefully lay the charges and set them off from outside," he said.

Anita looked at him as if he was mad, and then jumped down onto the floor. When nothing happened, she signalled for the others to follow. Anita walked as softly as she could in her army commando boots towards the huge mountain of sleep pods, all piled up on top of each other. When she reached the end, she saw an enormous metallic egg that was pulsating in the dim light. She turned around and saw the support man with his rucksack start to unload bricks of C4 explosive. He looked at her and motioned for her to leave the place.

Before she left, Anita opened the sleep pod closest to her and found it empty. Seeing Claude at the entrance door, she pointed upwards for them to leave by the staircase, as quickly as possible. Once back inside the church, Claude asked what she had seen.

"It's one bloody great pulsating egg that looks about to burst, but when I looked inside one of the pods, it was empty," she said.

"Come, put your mask on, we need to find his assistant, as they need to take more explosives down there," he replied.

When they walked outside, they found a small crowd being held back by the police and, ignoring all the questions, jumped back inside the van and took off their helmets.

"It's a big egg-shaped thing? You're going to need more explosives to destroy it," Anita announced.

"Yes, I guessed that from the gunfire I heard. I'm assembling two more backpacks of C4 to take down there," he replied, sweating as he completed his work.

"You've done your part, so now it's up to us to finish the mission. Can you turn the van around while I'm gone, in case we need to make a quick getaway," he said and left by the rear doors.

Anita climbed into the driver's seat, started the engine, and found the road was blocked by an even larger crowd. Finally, Claude got out to move the crowd and the van was turned and parked again. When he looked at the sign on this side of the van it said 'Gateway Hotel Food Deliveries.' He climbed back inside as they waited for the men to return. Ten minutes later, the two men appeared dressed in red overalls who went to speak to the two police officers.

"There may be a big explosion from the gas main. You need to move all these people away from the site," he said. When rumours spread about an explosion, the police made the crowd disperse down the road. As soon as the men were in the van, the driver pulled a detonator out of his top pocket and arming the charge, pushed the red button and waited.

Nothing happened outside the church, but behind in the graveyard they heard a muffled explosion, and they all smiled. Claude looked at Anita and gave her a high five. The driver started the engine and drove away down onto the Chelsea Embankment following the main road east into London. Continuing on the way to City Airport, they stopped at a Gateway Food centre. When the two men got out and another two got into the cab, Claude asked what was happening.

"Oh! That's Bill and Ben. They have a two o'clock flight back to Brussels. Now we have your overalls to put on as you have become the loaders today for this private jet," he said, passing them all clean and pressed white uniforms in a plastic bag for them to wear. After they changed, they were instructed to take two pallets of airline food to load into the van and then return for more.

"It's not all for your jet. We'll do a supply at another plane so you can see how it works," he explained. When they finished, they were given plastic IDs to wear around the neck and they drove off to the private jet parking at the airport.

"We enter at the Private Jet Centre where we supply the small jets. We already passed by your plane and dropped off two people, who will take your place once loading is finished. Make sure you hand over the ID when we make the switch," the driver said. Once inside, they drove around the park, followed by an air marshal to the first plane, while Anita and Claude watched. Then they continued to Janet's plane where the cargo door was already open and the captain was waiting impatiently.

"Hurry up," he shouted, as Claude wheeled the pallet to the door and was dragged inside. Then a man jumped down and started loading the boxes of food. When he returned to the van, Anita was told it was her turn. She wheeled the pallet to the door, only to disappear for a second and a similar-sized woman loaded the boxes onto the jet. Claude and Anita waited inside the cargo hold until the door was closed and they heard the van drive away.

Shortly after, the engines of the jet started and they began to taxi towards the runway ready for take-off.

"Looks like we're travelling cattle class for our departure, but really it wasn't such a bad day," said Anita, leaning back against a suitcase.

"You firing that elephant gun was the best part," he replied.

"Blowing up the churchyard, was fun," she said… but her words were lost as the plane climbed out of the London gloom into the sky. It was only after the plane levelled off that a young female co-pilot came to open the cargo door and let them out.

"Oh! We have two stowaways on board, what a surprise," she said, helping them out into the cabin. Sitting in one executive chair was Janet and in the other was Jana, cradling her baby.

"I trust you both had a successful day in London?" Janet asked as the plane burst through the clouds into sunshine at last.

"Shall I bring the champagne now, ma'am?" the girl asked.

"Yes, why not, I want to hear your story first. Watching the news, there was an explosion at a church graveyard? I hope you didn't leave body parts all over West London," she asked.

"No, it was mostly underground. Another giant egg, but we don't know if there were human or alien parts," Anita replied, smiling.

"Amazing you didn't get caught. There was no police backup today at all," Janet said, as the champagne arrived and she passed the flutes around to everyone. Then Janet asked the co-pilot, "Can you ask the pilot to come and see me once we're in French airspace?"

Janet looked back at them and continued, "Now, where were we. Yes, we have another problem and perhaps another mission for you to consider. Two days ago, James was kidnapped by the French military from Montserrat and taken to Guadeloupe. It's a French island about fifty miles south of Montserrat and I need professionals like you to find him and bring him home. What do you think?"

"Well, of course that's a challenge, as neither of us has any real ID or a passport," Claude replied.

"Don't worry about that. I can get you French or even British passports, once you find him," said Janet, as the pilot arrived.

"Good evening, Gerald. I need some info on our routing today," she asked.

"We are in French airspace flying SW to the next waypoint at La Rochelle. After that we change over to Spanish controllers in Las Palmas," he advised.

"Now, if I want to file a new flight plan from St Johns Antigua to the International airport in Guadeloupe, should I tell the French now or wait until the Spanish," she asked.

"With your new guests onboard, let's wait until we reach Las Palmas," he suggested.

"Yes, good idea. Of course, it's only just come to mind as we will need to refuel. The prices in French euros are better than dollars in Antigua," she replied.

"If this will be for refuelling only, I will change the plan and order the jet fuel in advance," he said smiling at everyone.

"Our two new guests will be leaving us there as they need a few days holiday after their stay in London," she replied. Anita rolled her eyes at Claude.

"Understood. While in transit in darkness, people can slip away in the night," he replied and left the cabin.

"Janet, what are you doing? This time you're going to have to pay us as professionals," she exploded.

"Alright, name your price?"

"I don't know. I thought 20k dollars for me and 20K euros for Claude would cover it," she replied.

"My goodness. I thought this would be attractive as Claude here speaks French and a holiday for a young couple would be a good cover. I'm not paying that! We need you on Monserrat," Janet said.

"What's wrong with you people? What are you fighting about on a beautiful Caribbean island," she asked.

"You saw what we are fighting today. Didn't he tell you how many of these things have been discovered in Europe? We don't know but we think they may be on our island as well," Janet replied.

"Alright, give us an allowance for some new clothes, a holiday place near a beach that doesn't need ID, and we'll do it. James helped us when we first arrived and if he's in trouble, I would like to help him," Claude said looking at Anita.

"Anita, what do you say?" asked Janet.

"Yes, alright, put like that, we'll give it a try," Anita replied.

"Right then, Jana, can you ask if our co-pilot can prepare us some lunch," asked Janet.

"So are you going to tell us exactly what's happened on this island of yours that makes you so afraid," Anita asked.

"Yes, of course. We still have five hours of flying time until we land. I can show you on my mind tablet what we have seen in the past and future," Jana replied.

"So where exactly are you people from," Anita asked.

"The same as you. We all came back from the future to our new life in 2024," Jana replied.

THE END

AFTERWARDS

Jana was sitting on the terrace at Janet's house. The July sunset cast a golden light across the sea below her. She caught the scent of salt in the air below, with white clouds billowing across the tropical coastline. She could not believe how lucky they had been to have returned to the island again, even if it was a foreign land.

"I've put the girls to bed and they're asleep at last," Bee said passing her companion a glass of white wine.

"Thanks, but I still can't work out what went wrong. We let them leave while the plane was being refuelled and they just disappeared? That's just so much BS! It's been two weeks since we returned and still no news," she replied, holding out an empty glass.

"When Sam went down to that frog island, we all thought there would be some news. Instead, he finds the beach hut empty. Finds they never brought any new clothes and just disappeared," Bee asked.

"I don't believe any of that crap. They must have been taken hostage just like James. Then moved off the island to some secure location. Maybe they're in Paris already," Jana replied, laughing.

"So, what do you think of the news from London after the new government was elected," Bee asked.

"Oh that! About what was expected. If you don't approve of the Great Reset, you must be racist or something more horrendous like the Far Right. Why do they all keep accepting donations for new clothes? Serves the people right. This new lot only want to serve themselves. Always the same when dictators get elected," Jana replied.

"How can they be so stupid to think that climate change can reduce the world's population by twenty or fifty percent? Remember, we know that after the comet strike in 2030, the population was reduced by 80 percent and then collapsed with the CME," she replied.

"Yes, we may have a one-world government, except it may not be controlled by us on Earth," Jana said.

"Let's talk about more positive things. We're making good progress in the new fields," said Bee.

"Good. And is Kiya still your guiding force in these endeavours?" she asked.

"Yes, and Justin has been most helpful as well," Bee replied.

"I'm sure he was on this submarine in the Arctic," Jana said pointing to the image on her laptop.

"Yes, of course. Look at the final clip of the video. That's Justin's face on the ice, alright. Even Susan agrees," Bee replied.

"We still don't know what's going to happen on the island," Jana said.

"I thought you were certain about these things in the future," Bee asked.

"Yes and no? There are a lot of things that can change future events that cannot be programmed or expected. I mainly look at events in the past," she replied.

"Right then, I'm going to make dinner tonight. I hope you will come and join us," Bee replied.

"Yes, of course. I'm going to take a dip in the pool first," she replied, and got up to leave.

Jana sat up on the top step of the pool inside the house. She had stripped off her clothes and sat in her underwear. She knew that what she was going to do was dangerous, but she had to find James.

Slowly she concentrated and tried to see where he was. She was only let in for a fraction of time, as it became clear that James and the others were in the fifth dimension.

Of course, she thought, although James no longer had his medallion, he still had access to another dimension on his arm. This dimension would allow him to move around, while other people would be frozen in time.

To be continued...

ACKNOWLEDGEMENTS

This book continues from the last book, now set in the first half of 2024. The story provides answers that were difficult to believe from the two previous books in the "Eve Not Adam" trilogy. You will find little time travel except when the characters return in 2024. The story starts in spring of 2024, runs through to July, and refers to events during the first half of that year.

Below are just a few of the sources I found helpful.

With thanks to the following for the inspiration.
- Steven M. Greer – *Extraterrestrial Contact*, 1999.
- Garrett M. Graff – *UFO The Inside Story*, 2023
- Vernon Coleman – *Endgame – Hidden Agenda*, 2021.
- Matthew Goodwin – *Values, Voice and Virtue*, 2023
- Paul Morland – *The Human Tide*, 2019
- Tim Marshall – *The Future of Geography*, 2023.
- David Reich – *Who are We and how We got here*, 2018.
- David Wallace-Wells – *The Uninhabitable Earth*, 2019

- G.L Davis – *Harvest – Alien Abduction*, 2020
- Tim Schwab – *The Bill Gates Problem*, 2024
- Bjorn Lomborg – *False Alarm*, 2021
- David Craig – *There is No Climate Crisis*, 2021.
- Paul Golding – *The Battle For Britain*, 2023.
- Stevin E. Koonin – *Unsettled*, 2021.
- Joseph McMoneagle – *Remote Viewing Secrets*, 2000.